the stories we tell

ALSO BY CHARLENE CARR

A New Start Series

Skinny Me
Where There Is Life
By What We Love
Forever In My Heart
Whispers of Hope

Behind Our Lives Trilogy

Behind Our Lives
What We See

Standalone

Beneath the Silence
Before I Knew You

For the child who grew within me as this book grew without.

It's been a trying journey, giving birth to this book as I prepared to give birth to you. May you one day learn the truths these characters learn. That love takes work. That trust is fragile, but can always be rebuilt. That there are two sides to every story, and forgiveness is as much for the forgiven as for the harmed.

All these things we hold onto will one day be tossed away: the framed pictures, the old bottles of hotel shampoos, the little scraps of writings—of thoughts and ideas captured tenuously—will pass onto other hands or pollute landfills, just as we'll pollute the earth, leaving our medicated and genetically modified cells to leach out of us.

And yet we hold on.

We hold onto it all, as if by doing so we hold onto ourselves.

We tell ourselves a story: We matter. This matters.

What uselessness.

What beauty.

The Stories We Tell

A Tale of Life and Love in Three Parts

BOOK THREE OF THE BEHIND OUR LIVES TRILOGY

CHARLENE CARR

Published in Canada by Coastal Lines
www.coastallines.ca

Library and Archives Canada Cataloguing in Publication

Carr, Charlene, author
The Stories We Tell / Charlene Carr.

Book Three of the Behind Our Lives Trilogy

(The Stories We Tell, Paperback)
ISBN: 978-1-988232-13-3

This novel is a work of fiction. Names, characters, places, and incidents either are the product of the author's imagination or are used fictitiously. Any resemblance to actual events, locales, organizations, or persons living or dead is entirely coincidental and beyond the intent of the author.

Typography by Charlene Carr
Cover Design by Charlene Carr

First Edition, December 2017

This work is also available in electronic format:
The Stories We Tell
ISBN: 978-1-988232-12-6

For more information and a chance to join the author's Reader's Group visit:
www.charlenecarr.com

CHAPTER ONE

Lincoln breathed deep the scent of cinnamon and coconut. He smoothed the back of his fingers along Kali's arm then squeezed her closer. She lifted her head and smiled.

He never thought he'd have this feeling again.

That night, sitting in the hospital room, watching Joseph's eyes meet Lucy's, realizing the child she'd just lost was Joseph's, not his, realizing two of the people he loved most had betrayed him, he'd broken.

He wasn't broken anymore.

Lincoln tilted his head and Kali raised her lips to meet his so intuitively he couldn't even be sure he'd been the one to initiate the motion. The kiss was soft, intimate, but he wanted more; to lift her from the couch and set her down in his bed, to peel away her clothing piece by piece.

He'd agreed they'd take it slowly. That meant moments like this, her wrapped in his arms as they lounged on the couch with fingers interlaced, intoxicating kisses that left him yearning.

Slow.

He let her be the one to inch them along. Their lips parted and he cupped her chin. "How are you feeling?"

She shrugged and pulled away, her body going rigid. "It is what it is, right? The verdict's already been made. The radiation worked or it didn't. I'm getting better or I'm not. Today won't change anything."

"You'll know."

Kali bit her lip and a pang of desire shot through Lincoln.

"Maybe I'll know. Maybe there'll just be more uncertainty. More waiting." She rested her head against his chest and threaded her fingers through his.

Lincoln stared at their hands. "I bet the swelling's gone down."

Silence.

"You said your vision seems a bit better, right?"

More silence.

"Kali?"

"I said it didn't seem to be getting worse." She pulled her hand away and withdrew from him. Two steps forward. One step back ... at least it was progress.

Kali settled against the couch and angled toward him. "This appointment is about checking to see that things haven't gotten worse, not to see if they've gotten better. Good news would be good. Of course. But I have to be realistic. And the reality is there's a very good chance I'm not getting any sight back." She hit her fist into her palm, a look of determination covering her face. "But Alika is helping me research ways I could possibly go back to my old job, even as things are. And if that doesn't work out there's training and other opportunities." Kali counted off the options on her fingers. "Counselling. Teacher's assistant. Workshops. This could be a whole new future."

"I know." Lincoln pushed out a smile. "Just hoping."

"I know you are. And thank you." Kali settled back against him.

He *was* hoping: that Kali would get better, that the tumour would go away, that her vision would come back. But he was also scared. Kali was here, in his arms and in his apartment because she needed him. Because she had no better option. And whether these next appointments brought good news or whether she learned to make her life work with the bad, soon, she wasn't going to need him so much anymore ... maybe not at all.

Which, again, should be good. *Was* good. If she stayed even when she didn't need to, it would mean this thing they were growing was real. But if she left the apartment? Made it on her own? She might go back to wanting the distance she'd wanted the first time she moved out. She may require him to schedule weekly visits if he wanted to see Theo. Would she even be okay with that? Would she want him at all?

Lincoln took a deep breath, willing his thoughts to disperse. Kali wasn't Ginny. Kali wasn't Lucy. But she had similar tendencies. She shut him out. She was independent. Her love ... no, not even love ... her affection didn't come easy. And he'd opened up to her, too much, maybe. If his heart broke a third time, he wasn't sure it could ever be put back together.

Kali leaned forward and rested her hand on Lincoln's cheek as she kissed him. The act was sensual but far too short. She pushed up from the couch and smiled, such a contented smile. "I better go check on Theo and Marvin. Make sure he's not scamming his Grampie into story after story." She shook her head. "Marvin, here. Indoors. For three weeks now." She laughed. "And not going crazy."

Lincoln swallowed. "He's had his moments."

Kali tilted her head side to side. "But he's here."

"Yeah."

"The counselling must be helping. But I think it's more than that. I think he wanted this, somewhere deep inside. I think it's Theo too—giving him a second chance; showing him he has love to give, that he's still valuable."

Had Lincoln ever seen a smile like the one she was wearing now? Certainly not in those first couple of weeks. The night of the firecrackers, maybe ... both nights of the firecrackers—the first on Canada Day when she'd tried to teach him how to dance and he'd misread the signals, the second on his birthday, when they'd transitioned to the start of something more. He'd thought by now ...

Her smile faltered. "What is it?"

Lincoln clasped his hands. "What's what?"

Her brow rose. "Your face." Kali sank back onto the couch. "Is it getting too much? I never thought ... well, I never thought. Marvin needed somewhere to stay. To heal."

"No. It's not—"

"Tonight's the last night you're here." She shook her head and patted the couch. "Tomorrow I'll change the sheets. You get your room back. Theo will climb in with me and Marvin will—"

"Kali."

"Marvin will squeeze into Theo's bed. Or we'll find a mat. He may prefer that anyway." She paused a moment. "This won't work long term though. I can already feel him getting antsy. Some of that may simply come from being under a roof day in and day out, but I'll find us a better situation."

Lincoln took a deep breath.

"Once things are figured out, with the job or finding a new one ... I'm already saving as much of my EI as I can, and when disability—"

Lincoln grasped her hips and pulled him toward her. "That's what's bothering me." He let out a faint smile. "It's cramped, yeah, but I'm not looking forward to you leaving."

She stared at him. "I'm not saying I want to leave."

"But you want your life back. Your independence."

"Of course."

He could almost see her choosing her words. Lincoln's stomach twisted.

"You're basically supporting me. And my kid. And Marvin. Your life revolves around ours. That's not right."

Lincoln shrugged. "It feels all right."

"For now. For you."

"But not for you?"

Kali shook her head. "Not forever."

"So you get your job back, or a new one, or support comes in, and you leave?"

"I don't know."

Keep quiet. Don't push her. Don't. "And if you leave, what then? Are we still?" He gestured a hand between them.

Kali's eyes clouded over. Fear? Frustration? Why didn't he keep his mouth shut? This was pushing. This wasn't taking it slow.

"I don't know. Day by day, right?" Kali stood again. She stepped from the couch, then hesitated. "I really should check on them. It's getting late."

Kali lingered a moment more. She opened her mouth,

closed it, opened it once more, then shook her head and hurried down the hall.

Lincoln stood and crossed to the window. Was it weak, asking her those questions, pushing her? Or was it what anyone would want to know?

He thought of his life in the months before he'd met her. Empty. Listless. He was a different person now. He was happy. His life had purpose. If she left, would all that disappear?

No. It wasn't just her. He knew that. Not just Theo, either. He'd worked to get where he was today. To actually feel happy. To not want to hide away from life. She and Theo had been the catalyst, but he'd done his own work too. It felt good, of course—being needed, relied on, cared for. Loved. If not by Kali, not yet, Theo loved him. Of that he was certain.

And if Kali and Theo moved on with their lives, if Kali's stated effort to 'give it a try,' fizzled away to nothing, it didn't mean Lincoln had to go back to the life he'd been living before. It didn't mean he'd automatically retreat to the woods. But would he want to?

Lincoln gave his arms and head a shake. He needed to stop thinking so much, a habit he'd developed in the months after Lucy—hiding in this apartment, ready to give up on life.

He crossed to the door and yanked on his boots. A thick blanket of fog covered the city; the perfect atmosphere to step into the night, breathe deep the cool air, and let all thought drift away.

CHAPTER TWO

Six hours later, Lincoln stepped into the apartment and settled onto the couch as quietly as he could manage. In four short hours he'd need to take Kali to her appointment. He closed his eyes and didn't open them again until the quiet, familiar noises of the kettle, a mug on the counter, and a spoon stirring gently roused him. He groaned, stretched, then rolled over to see Kali standing across the room, a coffee cup in hand.

"You were out late."

"Went for a walk."

Kali leaned against the wall. "Until almost three in the morning?"

"Visited a bar in between."

"Ah." She nodded, one hand wrapped snugly around the mug, the other rubbing the back of her neck. "Which one?"

"Tom's Little Havana."

"Have fun?"

Lincoln pushed himself up and swung his feet to the floor. "Some interesting conversations." She rested casually against the wall, her delicate ankles crossed, her eyes, still heavy with sleep, gazing at him. He could watch that sleepy gaze every morning for the rest of his life.

"I was a bit worried." Kali straightened and smiled. "But it was probably good for you. Get out of your head."

Lincoln opened his mouth to question.

"Maybe I should have done that." She took a sip of her coffee and gave a little shrug. "Walk the night. Meet strangers who know nothing of my life. Get out of my head."

Something in Lincoln's chest clenched. "It's going to be fine."

Kali nodded. "We hope." She turned, vanishing from Lincoln's sight. He reached for his phone. Forty-five minutes before they had to leave. Enough time to shower and eat.

AFTER FINDING A SPOT large enough for the truck, Lincoln rested his hand on the small of Kali's back as they travelled the sidewalk. She was tense. Quiet. He tried to catch her gaze but she focused straight ahead, which meant as far as she could see, he wasn't even there. Her cane tap tapped ahead of her. She took it everywhere now, preferring it to using his arm as her guide.

They walked through the crowd of people milling in front of the hospital doors. A man, broad, with a limp, paced the area. Broad wasn't even the word; he was massive. Almost two of Lincoln's arms would fit inside his one. But he looked timid, nervous. Near him, a woman brought a cigarette to her lips, her hands trembling so hard it took three tries to light it. Another man sat on a bench, head in his hands, shoulders shaking. Lincoln looked away and tried to pull his mind from thoughts of these people. Were they waiting for someone they loved? Had they just received news that would forever leave their lives shattered?

He brought his gaze back to Kali. Would that be them in an hour? Nervous, uncertain, wishing to be anywhere but here? It could be bad news, that the treatment did nothing, that the tumour was still growing, that Kali would lose her sight entirely and maybe, sooner than should be possible, her life. Lincoln stared at her back, the slight sway of her hips, the tall stance of her shoulders. It couldn't be that. It wouldn't be that. She was going to be fine.

Kali made her way to the clinic doors, tap, tap, tap. Her head held high, her steps sure. She pushed open the door before Lincoln had a chance to hold it for her.

"Do you want me to—?"

She cut him off with a shake of her head. "No." She kept her chin raised. "Thank you, but go on home." She pushed out a smile. "It's going to be hours. I'll give you a call when I'm done."

"I don't mind." Lincoln put a hand on her shoulder. She grasped it and gave a squeeze.

"No. There's no point us both wasting the day here."

"It's not a—"

"Go home, Lincoln. I'll call you when I need you."

He wanted to protest, tell her again he didn't mind waiting, tell her she might need him, want him, when she came out with the news. He kept silent and caressed her arm as he let his hand fall.

MARISSA, KALI'S FAVOURITE radiation therapist, offered a wink. "It's been nice not seeing you so much."

Kali pushed out a laugh. "I hope we see each other less and less as the years go on."

Marissa gave Kali's shoulder a squeeze. "Me too. How have you been?"

Kali swallowed. "Surviving." She paused. "There's been good."

"There always is." Marissa led Kali to the MRI room. "You remember the drill? No jewellery, zippers, buttons, nothing metal."

Kali nodded. She climbed onto the MRI bed and waited for the machine to move. She should be used to it by now, but still the tight space and clanking made her jaw tighten. Wind rushed through the tunnel, chilling her. She clenched and unclenched her fists, started at 300 and counted backwards by threes. It should calm her. 297. It would calm her. 294.

AT LAST IT WAS OVER. Once out of the tunnel, Kali eased herself onto her forearms.

"Not so bad?" Marissa entered the room and offered Kali a hand to help her off the table.

"Better than a root canal." Kali put a hand to her head, fighting the dizziness that threatened.

Marissa's brow furrowed. "We're going to get you all figured out today, okay? Dr. Manning will be ready for you soon and then on to Dr. Jones for the MRI results."

"Yeah." Kali knew all this, knew many people had to wait, knew it was a favour. And she was thankful. But some days, today, it felt impossible to believe all of this was okay, impossible to smile. It was bull, what she'd told Lincoln, that whatever had happened had already happened, that today changed nothing. Today changed everything ... or at least had the potential to.

"Back to your fella?"

"Huh?" Kali turned to Marissa. "No, uh, he's gone. The Sunshine Room. I think I'll wait in the Sunshine Room today."

"Great." Marissa's smile was broad. Her shiny black hair glinted in the light. "You want me to send some—"

"No." Kali raised her hand. "I need time alone."

"Right." Marissa nodded, her dark lashes lowering over her even darker eyes. She squeezed Kali's arm. "Someone will come get you when Dr. Manning is ready."

KALI STRETCHED OUT on a couch in the Sunshine Room, thankful she had it to herself, though she almost wished she'd asked Lincoln to stay. She could be curled up in his arms right now, feel the rise and fall of his chest against her back, the caress of his fingers along her skin. She took a deep breath then released it slowly. She repeated this, again and again, until a nurse she didn't recognize led her to the neuro-ophthalmology wing. After a round of tests, Dr. Manning's less than confident smile sent Kali sinking back into her chair.

"It's bad?"

"It's not better, which is what we had hoped. It's somewhat worse." The doctor smoothed back her non-existent stray hairs. "But that doesn't mean much. It's not unusual, Kali. The treatment can cause swelling and for some it takes longer to settle than others. Most likely you'll come back in a month and we'll be looking at an entirely different scenario."

"Improvement?"

Dr. Manning pressed her lips together. "Hopefully. At least no further decline."

"Okay."

"I don't even always see someone this early after treatment. We were hopeful. For your job. For—"

"I get it." Kali stood. She put out her hand. "Thanks. I'll see you soon."

Kali made her way back to the Sunshine Room and closed her eyes. It didn't mean anything. Most likely her reduced vision was due to swelling. Most likely it was fine.

A LITTLE OVER AN HOUR later she was in Dr. Jones' office, waiting. She sat, her hands clasped. *Let it have shrunk.* The clock on the wall tick, tick, ticked. *Let it be a miracle. Let it be almost gone, or dead. Let it be dead.*

Tick. Tick. Tick.

Kali startled as the door pushed open.

Dr. Jones sat. She could see the news on his face before he uttered a word.

"So it's larger? It's grown?"

"It appears larger. But as I said, the swelling—"

"You don't know. What you're saying is you don't know."

"Not conclusively." Dr. Jones folded his hands. "You know we often don't have definitive answers."

"So it could be enlarged because it's growing, because it's taking over my brain. I thought at least—"

"Most likely," he held out a hand, "the tumour cells are dead or dying, and in four to six weeks we'll see an entirely different picture. There's no reason to think the worst."

She knew that. Of course she knew that. But she'd

thought. She'd hoped ... "Does this lessen the chance of ever regaining the vision I've lost?"

"Not necessarily."

"But maybe."

"I can't—"

"You can't say." Kali looked to the ceiling. Where was the peace she'd found? Where was the woman who'd accepted her fate, who decided life could be lived and lived well even if her vision remained as it was, even if it got worse?

"My professional opinion is that you're never going to regain all you've lost. And you're definitely never going to come in and see this magically gone. Whether it's residual meningioma, dead meningioma, or scar tissue ... all of them will affect your vision."

"But the hope is dead or scar ... so no growth."

"That is the hope."

Kali stared at him, seeing the basketball player in the church parking lot. Seeing the way he used to lean against his car with a group of girls and guys surrounding him. Did he ever imagine he'd be sitting across from the little girl who'd watched from a distance, telling her that her optic nerve and chiasm would always be scarred? Did he even remember she was that girl? He'd never mentioned it.

Kali had caught his ball once as it rolled to the sidelines, thrown it to him. And he'd grinned. That casual, careless grin. Shelley had elbowed her and Kali smiled back. Even though she wasn't interested in guys, and certainly not one five years her senior, she'd never forgotten that grin.

"Kali?"

"Mmhmm?"

"You're going to come back in," he looked to his calendar,

"in five and a half weeks. Until then, we're going to hope for the best."

Kali stood.

"I see you're using the cane."

Kali looked at it, she hadn't even realized she'd taken it out of her satchel when she'd stood, hadn't realized she held it in her hand.

"That's good. That's wise."

Was it? Or was it giving in?

CHAPTER THREE

Nothing had changed. Not really. Not at all.

Kali's eyes widened at the sight of Lincoln. He'd waited or come back without her call. She sighed, thankful, and tap, tapped over to him; not that she needed the cane in these halls, but she might as well get used to it being a permanent feature in her life. What was that saying? Practice makes perfect. If today's results were any indication of future ones, she needed to reach perfection.

Kali stepped into Lincoln's embrace, letting him hold her a moment, letting herself be weak and sad and angry. She stepped back, her hand lingering on his arm. "You didn't wait this whole time, did you?"

He shrugged.

"That's," she shook her head, "thank you. If I'd known I would have ..." But would she? She'd wanted to be alone after the MRI, after the appointment with Dr. Manning. She'd needed that. "Anyway, too late now." She sighed. "Let's get home."

Kali stepped toward the door, trusting he would fall into step behind her as she entered the hall. She tapped her way down to the main hospital doors and out into the sun. Lincoln had waited. For hours. Alone. And in addition to all that ran through her mind, she felt awful for it. But she'd told him to go home. To leave. It wasn't her fault.

Kali walked faster. She wanted to be home, where things felt normal—or closer to normal than being here, surrounded by patients. A patient herself.

A path opened in the crowd for her and her cane. She tap, tapped to the sidewalk faster than she ever had before, then up the street to the truck. She turned. Lincoln was far behind. He jogged to catch up.

"That man. He was there before and he, he stared at you."

Kali held out her folded up cane. "Everyone stares."

"No. Like he knew you."

"What man?" She looked past Lincoln.

"He—" Lincoln shook his head. "He's gone. I tried to stop him but he hobbled away."

"Hobbled?" Kali's stomach flipped.

"Yeah. Hobbled. Limped. I don't—"

"What'd he look like?" Her throat tightened.

"Tall. Huge. Muscular, not fat. Black." Lincoln shrugged. He eyed Kali, his head tilted. "I guess if he wanted to talk to you he wouldn't have walked in the other direction."

Kali turned her head from his gaze, her pulse racing. She yanked open the door and stepped into the cab. "Yeah, I guess not."

KALI STARED AHEAD, THE majority of her focus on keeping her breath even. Twice now. Twice in what, less than three weeks? Derek was back. But if he was back, why hadn't he shown up by now? Had he been waiting by the hospital, hoping to see her end a shift? For three weeks? No. Someone would have seen him, recognized him. Shelley.

Had he been back for three weeks and not searched out Marvin? It wouldn't be that hard finding someone who knew Marvin, who knew he was off the street and living with her. Her and Lincoln.

Kali glanced to Lincoln, who glanced back, smiled. He probably thought she was silent because of the test results. Her chest throbbed. Breathe in. Breathe out. Was Lincoln the reason Derek had kept silent?

"Is everything all right?"

Kali kept her eyes ahead. It was too much. No one person should have to deal with this much.

"I mean I understand if you don't want to talk about it. It couldn't have been good—"

"It just means more time. I'll go back in a few weeks."

She could hear the faint sound of Lincoln's swallow.

"So, swelling then, or ..." his voice trailed off.

Kali couldn't do this. She couldn't answer questions. Not now. She could hardly breathe. She focused, her breath slow and ragged before she managed to bring it under control again. Was she jumping to conclusions? There must be dozens of big, black, muscular men throughout the city. But who limped? And who stared at her, waiting around outside the hospital three weeks after she thought she'd seen him?

Her husband, who abandoned her not once, but twice.

The man she married had died that day in the frigid Atlantic, died alongside his brother as they'd been bashed against the rocks.

The man who'd been thrown high enough on the treacherous shoreline that bystanders had managed to grasp his arm and pull his bloody and bruised body out of the sea wasn't Derek. Not any longer.

He was someone different. Less.

In the week following the accident he'd hardly spoken. Not when told of Jason's death. Not when told the boy they'd saved was doing well. Not when the media tried to get interviews of the local hero.

Kali had nursed him in the hospital as much as she could, and then back home whenever she wasn't in school or working. He'd been silent with her too. At first she'd almost loved the silence. Been relieved by it, at least. It meant she didn't have to speak either, to comfort him with false words when all she wanted to do was scream.

Everyone expected her to praise him, to tell him Jason's death wasn't his fault, to tell him he was a hero. But praise was the last thing on her mind. She was angry. Livid. Being a hero was one thing. Being an idiot was another.

Protect your own. She knew that. Jason knew that, which is why he'd jumped in after Derek. But Derek? Derek had to be the hero. Always the hero.

It was partly her fault for not seeing where that compulsion could lead. From the day she'd met him, Derek had always tried to save things. A woman at the club who'd gotten into a fight with her boyfriend and was left stranded; twenty bucks from his hand to this stranger's to make sure she got home all right. A baby bird a few weeks later, fallen from its nest. The community rec centre, where he'd stood with a placard and collected signatures, determined to show the community wanted and needed the space. His father—who he fed, made sure went to the doctor twice a year, and whose forms he filled out to ensure money kept coming in.

Kali had found these things endearing, if slightly off-putting. She wondered at times if he thought he was saving her in some way. From what, she didn't know.

She'd never specifically encouraged his philanthropy. Just endured it with a smile, deciding there were worse things than an afternoon's plans derailed by a lost dog Derek couldn't abandon until the owners were found.

A boy, lost among the waves ...

It was admirable, people said, when Kali stood at Jason's grave, a grave Derek couldn't bring himself to visit. He was a hero, they said, the way Derek leapt into the water without a thought.

They were wrong.

He was an idiot. It wasn't his place. He had his own child to think about. Kali squeezed her eyes shut. Her hands clenched.

That boy who'd slipped into the waves had a father. A father who stood watching as two strangers risked everything, as one lost his life, as Kali and Derek lost the future they'd dreamed of: the normal, happy life she'd finally let herself believe was possible.

The father kept saying, I can't swim. I can't swim. Even after the boy was back in his mother's arms, after Derek was lying on the shore, after the last time anyone saw Jason surface. He hadn't said it before Derek jumped though. It couldn't be her husband's excuse. His only excuse was his own misshapen need to be the hero.

"Kali?"

He'd called her name the night she'd kicked him out, the night she told him if he was leaving, fine, but never come back. The night, despite her threat, he'd walked away.

"Kali?"

She could see it clear as day, Derek standing at the bottom of the steps of the small house they'd rented, yelling her name like some crazed idiot as she threw his duffel bag out—or drug and kicked it out, rather, like a crazed idiot herself. Like the ridiculous couples on cheap reality TV, making fools of themselves on Judge Judy or screaming, mindless of the cameras on Cops.

She'd been six months pregnant by that point. Six months pregnant, and had spent the past two not being excited about the child inside of her, not resting, putting her feet up after a long day of classes and shifts at the hospital. No, she'd been nursing Derek. First his body and then his mind. But she couldn't reach his broken spirit. She didn't know how.

He'd given up. Checked out. Sunk into himself in a way that half terrified her, fully enraged her. It was indulgent. Selfish. So he'd lost a brother; it was his own damn fault. Nobody else felt compelled to jump into the water that day.

And then he came home one Thursday afternoon with his eyes bright, smiling. He told her about his plan as if it was wonderful. A plan that meant abandoning her and his soon-to-be child even more than he already had.

Selfish. Indulgent. Damn ridiculous.

"Kali!"

Kali startled out of the memory—shock, then confusion breaking through the anger that coursed through her. She unclenched her fists and turned to Lincoln. "Yeah?"

He wore a question on his face as he gestured his head toward the window. "We're home."

Home? Kali was expecting to see the small house she and Derek had rented. The brown painted porch. The wilted flowers out front. She looked instead at buildings and streets that seemed foreign. She blinked, and the reality of life came back to her.

"Oh, right." Kali undid her seatbelt. "Okay."

Lincoln reached his hand across the space between them and rested it on her arm. "What's going on?"

"Nothing. I'm fine."

"You're not fine."

Kali smiled. Her pulse still raced. The blood coursing through her along with the anger. "Just frustrated." She gave a little sigh. "I guess I was hoping for good news more than I realized."

Lincoln stared at her. She stared back, smiling, as her mind raced and her chest tightened again. If it was Derek, if he was here, what did he want?

Had it been him weeks ago? If it had, what was he waiting for? Why hadn't he contacted her?

What did he want?

Lincoln broke their gaze and opened his door. Kali opened hers. He walked around and waited, clearly expecting her to reach for the cane, do the little flick Theo loved as it snapped into shape. She put her hand out instead and he offered his arm without a moment's hesitation. She held it tightly as they made their way up the porch, through the building's main door, and onto the small stairway.

It was silly, holding on at this point. She knew the steps; she had a railing on the other side of her. But if Derek was back–she glanced to Lincoln with a smile she hoped looked genuine. He smiled back–she didn't know how long this arm would be here, and she didn't want to let it go.

CHAPTER FOUR

Over the next few days, Kali's senses were on edge—the ones she had left, anyway. Every time a car door slammed she flinched and had to coach herself not to run to the window. She succeeded most of the time, but not always. She found herself staring at Marvin, wondering if he'd seen Derek, if he knew he was here, safe, alive. He had to be alive, which mean he could be here. If he was dead, surely someone would have contacted her. Technically, he was still her husband.

Was that why Marvin had been so content these past few weeks? Why he could stay inside and had hardly any episodes? Obviously the counselling was part of it, but unless the psychologist was a miracle worker, it was only a part.

Marvin she stared at. Lincoln she avoided. She should tell him. She knew she should tell him. She wanted to tell him. But what would she say? *Oh, remember that husband I let you think was dead? Well, he's not, and I'm pretty sure he's back. Yes, I'm married. Technically.* It was cruel, letting him believe the lie, but would it be more cruel to speak the truth, especially when she wasn't certain Derek actually was back?

She'd be hurting Lincoln for nothing. She'd be risking everything they were trying to build for nothing.

Kali startled as she became aware of Theo's presence in the room. She turned to him and smiled. He was talking more and more, which was wonderful. But what about when the dreaded question came—*Where's Daddy?*

What would she say? What could she?

That his Daddy abandoned them? That Kali sent him away? Both answers were true, but neither gave the whole story.

"Mommy?"

The sound, still so new, sent shivers of joy through her. "Yes, sweetie?"

Theo's forehead furrowed. "You still sad?"

"Oh." Kali let her breath out slowly. How long had he been standing there, watching her, before she'd sensed his presence? "I'm okay."

"But you no see good still?" He put his hands up the way she'd shown him weeks ago, one blocking his sight entirely, the other cutting off the peripheral.

"No. I still can't see well."

He pointed to the cane on the coffee table. "But that help you see better? With your hand?"

"It helps."

"So you kinda see better?" He tilted his head, a hopeful smile on his face.

Kali swallowed. Her brow furrowed. "Kind of."

"So don't be sad no more, okay?"

Kali walked over to him and crouched down. "I'll try, sweetie."

"Cause maybe one day you see good again some times."

Kali rubbed her hands along Theo's arms. He looked so serious. So concerned. "You don't need to worry about it."

He shook his head.

"Theo."

"You my Mommy." He pushed his finger into her chest, then into his own. "You sad. I sad." He paused. "You don't be happy till you see again?"

Kali's stomach twisted. She took Theo's hand and led him to the couch. It wasn't right, him holding her fear like this. Her pain.

She'd been doing better these past weeks. Thinking about her loss less. Partly because of the CNIB and the hope she'd found of a life worth living, whether her sight came back or not. But since that day at the hospital, fear of Derek had taken over. Consumed. Because of what Derek being back meant for her and Lincoln, obviously, but also what it could mean for her and Theo. She had her rights, but Derek also had his. What if he tried to take her son away?

If she was honest with herself, that's part of why she'd kept such distance. She didn't want Derek falling in love with Theo; not while he was in the military, in some other province or overseas. She didn't want her son shipped between them. She didn't want to see Theo's face as he sat missing his father. She didn't want to risk the chance that some judge would decide Derek was better for Theo than her. It'd be unlikely any would, but possible. And that possibility kept her up at night. Especially now. What if he had a girlfriend, or worse, a fiancée? What if he was here to ask for a divorce and then right after, to ask for his son? What if he could give Theo a life she never could?

Kali sighed. "I haven't been the best Mommy lately."

Theo shook his head and poked her. "Good."

"I was really sad for a long time. And angry too."

His brow furrowed.

"Not at anyone in particular. Just at life. You know what hope is?"

Theo tilted his head. "When you want nice things?"

Kali smiled. "Kind of. It's more like believing that good things will happen or come to you ... I thought hope didn't matter. I thought it meant nothing." Her smile wavered. "I know you may have heard me say that once, but I was wrong."

Theo's lips pursed.

Kali resumed her smile. "Mommies can be wrong too. Very wrong. Just the way you learn new things every day, so do we. Sometimes we think we know things, the truth about life, when we have no idea." Kali took his hand in hers and gave it a squeeze. "Things happen. Bad things. Good things. And maybe luck is involved or fate or ..." she paused. "You have no idea what I'm talking about, do you?"

Theo tilted his head.

Kali squeezed him into her side. "You will one day. And when you do, I want you to remember, the bad things, when they happen, they don't have to be as bad as you think ... we have a choice about how bad we let them be. I didn't realize that before." She took a breath. How could she learn something then forget it so quickly? "Think of Lincoln. You love Lincoln, right?"

Theo nodded.

"Well, if all the bad things hadn't happened, the rats in our apartment, me being ... sick, maybe Lincoln wouldn't be with us now. And maybe Grampie wouldn't have come to stay, and ... who knows, maybe you wouldn't have felt safe to talk, and that's one of the best things ever."

He stared at her, expressionless.

"I don't know if I'm explaining this well. I don't know if I can ... I know it seems like I'm still sad. I'm not so much though. I guess I've just had a lot on my mind. But I'm going to try to do better. I'm going to try to remember that good can come from the bad. I'm going to try to hope. To dream. To expect good."

Theo continued to stare.

Kali squeezed him tighter then pulled back; he may not understand any of this, but he was hearing it. "I want you to do that too, expect good. I want you to try to be happy and not worry about me. Think instead of good things. Of wonderful things. Like going to the park and ice cream and pizza and the beach. Can you do that for Mommy?"

Theo's brow furrowed again. "And playing catch with Lincoln? That's a good thing."

Kali laughed. "Exactly. That's a great thing."

Theo nodded, his face still serious. "I try. You try too."

"Yeah." Kali nodded. "I'll try too." She'd try not to think of Derek, worry about Derek. He'd come or he wouldn't. And she'd deal with the fall-out if he did. She'd survived this far. She'd keep surviving.

AFTER A LONG DAY AT work, Lincoln stood outside his apartment, not ready to go in. The past few days being home felt like tiptoeing through a minefield ... not that there'd been explosions, per say. At least not obvious ones. The tension had been more subtle than that. Expressions of concern gave him annoyed looks. Efforts to touch resulted in shrugged shoulders and sly maneuvers away.

It couldn't just be the news that her tumour hadn't shrunk ... Kali had been expecting that news. Lincoln rubbed a hand along the back of his neck. But what did he know? Perhaps it could. Perhaps that's all it was.

She had been hopeful. Had started to see life for its possibilities, even if her sight wasn't coming back. But maybe that had been the lie. Maybe all she wanted was her sight to return, her life to return.

Lincoln had tried to talk to her about it this morning and she'd worn that forced smile. Told him she was fine. They were fine. All was fine. Each sentence a lie. She'd squeezed against the counter when he'd walked by her, ensuring they didn't touch. She'd flinched when he reached past her for the carton of juice.

Lincoln stared at the building's door. Behind it, a flight of stairs, and after another door would be Kali. Kali who, after finally letting him in, was pushing him away again. Kali, who had been on edge ever since she'd walked out of those hospital doors.

Lincoln's whole body felt heavy. Exhausted. He wanted nothing more than to lie back and relax, but the thought of walking inside, having to tiptoe around her, was the most exhausting thought of all.

He turned from the house and made his way to the Common. Lying in the grass or walking the open green space would only delay the inevitable, but it seemed the best option.

Just past the Oval, Lincoln stopped. Marvin's cart was safely stored in the backyard behind Lincoln's place, the items he couldn't part with in boxes in his room, but the man still walked the city several hours a day or spent time at the Common, which seemed to be his second home. Lincoln stared. He'd seen him here countless times. Both before he'd moved in and since. But not like this. Marvin was laughing, his hand on the arm of someone mostly concealed by a tree. Lincoln walked closer as Marvin wrapped his arms around the man then pulled back, gesturing for the man to sit down beside him on the grass.

Lincoln watched, motionless, as the man took his time sitting, favouring one leg. He was smiling, looking at Marvin with something ... affection? Nervousness?

Lincoln could no longer see Marvin's face, but his motions were relaxed. Smooth. Not the jerky, uncertain movements he made when talking to a stranger or in an uncomfortable situation. A strange chill passed over Lincoln. No denying it, this was the man from the hospital. The man who'd been watching Kali. Kali ... who'd been a different person since that day.

The hair rose on Lincoln's neck. Something wasn't right. Marvin's laugh carried through the park. He could see the man's softer laugh but not hear it. A nephew, maybe? A family friend?

Kali's face when he'd mentioned the hobbling man flashed into Lincoln's mind. Fear. Alarm.

Something wasn't right.

Lincoln turned toward home, his strides long, his mind whirling. Maybe he was being silly. Paranoid. But he couldn't push away the feeling that whoever this man was, his presence was about to change their lives.

CHAPTER FIVE

Lincoln slowed his pace as he took the stairs to his unit door. He stood outside it for seconds, minutes, he couldn't be sure. His hand hesitated on the knob. Marvin led a whole life before Kali stepped into it, but the man with the limp was connected to Kali some way too. He'd stared at her that day outside the hospital.

Lincoln turned the knob. Inside, Kali sat on the floor with Theo, both of them bent over the track Lincoln made for Theo's dinky cars. They were smiling, and the smiles stayed as they looked up at him. Theo waved. Kali stood, a question replacing the smile. Lincoln stepped forward.

Was the man the reason she'd been so withdrawn these past days, the reason she'd recoiled from his touch? She'd never mentioned anyone but Derek, but that didn't mean ...

"What is it?"

Lincoln shook his head, released an awkward laugh, mentally trying to ease away the uncomfortable feeling in his chest. What they had was real. Growing. Slowly, but growing. He wasn't about to lose her to some past lover, and it was stupid to think he would. "Nothing. I just ... remember that guy I mentioned at the hospital?"

Kali glanced to Theo. "Why?"

"He didn't sound like anyone you know? An old friend?"

She stared, swallowed.

"Marvin was out sitting with him. Hugging him."

Kali wrapped her hands around her middle. Her face paled.

"Kali?"

"I never thought ... I really never. I mean I knew one day ... it was possible." She stared at Lincoln. "I'm sorry." She looked again to Theo. "Damn. Just—" Kali looked back to Lincoln. Past Lincoln. Her eyes widened. She stepped back.

Lincoln turned to the sound of feet behind him, a man's gasp. "Is that?" The man's voice was soft. His eyes misted. "Is—?"

"Go to your room." Kali snapped at Theo, who stood, his eyes as wide as his mother's had been. "Now!"

Theo stood, frozen, then ran from the room.

"Kal." The man turned to her, pleading in his voice as Kali backed away.

"You promised."

"I didn't." He shook his head. "You made a promise for me. I never—"

"No." She raised her hand.

Lincoln stood between the two. "Kali, who—?"

The man looked toward the hall. "Kal, he's my boy."

His boy?

Lincoln turned to the sound of Marvin, who stood against the door jamb, his face aglow. "It's my Derek."

"Your ..." Lincoln ran his hands through his hair and looked between Kali and the man. "You're ..." He opened his mouth, closed it, shook his head, then turned to Derek as he spoke to Kali. "You said he was dead."

"I didn't." Kali's voice squeaked. "I never said ... you assumed."

Lincoln whipped his gaze to Kali. "You never corrected me."

"Hey, man." Derek's voice was soft, softer than Lincoln would have expected the voice of a man that large could be. "Not to be rude, but do you mind if I have a few minutes with my wife?"

"Your ..." Lincoln backed away. "Your ex, you mean? Your ex-wife." He looked to Kali, who looked away.

"No, I mean my wife."

Lincoln retreated to the kitchen, stopping only when he bumped into the table.

He could hear Derek mumbling something, then Marvin shuffling down the hall toward Theo and Kali's room.

"What are you doing here?" Kali's voice was clipped, angry, and just loud enough for Lincoln to hear.

"I was called."

"Called!" Her voice rang louder now. Clear. Lincoln looked toward the living room and then to the hall. It was wrong, he knew, standing here, listening. But he couldn't make himself move. Kali's husband wasn't dead. Kali's husband was still her husband.

And he was standing in Lincoln's living room.

"The police station. They said Dad had been taken in, said he was beaten and ..."

The voice lowered and Lincoln leaned forward. He shook his head, rubbed a hand along his neck, then turned toward the hall. He couldn't go to his room. One of them may see him from the living room and know he'd been listening. He continued down the hall. The bathroom or Kali's room—where Marvin and Theo would be talking about what—the fact that Theo's Daddy had come home?

Lincoln stepped into the bathroom, sat on the edge of the tub, and let his head sink into his hands.

HOW LONG HAD HE been sitting there, back hunched, hands over his ears? Ten minutes? Twenty? An hour? A gentle rapping made his gaze dart to the door. He waited as the taps sounded again. "Lincoln?"

Kali spoke, her voice soft and uncertain. "Lincoln, are you in there?"

Lincoln nodded. Of course he was in here. Where else would he be?

"Lincoln, can I come in?"

Could she? He hadn't locked the door, so of course she could.

"He's gone, Lincoln. And I'm sorry. I—"

Lincoln stood and crossed to the door. He pulled it open to see her standing, hands clenched in front of her chest, her face that of a stranger's. He hardly recognized the sound of his own voice. "He's your husband. He's alive and he's your husband."

She swallowed a long draught of air. "Technically."

Lincoln stared at her.

"We're legally separated. We have been for years." She gestured down the hall. "Can we talk?"

Legally separated. It wasn't divorce. It wasn't anything, really. Was it?

Lincoln looked down the hall in the opposite direction.

"Where's Theo? Is he—?"

"He's in the room with Marvin. They're reading stories. I sent Derek away. He's coming back tomorrow, but I sent him away. For now."

For now.

Her voice sounded distracted. "I need time. To tell Theo. To explain."

"And then?"

"Come." She gestured down the hall again. "We need to talk."

Lincoln kept staring. She looked so vulnerable. So weak. But she wasn't. She'd been strong when he met her. Strong so many times in between. He tried to scan through every moment. Every time she could have told him the truth and every time she hadn't. That first night Derek's existence had come up ... he could hear the words again, when he asked if she'd been married: *I guess I still am.* That was it, the moment she'd come closest. But then he'd pried further. An accident? An illness? And she'd described what happened at Peggy's Cove, the way Derek had jumped into the water to save a child, the way his brother had jumped in after him. Lincoln had thought it strange, how she'd talked about it. *My stupid husband*, she'd said. Strange too, the way her body tensed with such anger ... but he didn't know anything about what it was like to lose a spouse, especially in that way. He could imagine how she'd be angry, how giving into anger could be easier than giving into grief. She'd redirected the conversation and he hadn't pried further, thinking the grief was taking over, not wanting to push.

She'd been covering a lie, not grief.

She could have told him other times, too. Multiple times.

Lincoln closed his eyes—was this how little she thought of him? When they first kissed, when she'd stood across from him in that hotel room, pushing him away, was Derek the reason? Was he at the centre of the 'complicated life' she never fully explained?

Lincoln opened his eyes. She could have told him then. She could have told him just days ago, when he'd mentioned the man staring at her, the man with the limp. She must have known. He met her gaze as she stood outside the bathroom, urging him to step into the hall, to talk. She'd known. It explained it all—the preoccupation, the aversion to his touch. She'd known and said nothing. She'd known and let him find out like this.

"No."

"What?" her voice came out soft, questioning.

"No. We don't need to talk."

"But—" She put her hand on his arm and he yanked himself away as if he'd been burned. "I need to go." He pushed past her.

"Lincoln."

"Kali," he turned, his voice sharp, his chest tight, "so many times. So many chances." He shook his head, remembering the way she'd leaned her head against his chest, looking into his eyes, the way their lips met. How they lay like that for hours some nights after Marvin and Theo were asleep, talking or touching. How patient he'd been, how he believed her hesitancy to progress their relationship, to be intimate, had to do with the memory of her dead husband, the fear of letting herself be with someone else, someone new.

He'd thought his tenderness and patience would win out, that one day she'd trust him enough. Love him enough, the way he loved her ... but this wasn't love. It was true, she'd never said Derek was dead, but she'd known it's what he thought. She'd known she was letting him believe a lie. "Why didn't you tell me?"

"I didn't think he was coming back."

"But you knew he could."

"I didn't think ..."

Lincoln's arm tensed. He wanted to hit the wall, tear something apart. "Yeah. Exactly. You didn't think." He backed away from her. "Or maybe you did. Maybe you thought that would scare me away? That I'd kick you out if I knew I was shacking up with a married woman?"

"We weren't shacking up."

"Or you just didn't care. It was only about what you wanted, what was easy for you, convenient for you." Lincoln stopped, his breath coming quick. "You're so selfish it makes me sick."

"Lincoln."

"No." He turned away. "I can't be here. I can't go through this again." Lincoln held his hands out, as if trying to push it all away. "I can't look at you right now."

He strode down the hall, the front door slamming behind him. She'd lied. Again and again. Constantly. And he was the fool who'd believed it. Who'd thought what they had, maybe, was love.

CHAPTER SIX

Kali flinched as the door slammed shut. She stared at it, willing it to open, willing Lincoln to walk back in, sit on the couch, hear her out.

But he wouldn't. Not yet. And it made sense. She'd had time to tell him. Lot's of time. Was he comparing this to what Lucy had done, the lies and betrayal? This was nothing compared to that. Nothing.

Kali stared at the floor. Or maybe it was worse. She was married, and in Lincoln's eyes, she'd turned him into a cheater, made him what he hated. She was married. She had a husband. And though she hadn't lied exactly, she certainly hadn't been truthful. She'd let him believe a lie.

At first, when she was merely staying in his place for a few weeks until she found somewhere better—basically a stranger—the truth hadn't seemed relevant. Later, she'd been too scared and embarrassed to tell him the reality—she was an abandoned woman. Her husband didn't want her ... at least not enough.

But she could have told him anyway. She should have, especially when they transitioned from strangers to friends to would-be lovers. If Lincoln couldn't forgive her, she only had herself to blame.

Kali turned to the couch, eased onto the cushions, and took a long breath. Derek was back—somewhere out in the city. Lincoln was out there too, walking the streets or driving aimlessly. He had to return eventually, but the way he'd looked at her, it might never be the same.

She'd been selfish, unappreciative, cruel. Not only in not telling him, but in letting her preoccupation with Derek affect Lincoln—turning from his touch, avoiding his gaze. Not because she didn't want that touch, but out of fear if she looked at him too long, if his arms wrapped around her, the words would come tumbling out, and then anything could happen. He could understand, or he could leave. A gamble she couldn't bring herself to take.

Kali wrapped her arms around her as she paced the room, her cheeks moist. She'd screwed up. Again and again she'd screwed up. With Lincoln. With Derek. With Theo—with what was best for him.

She lived again the moment Derek stepped through the door, the way he looked at Theo, amazement in his eyes. The way her heart seemed to leap in her chest before it started racing. He was as handsome as he'd ever been, more even, than she remembered, than he'd been the last time she'd seen him. Then though, the strongest emotions had been hate, anger, all swirling with grief like a second layer of skin.

Time had mellowed those feelings. The anger was still there, but not the hate. Regret, questions, sadness, but no hate.

Derek looked hopeful as he'd taken in the sight of his son; amazed, yearning. He looked like a man who was ready to stay. And it's what he'd said, too, in the heated conversation that followed when Lincoln and Marvin left the room. He was here to stay. Here to be a family, in whatever way she'd allow.

When she pushed him, spoke through clenched teeth that if he was going to try to take Theo away from her he'd better think again, he'd practically blanched. Never, he'd sworn, his hands grasping her shoulders. He was here to be with Theo, to spend as much time with him as he could, but he'd never take him away. And as he said the words she'd felt foolish for her fear. For her anger. For not giving him a second chance. Most of all, for cheating her son. Because behind all he'd done wrong, Derek was a good man. She knew that. And if she'd let him, he would have been there for Christmases and birthdays, if possible, and any other time he could have gotten away. He would have been a father to his son. She'd stolen that from Theo. Guilt covered her like a shroud. She needed to do better. She would do better.

They'd stood face to face, Kali's chest heaving, Derek's calm, his expression hopeful and determined.

Her mother's funeral was the last time they'd stood this close. She hadn't invited him. She hadn't asked how he knew about the death, the service. He'd stood at the back of the church as the scant mourners made their way out. Two years and five months. That's how long it'd been since she'd lain eyes on him. He stood like a shadow off to the side as she greeted people, accepted hugs. When the last person departed, he stepped forward. She turned from him, like the coward she was, and rushed to the waiting car. At the cemetery as Kali stared at the grave, Theo in her arms, after everyone but Shelley and her husband had retreated, Derek finally approached. Limping. He walked slowly, hesitantly, as Shelley squeezed Kali's shoulder and stepped away.

"You're back," Kali had said, still staring at the grave.

His voice was rough, shaky. "For a few days. Bereavement leave."

She held back a scoff. Bereavement? For him? She'd wanted to scream, tell him how hard it'd been, all those nights alone as Theo cried, as she struggled to study and manage a job and a newborn. Marvin had helped out, mailing his pension cheque to her each month, and eventually she'd had to cash them, promising herself as soon as she had a regular income she'd pay back every cent. Her mother had been the one to make survival possible, taking Kali in when she could no longer pay rent. Watching Theo while Kali was at school or work.

And here Derek was, at last. For a few days. On bereavement leave. She didn't need him for a few days. A few days would do nothing.

"I'm sorry, Kali." He stepped closer and she retreated; her vision filled with the way he'd jumped into those crashing waves without a thought, abandoning her, and how he'd abandoned her day after day for the months following, succumbing to his own grief until, at last, a smile on his face, the first she'd seen in weeks, he'd told her he was leaving.

Derek's voice cracked. "Can I hold him?"

She shook her head, hating herself as she did so. Then she remembered her stay in the hospital, the flowers and chocolates and stuffed animals, but no Derek.

She'd told him not to come. Told him he wasn't wanted, but she'd hoped. Hoped he'd disregard her words, figure out a way to leave the army—not for a few days, but forever—hoped he'd come back to her. To them. He hadn't. Instead, he'd left her crying in that hospital bed, a newborn in her arms, terrified of what the future held.

"It would confuse him," she whispered. "He's confused enough, with Mom being gone."

Silence, and then Derek cleared his throat, a sound familiar and foreign all at once. "Can you turn? Just let me see him. I got a glimpse in the church, but—"

With resignation, she shifted Theo in her arms and Derek's face softened, his eyes widening. He leaned in and waved. "Hey, buddy. How's it going?"

Theo curled his head into Kali's shoulder and she held him tighter, wishing he'd say hello, smile, anything. It'd been five days since a sound had come out of him. No tears. No laughter. Everyone she talked to told her not to worry; it was just the shock. But she worried.

Kali looked behind her toward Shelley, waiting by the car, her husband's arm around her. She wanted that. A husband who stood beside her. She wanted to ask Derek to stay. She wanted to say she was sorry for the things she'd said, that they needed him, Theo needed him. She also wanted to scream in his face, throw things at him, let him know how much she hated him for promising the world, a happy future, then tearing it all away. She simply held Theo tighter. "I should go. People will be waiting."

"I'll drive you." Again, the tenderness in his voice—so familiar. So foreign. "I rented a—"

"No." Kali turned from the grave site. "No. And don't come, either."

"Kal—"

"Please." Her chest clenched. It'd be so easy; they were

just words. *Come back. I need help. I can't do this on my own.* But if he didn't? If she showed her vulnerability and he said no, it would be admitting she was weak. Admitting she couldn't do this. She wasn't weak. She *could* do this. She would. She had no choice. If he wanted to be back in their lives, he shouldn't need to be asked. He'd just be there.

"I can't take all the questions. Not today." She glanced toward Shelley then back to Derek, their gazes locking. *Fight,* she willed, as her face remained firm and determined, as she held her chin high. *Fight for me. Fight for your son. Do it now and I'll forgive you. Do it now and we can go back to our lives, the future you promised.*

He nodded. "If that's what you want."

"It is."

Derek stepped toward her. "So, you're okay then? You two have everything you need?"

Kali's throat tightened. Everything they need? They needed money. They needed help. Theo needed a father. She swallowed, her chin still high. "We get by."

Derek tilted his head, a question on his face. "You don't need to merely get by."

Kali's anger flared. "Well, what do you suppose we should do?"

Again, his face seemed a question he wasn't willing to ask. "You've gotten my letters?"

She nodded. Not that she'd read any but the first. It was stupid, immature, childish, to leave the envelopes unopened, tucked away in a drawer. But she didn't need words on a page. She needed a husband. A father.

"All right then." Derek took a deep breath. "Well, I guess I'll keep doing what I'm doing." He glanced to Shelley then back at Kali. "If you need anything else, anything more, you'll let me know."

Disgust bubbled up in Kali like bile. She needed money. She needed help. Not birthday and Christmas presents and cards. Not four letters in two years. She turned without a word, holding Theo tighter, and stepped toward the waiting car.

She'd never seen Derek again; never heard his voice. Not until he stepped into Lincoln's apartment less than an hour ago.

KALI JUMPED AS THE door opened. She stood, her hands clasped in front of her.

"You want to talk?" Lincoln crossed the room and sat on the opposite end of the couch. "So talk."

Kali pushed out an uncertain smile. Her throat tightened. She eased back onto the couch. "Where do I start?"

Lincoln's voice was rough. Tight. "Could be why you're married, not divorced. Or, I know. How about the fact that your husband didn't die when he jumped into those waves, and you just failed to mention that?"

KALI NODDED BUT DIDN'T speak. Her brow furrowed, her lips pursed. She stared at him. Not obstinately, not with annoyance, pride, dismissal, or anything else he'd seen of late. She just stared, looking small, young, uncertain.

Lincoln couldn't say why he was back. He hadn't been

gone fifteen minutes. He certainly didn't want to be here, sitting across from her, listening to her story.

No, he knew why he was back. He needed a chance to understand. He needed an explanation. Kali had made him what he hated—a cheater. He deserved to know why.

He eased back into the cushions, waiting for her to speak.

Four years separated. Could that really be cheating? That was one of the questions that brought him back. She'd lied. But whatever the reason, Derek certainly wasn't in her life anymore, and from the look on her face when she'd seen him, the tone in her voice as they'd argued in the living room, she didn't want him to be.

"I was about four months pregnant." Kali's voice was quiet, softer than he was used to. "We'd been married about six months. We didn't plan for a baby so soon. I still had over a year left of school. But it happened."

She rubbed a hand along her abdomen, as if remembering the feeling of a life inside her. Her gaze pointed toward the window rather than at Lincoln. "That afternoon we decided to take a drive out to Peggy's Cove. Jason's fiancée was from Ontario and she'd never seen it." Kali paused, her eyes glazing over. "It started out as such a nice spring day. The sun blazing, flowers in the earliest stages of bloom. I was over my morning sickness—mostly. So everything seemed brighter, more beautiful. We laughed on the drive up. Jason was hilarious. Always. And I hadn't been to Peggy's Cove since I was a teenager. Seeing it through Suzette's—that was Jason's fiancée—eyes made it even more special. You know?" Kali looked at him. Lincoln barely nodded before she looked away again.

"We were out on the rocks. I remember Jason holding

Suzette back, saying the warnings were no joke. Stay off the black rocks.

"Some tourists were there, letting their kids run around. Jason shook his head, gesturing to them. I can't remember exactly what he said, but something about how foolish it was. The waves aren't bad, Suzette had laughed, and minutes later a rogue one sprayed up."

Kali seemed to stare into another time and place. Her voice shook. "One of the kids, a boy, a twelve-year-old, got swept into the ocean. Derek ran to the edge of the rock and leaped. He didn't say anything. He didn't look back. He just ran. He knew. Anyone who lives here knows. You don't go into that ocean. Not there. We all rushed. Jason, Suzette, the parents, onlookers. And amazingly," Kali's breath halted, as if she was there, seeing it again, her husband under the water, then coming up, the boy in his arms.

"He caught the kid. They thrashed there in the waves as Derek held the child's head above water, treading, trying to swim back and getting pushed away over and over. Jason rushed forward as Suzette screamed, trying to hold him back. She clung so hard she fell forward when he escaped her grasp and I ... I don't even know. I can't remember. Did I scream? Did I cry? I remember helping Suzette up, her arms around me, her screams.

"Jason reached Derek and the boy and together, with one arm each around the child and one arm struggling through the waves, they got close enough. Other men clustered around by then, the boy's father, his uncle I think, some tourists, close enough to reach. They made sort of a chain, bracing themselves on the rocks, and they got the boy. Then they got Derek. Then another rogue wave and Jason was gone."

CHAPTER SEVEN

Kali's hands covered her face, her shoulders shook, tears streamed below her fingers.

Lincoln shifted over and wrapped his arm around her. Kali wiped her hands across her face. "We never saw Jason again. Not alive, anyway. Two days later divers finally ... it had to be a closed casket." She choked and gasped. "I'm sorry. I haven't let myself relive this in years. But it's like ... it's like ..."

"Yesterday?"

Kali looked to Lincoln and nodded. He reached past her and grabbed a tissue from the side table. She smiled weakly, wiped her eyes, blew her nose, then pressed her hand to her forehead. "Those men, they had to hold Derek back. It took three of them, pulling him farther and farther from those black rocks as he fought, yelled, tried to jump back into the ocean to save his brother."

Kali sat straighter and turned to Lincoln. "He was different after that. Everything was different. The news called him a hero. He hated that. I hated that. Jumping into that ocean, it wasn't heroic. It was reckless. Stupid." Kali's voice rode a wave of emotion so strong Lincoln could almost feel it, the fear and tragedy of that day, the anger and thankfulness and confusion. "He got his brother killed. He could have killed himself. And for what? Strangers. A foolhardy boy. Neglectful parents."

She shook her head. "I don't think Derek saw that side of it. I bet to this day he thinks it was the right thing to do. But it wasn't. It killed his brother, and that's what he couldn't get past. Couldn't forgive himself for. I can't even count the number of times in the weeks and months after I heard him muttering it should have been him. He should have been the one to die. Right in front of me, he'd say it, as his child got bigger and bigger inside me every day, he'd say that. Like we didn't matter. Like Theo didn't matter." Her body shook again, the tears resuming.

"Everyone said he was a hero. They wanted to do news pieces, but he wouldn't talk. He stayed in his room once he was out of the hospital, letting me do everything. He didn't go to work. Jason and he had just opened a small mechanic shop, but it stayed closed. He didn't make a meal or help out around the house. He barely showered or changed his clothes. Amazingly, he had nothing but some nasty scrapes and bruises from the rocks, a mild case of pneumonia. On the outside there was nothing wrong with him, but inside he wasn't Derek anymore. The man I'd married had died."

Kali took a breath. She straightened in her seat.

"Then one day I came back from classes and he was gone. I was hopeful. I thought it was a good sign: that he was ready to come back to life. And he was." Her mouth tightened. Her voice lost its sadness as anger took over. "He stepped in the door with a smile on his face and told me he'd enlisted in the army. He said it was the perfect plan. That he'd save other people's brothers, that he'd help protect us all. He said the income would be good too. But what was income when he'd be away for months at a time? When he might die?" Kali shook her head. Her jaw tensed and twitched. "With all of his basic training and land course and occupational training and whatever else, it'd be almost eight months before he'd even be posted anywhere. I was due in less than four. But that didn't seem to matter to him, the fact that he'd be deserting me for the last three months of my pregnancy. The fact that his training meant he'd miss the first four months of his child's life." Kali turned her gaze again, staring at the wall or the floor, Lincoln couldn't be sure.

"I told him no. But it was too late. He'd already done it, signed up, without talking to me." Kali shook her head again. "I lost it. Said if he was leaving, to never come back. We were done." Kali paused. "He left. And that was it."

Kali leaned back against the couch and returned her gaze to Lincoln. He took a breath. "You never saw him again? Until today?"

"He came to my mother's funeral. We talked for maybe five minutes. That's all."

"In over four years?"

"He sent cards and letters from time to time."

"The last card was sometime before we moved in with you. I didn't bother getting my mail forwarded. Almost everything is online these days. So who knows if he tried again?"

Lincoln's fists clenched. "And he didn't send money or ... He didn't want to see Theo?"

"Money? No." Kali's voice came out clipped. "Theo.

Yeah. At least at first. I only opened the first letter, about a month after Theo was born. He wanted to see him. I stopped opening them after that. I didn't read the Christmas or birthday cards either, just saved them while giving Theo the gifts they came with. In that first letter Derek said he could come home on leave for a visit, or fly us up to see him. I never replied. When he left I told him I never wanted to see him again, that he made his choice and I made mine. If he thought he was abandoning us, he shouldn't worry about it. We weren't his anymore. There was nothing to abandon."

Lincoln nodded, unsure what to say. It couldn't be this simple. He wanted to hate the man. But the way he'd looked at Theo earlier today, the way Marvin had wrapped his arms around him, it couldn't be this simple. Also, it seemed unlike Kali, to keep her son from his father. To hold onto hate so hard ... or whatever she was holding onto. Maybe it was fear? That if Derek got to know Theo, fell in love with Theo, he'd take him away?

"What did you say to Theo about the cards? The presents?"

"Nothing. I gave him the presents. The last ones came when he was three, but there wasn't much to explain. A present's a present. He didn't care where they came from. Like I said, I kept all the cards for when he was older, when he started asking questions."

"And Marvin, did he think ... he knew Derek was alive?"

"Oh yeah. Yeah. They might have kept in some contact. I'm not sure. I told Marvin I didn't want to hear about him. That I had to move on. But they must have had some contact ... the police knew where to call."

Lincoln nodded. "So, that's what brought him back?"

Kali shrugged. "I guess so."

"How long has he been back?"

"A few weeks." She leaned toward him. "I didn't know. I thought, maybe ... outside the hospital that day, and I thought I'd seen him from a distance once. But I didn't know."

Lincoln shifted so he faced her head on. "But you suspected. And you didn't tell me." He paused, the anger and betrayal creeping back like a cat ready to pounce. "Why didn't you tell me?"

Kali looked to her lap, silent.

"Do you love him?"

She raised her head and their gazes locked as several breaths passed. "I did."

"Do you?"

She inhaled and shook her head. But the movement was slight. Uncertain. Lincoln's chest constricted.

"Could you? Again?"

Silence surrounded them.

"I never stopped. That kind of love ... it never stops."

LINCOLN TURNED AWAY, his hands on his knees, his throat constricting as if a vice had wrapped around it.

Kali reached for his wrist, her voice desperate. "But not like that. Not like ... it's what I said before, about hate and love, the way they intermingle. He was my first love. He's Theo's father." Her eyes closed. "He says he's back. That he wants a chance to actually be Theo's father. I've had a lot of time to think about it over the years." Kali hesitated. "I think I was wrong. Proud and hurt and stubborn and wrong to keep Theo from him. And as soon as he said it, that he was back, that he was sorry, that he'd do whatever it took to be a father, the hate, the anger, it was still there, but the love was too. For my son's father. Nothing more.

"I don't want to be with him but I have to try to let Theo get to know him, to let go of enough anger for that. It doesn't change anything for me and you. It doesn't have to. But I have to try. I owe them both that."

Lincoln pulled his arm away. "It's getting late. Theo and Marvin must be hungry."

"Lincoln."

He stood.

"I'm trying to be honest. I can't say there isn't love somewhere inside me for Derek, but it doesn't mean ... anything. Not for you. Not for us. I told you I wanted to try, to see where things go between us, and I think they've been going well. Derek, he doesn't change that."

Lincoln turned from her. She was wrong. It changed everything. He turned back. "He's coming again tomorrow? To see Theo?"

Kali nodded.

Lincoln stepped toward his room. "I haven't been to the lot in a while. Seems like a good time to visit."

"Lincoln."

"You all need time. To figure things out."

"Lincoln," Kali stood and stepped toward him, "this is your place. You don't need to leave."

"Yeah." Lincoln sighed. "Yeah. I do."

CHAPTER EIGHT

Kali sat in the living room—alone again. She wanted to run: find some trail and let loose. Or dance: find some club and move till her feet ached and sweat streamed off her body. But she couldn't do either. She may never do either again. She tried to picture it, her feet hitting the trail, her body strong, confident for two steps, three, five, but eventually there'd be a bump, a rut, and she'd go tumbling. And on a dark, crowded dance floor? Within minutes she'd be a hazard—to herself or someone else.

Not that any of that mattered. Not now. She couldn't leave even if her vision were crystal clear. She had a boy in a room up the hall who was waiting for her—confused, probably. Scared, maybe. She stood.

Kali knocked on the door then eased it open before she'd gotten a response. Theo sat curled up in the bed, his eyes wide and trained on her. Marvin sat beside him, a storybook in hand and a pile on the sheets between them. Kali looked to Marvin—had he told Theo? Did her boy know the father he'd never asked about was here, back, waiting to see him?

Marvin shook his head lightly then stood. "I don't know

about you two but I'm getting mighty hungry. Think I saw a frozen pizza in the freezer. Should I put that in?"

Both Kali and Theo nodded—hers slight, his boisterous. Kali crossed the room and settled into the spot Marvin had left. "How's it going?"

Theo shrugged.

"Looks like Grampie read you tons of stories."

A nod.

"Did you two talk much?"

Theo tilted his head. "He said not to be nervous. Everything gonna be okay."

Kali smiled. "That's true. Everything will be okay."

"But why you yell at me? Who's that man?"

Kali let out a long breath. She held her shaking hands against her stomach, willing the motion to stop. "You know what a daddy is, right?"

Theo nodded. "Most kids have a daddy." He paused, staring at his hands then looked up. "Not me, though ... but," he smiled, "Lincoln's kind of mine, right? 'Cept I don't call him Daddy?"

Kali smiled, her whole body tense. "He's a little like a daddy, yes. But Lincoln's not your daddy. That man. He's—" Kali swallowed. *Like a band-aid. Just—* "That man's your daddy."

Theo shook his head. "No. Daddies live with you."

"Sometimes." Kali bit her lip. "But sometimes they don't."

Theo tilted his head. "Why I don't know him?"

"He's been away. He left before you were born."

Theo's forehead scrunched. "He don't like me?"

"No." Kali leaned forward, her hand on his arm. "Of course he likes you. He loves you. So much."

Silence.

"He don't like you?"

"It's not that he—"

"Then why he away?"

Kali tried to find the words, knowing none could fully explain the truth, knowing there was no one truth. "We saw life differently, your daddy and me. But he's back now and he wants to get to know you." Kali faltered. "Because he loves you so much and he can't handle missing any more of your life."

Theo gave a slight nod. "He live with us now?"

"No." The word burst out of Kali's mouth. She took a breath and continued. "No. But you'll see him sometimes. And maybe one day ... I don't know, but maybe one day you'll live with him some of the time."

Theo's brow furrowed again. "And you too?"

Kali shook her head. "We don't need to worry about that yet. All you need to know is that your Daddy is here now and wants to get to know you. He's going to come by tomorrow to meet you."

Theo pointed at Kali.

"I'll be here too. And Grampie, probably."

"And Lincoln?"

Kali offered another smile. "No, I don't think so."

Theo pressed his lips together, head down, then brought his gaze back to Kali. "Is Daddy nice?"

Was he? He used to be. The nicest man Kali had ever known. The sweetest and most thoughtful, the one who could make her laugh like no one ever had ... but that was before the accident. Kali had no idea who he was now. She pushed out a smile. "He's super nice. You're going to love him."

"You love him?"

Kali swallowed, Lincoln's face in her mind as she'd answered that question just minutes before. "Of course I love him. He gave me you."

BIRDS CHIRPED ABOVE AND below and all around Lincoln. He stretched and rolled over in the small bed. He stared at the ruts in the wood ceiling above him then turned to the alarm clock—not set to go off for another four minutes. Four minutes when nothing and no one wanted or relied on him. Four minutes he could pretend everything was fine.

Lincoln pushed himself up and looked around his cabin in the sky. It felt good—the silence and solitude of the last hours. Four people in his Brunswick Street apartment had been cramped. Still, if he could choose between the two, he knew which choice he'd make ... if he'd have a choice.

Lincoln hit the alarm the instant it started to buzz then leaned back against the pillows, closing his eyes and letting the birds' song wash over him. This was the life he'd wanted until Kali and Theo, the life he'd believed he'd needed. Instead, he was back in a job he'd been overqualified for even at age sixteen, working for the cousin he should have been working with. But getting to see Kali and Theo every day made it worth it, completely, until now.

Kali's words from the night before came back to Lincoln. *I never stopped. That kind of love, it never stops.* But she also said she didn't want to be with Derek, that as far as she was concerned nothing had changed between her and Lincoln. He believed she meant the words. But would she mean them after today, or next week, or a year from now?

If no part of her wanted to be with Derek, why was she still married to him?

Derek would probably want her back. How could he not? He'd claimed her, right in front of Lincoln. *My wife.* And if the choice came between being with her husband—her son's father—or some guy she'd met on a street corner ... Lincoln seemed like the unlikely choice.

KALI PACED THE LIVING room. She looked to the clock. 9:57. She'd already gone back on her part of the bargain, that if he left last night, Derek could meet Theo this morning at ten. She both hoped and feared that Derek would go back on his—to arrive at ten on the dot. But he'd never been late, not without a good excuse: a lost child, an elderly woman whose groceries had toppled over. Kali wouldn't accept those excuses anymore. Theo had to come first. And if Derek was late, it would tell Kali he wasn't ready to be a dad yet. Not that she'd keep Theo away from him entirely, but she'd be cautious. Incredibly cautious.

Her head turned to the sound of three strong raps on the door. She looked to the clock and watched the hand click to 10 o'clock exactly. He'd probably been standing outside the door, waiting. Despite her nerves, she couldn't hold back a slight smile. He'd done that when they were dating. Stand outside the door, waiting until the exact moment he'd said he'd arrive. She'd watch him from the window. Once, he was twelve minutes early to pick her up and leaned against the porch rail, waiting, until the precise moment he'd said he'd come.

Kali opened the door and a world of memories flooded over her. Under his arm was a bouquet of flowers and a wrapped gift she imagined could only be a basketball.

"For you." He smiled nervously, holding out the bouquet. "And ..."

"Theo's not here."

Derek's brow furrowed exactly the way Theo's did. His head tilted, and it was like seeing the man her son would become.

"You can see him. Today. But not now. Not yet. Like you said yesterday, we need to talk. And we'll need to set guidelines. We'll need to figure out how all of this is going to work."

Derek nodded and moved to step inside. Kali held out her hand. "Not here ... not," she turned her gaze and raised a hand to the side of her neck. "We'll go outside. To a cafe or some bench or—"

"How 'bout the park?"

Kali nodded. Could he hear her pounding heart? See the rush of blood that crashed through her?

Derek held out the flowers again. "This is Lincoln's place. I understand."

Kali took the flowers and stared at him as he took a step back onto the landing.

"I'll wait right here. You come out when you're ready."

She lifted her arm to close the door then let it drop. She

wanted to yell at him, curse him for leaving, for being so weak. She wanted to wrap her arms around him and shed tears of relief that he was alive, that he was back for Theo, that she wouldn't have to explain to a confused little boy that his daddy was living somewhere else, choosing not to know him.

Derek smiled gently when she returned, satchel slung over her shoulder, cane in hand. "You look good. No different really," he paused, "though more like a woman, less like a girl."

She hesitated before offering the slightest smile. "I could say the same to you. More like a man. You're broader."

That head tilt again. "You know what? I was wrong. You're even more beautiful."

Kali stepped to the landing then turned to close and lock the door. Derek's hand lighted on her upper arm. "Are you okay? I can't imagine ... all those years alone, and now this. Now—"

"I'm not alone. Not anymore." She stepped past him, one hand on the railing, the other holding tight to her cane. She didn't need it, not here, not usually. But today she felt extremely unsteady. "We don't need to talk about that. What we need to talk about is you. Why you're here. What that means. What your plans are."

CHAPTER NINE

When they reached the sidewalk, Kali turned to Derek. "There's a little park up the way, past the library. We could sit there."

Derek nodded and fell into step beside her. "Marvin said you have a tumour, but that it's not life-threatening, just vision threatening."

"Derek."

"I saw you at the hospital, saw you with him that day. I wanted to say something but couldn't. Not then. Shelley said you were with someone, or starting to be. She said I shouldn't step back into your life unless I knew for sure I was here to stay."

Kali stopped and turned. "Shelley knew you were here?"

"I went to the hospital. I knew that's where you last worked. She told me about your tests. She—"

"She knew?" Kali's voice raised. "For how long?"

"I made her promise not to tell you. She only knew for a couple of weeks. She was angry about that, really. But I begged her to let me tell you in my own time."

Kali kept walking. At a stop light she turned to him again.

"How long have you been back?"

"About three weeks."

"Why did you—?"

"I wanted to get things in order. A job. A place to live. I didn't want to show up and have you think ... I don't know. I wanted to be established. I wanted to show you I was serious."

The walk signal turned green and Kali tapped her way into the street. She kept her gaze ahead, knowing the potential perils of trying to do anything but. "You have a job? With the army?"

"I left the army. I'm working at a mechanic's up on Robie Street. I have an apartment on Chebucto. Less than a ten minute walk."

Kali frowned. They crossed the lawn and settled on a bench overlooking the park and the community garden greenhouse. She angled herself toward him. "So you're here to stay."

"I'm here to stay."

"I thought you couldn't just leave the army. I thought—"

"You can't usually. But my contract was up. I could sign on for another stint or I could leave. I decided to leave."

Kali took a deep breath. "Why?"

Derek smiled and gestured to his leg. "I'm not going to lie, part of it was this. There's a lot less you can do in the army when you're crippled."

"Derek."

"Anyway, that was part of it. But the biggest reason was you and Theo. I wanted a chance to make things right." Another smile. "I could have gotten a transfer to Dartmouth if I'd signed up again, but there'd always be a chance they'd transfer me somewhere else. I wanted to be in control of my destination. I wanted to make sure, no matter what, if you needed me I'd be there."

Kali looked at the bench between them, her head shaking. She returned Derek's gaze. "But why now? Why after all of these—"

"I broke, Kali. After Jason, I was devastated. Ashamed. Shattered. Depressed—though I didn't have that word for it at the time. All the things you held back from saying, all the things I could see in your eyes, I felt them too. It was rash and arrogant to jump into that water. I didn't think of you. I didn't think of our unborn child. I just jumped. I acted on my need to be the hero without a thought. Even worse, I did the same thing when I signed up for the Forces. I leapt—hoping for a way to save myself, to save all of us. But I didn't think about what that meant. I didn't think about the consequences. And as a result of those choices, I lost my brother—destroyed the amazing future he would have had—and then I lost you."

Kali's jaw clenched. Derek looked broken, contrite. Part of her wanted to reach forward, smooth her hand along his jaw like she had so many times before, but the anger still brimmed. He had abandoned them, even if she'd been the one to push him further away.

Would he have come home regularly if her anger hadn't flared, if she hadn't made the declarations she'd made? Would there have been phone calls and video chats in between? Would she have had support—both emotionally and financially? Would Theo know his father?

None of that mattered now. The past couldn't be erased, no matter how sorry he seemed. She'd been alone. She'd raised their son alone, and Derek hadn't sent her a penny.

Kali took a breath. "So, what changed?"

"Me, I guess. Over time. When I was recovering," he gestured to his leg again, "the army made me go to counselling. I should have had it long before, but I hid my scars well."

"It was an IED?" Kali glanced at his leg. "I received a letter from the army, but ..."

"Yeah." Derek nodded. "On a humanitarian aid mission. I was lucky. One of my friends ..." he shook his head. "It took a long time. I've been in counselling for the past two and a half years. Not as intensely of late as at the start, but it revealed a lot of things." He paused. "A lot."

Kali nodded then looked away. She rubbed a hand along her arm then turned back. "What things, Derek? What's so different? It's been over four years. Four years of near silence, four years of—"

"The silence was your choice, Kali."

Kali's jaw clenched. "You're the one who left."

"With every intent of coming back."

"What things?" Kali's voice rose. "What brought you back? If your contract hadn't been up would it have been another year, two, never?"

Derek's chest rose and fell, he offered the slightest smile. "You always said I had a hero complex."

Kali turned her gaze to the park.

"I had to figure out where that came from, why it was so important." He paused. "I think it had a lot to do with my mom, not being able to save her. Then my dad, too ... not being able to save him from himself. Not being enough for him."

Kali looked back to Derek, her jaw twitching. The words

weren't a surprise. She'd wondered these things herself. Wondered how much Marvin's breakdown, his giving up on life, had to do with Derek giving up on her, wondered if she'd been wrong to push him away, if his choices were more than selfish and arrogant and thoughtless. If she'd failed him by not seeing that something was deeply wrong, that he needed help.

"I honestly thought you'd be better without me, that if I stayed long enough you'd be destroyed, like everyone I loved was destroyed."

Kali's brow furrowed. "Your mom had nothing to do with you, and neither did Marvin. Saving him wasn't your responsibility."

"I know that now. But Jason, Jason was—"

"Jason made his own choice."

"Anyway," Derek folded his hands, "I thought if I provided for you, if I devoted myself to helping others, making up for all the people I couldn't help—"

"Derek."

"I know it was wrong thinking. But that's how I thought. If I did that, it'd be better for all of us. I'd see you when I could, but I wouldn't have to face ... my life."

There was so much to say. So many ways she could accuse, confront. Even the providing—she thought back to the rats, to the apartment before that one, with its mold and drafts. She'd said she didn't want him, didn't need anything from him, but when it got bad, when she wasn't sure where money for medicine was going to come from, or she spent her mornings checking traps. When she had to move herself and her son into an apartment with a stranger, she would have taken Derek's money—without a thought. He owed them that much.

"I'm truly sorry, Kali. We were supposed to be partners and when I signed up without talking to you I broke that partnership, that trust. I understand now why you reacted the way you did."

Kali pressed her lips together then sighed. "I was wrong, too. Keeping you from Theo. Making it all or nothing."

"I should have fought for you though, for all of us. I shouldn't have let you push me away with my tail between my legs. He's my son. You're my wife."

She shook her head. "Was your wife. I only stayed ... well, for Marvin. I needed to be family, but now that you're back."

He put a hand on her arm. "We'll talk about that later. The point is I should have fought. I wish I'd ... even when your Mom died, I could see how distraught you were ... but you didn't want me and I believed I'd only bring you down. I was in a bad spot, probably worse than before. It was just a few months after the accident. It's a complicated feeling, not being whole."

"What do you mean?"

Derek gave her a questioning look then lifted his pant leg. Kali gasped.

CHAPTER TEN

"You're an amputee?" Kali stared at the prosthetic where Derek's leg should be.

"I thought you said you got a letter?"

"I did ... it didn't go into detail. It said you were injured but not ..." Kali shook her head, guilt flowing over her. "I guess they expected we would be in contact once you returned to the country. It said you were alive. It said where you'd be recovering and how to contact you and your commanding officer."

The unspoken words hung between them. She never contacted. She never tried. Even when he came that day to the graveyard, she never asked. She knew he was alive, was thankful he was alive, but beyond that, she hadn't allowed herself to care.

Tears brimmed as she blinked them away. "I'm sorry. I had no idea."

Derek's voice was soft. "It's in the past. I made my choices. You made yours."

Kali stared at him, trying to imagine what it would have been like: that first morning waking up and realizing his leg was gone, the days after, adjusting physically and mentally to the loss. The pain. She'd nursed amputees before. Knew about the phantom pain, phantom itches. The loss of a limb too often equating to the loss of one's self. "I'm so sorry."

"It could have been worse. And like I said, it's in the past."

Kali let out a rough laugh. "Every thing's in the past." She gestured between them. "That doesn't mean it doesn't matter. That doesn't erase it."

That slight smile again, the one that used to make her melt. "But maybe we could erase it. Try to start fresh."

Kali pulled her gaze away. "How often are you wanting to see Theo?"

"As often as you'll let me. I don't want to be a weekend or holiday father. I want to be in his life. A consistent part of his life. But I understand that will take time."

Kali glanced back at him before returning her gaze to the park. "It will. And at first you can only see him with me there. Maybe for a while."

"That makes sense."

"You're a stranger."

"I know." Derek paused long enough that Kali turned to him. "Did you tell him about me? Does he know?"

"Last night."

"And before?"

"He never asked, so I never told."

"Never—?"

"He's only been speaking for a couple of months."

Derek's face paled. "Is he? Is something?"

"He's brilliant. He just ... when Mom died it was very traumatic for him. She died while holding him. He was trapped in her arms for hours. It was right around the time he started to speak. He stopped that day. The first time he spoke again, was at daycare shortly after, and there was an explosion."

"Oh, God. Kali."

"It's okay. Or, better." She smiled. "He's doing really well now. Lincoln actually—"

"Lincoln. The man you live with?"

"Yes. He was the first person Theo spoke to, and the second."

"And you two are—?"

"Figuring things out." Kali stood. "You can see Theo today. I'll assess how that goes, and then we can figure out when next, what next."

Derek stood. "Okay."

"I was thinking the playground on the Common. It's his favourite, but ..." She glanced to his leg.

"The playground is great."

Kali nodded, her whole body on edge, her hands tensed. She flipped out her cane and turned toward Mrs. Martin's. "All right, then. You ready to meet your son?"

DEREK STOOD ON THE sidewalk as Kali knocked on Mrs. Martin's door. Rather than rush out toward her like he usually would, Theo stood behind Mrs. Martin, his head peeking out around her legs.

"Hi, sweetie."

Theo glanced to Kali, his brow furrowed.

"Did he—? How was—?" Kali looked to Mrs. Martin.

"He was pretty quiet today. Contemplative." Mrs. Martin reached behind herself to rub her hand on Theo's head. It's not every day a young man gets to meet his father for the first time."

Kali smiled and reached a hand out to Theo. "You ready?"

His mouth scrunched to the side, his gaze past Kali as he took her hand.

"Thanks so much." Kali turned from Mrs. Martin to see Derek, an equally tentative smile on his face.

Theo tugged on Kali's hand. "Where's Grampie?"

"Oh," Kali smiled, "he's on his walk."

Theo looked to the ground, his little legs trailing behind as Kali walked toward Derek.

"This is your father. Your Daddy."

Theo kept his head down. Derek crouched with obvious effort. "Hey, buddy. It's great to finally meet you."

No response.

"I've wanted to meet you since the first day I found out your Mommy was pregnant."

Silence.

"I'm sorry I didn't come sooner. I wish I could have."

Kali let go of Theo's hand and rubbed her palm against the back of his neck.

"Wouldn't you like to say hello?"

Theo shook his head, gaze still down.

"Maybe you'd like to see this?" Derek lifted his pant leg, revealing the prosthesis attached below his knee.

Theo's eyes widened and he looked from the prosthetic to Kali and back to the leg again. "Where'd it go?"

"I had an accident."

Theo's eyes stayed wide. He looked to Derek's face. "It hurt?"

"It did. A lot. It doesn't hurt so much anymore."

Theo's lips pressed tight together.

"Do you want to touch it?"

Theo looked to Kali, uncertainty swimming in his eyes.

"You can if you want to."

He reached out, barely grazing the prosthetic, then pulled his hand back. "This why you no here? Not like a real daddy?"

Derek's brow furrowed. "It's part of the reason. Part of why it took me so long to come back. Also part of why I did come back."

Derek stood. "Your mom suggested we go to the park. Would you like that?"

Theo gave a tentative nod, then reached for Kali's hand. They walked in silence the first few minutes. When they stopped to wait for a crossing light, Derek spoke. "Did you know Grampie is my daddy?"

Theo tugged on Kali's hand and looked up at her.

"That's right."

"Yep. He's my daddy, and I'm yours. Kind of neat, right?"

Another tug. "Where's your daddy?"

"Oh," Kali smiled, "I never met my daddy. Not that I remember, anyway. I wasn't lucky like you."

Theo gave a slight nod and looked to Derek as the light turned. They continued in silence.

THE PARK WAS NEAR empty. Surprising for a Sunday afternoon. Only one other family with two kids played on the climbers. One other family ... Not that Kali, Derek, and Theo were a family. Not really. Not anymore. Kali swallowed. "I'm going to sit over here," she said to Theo. "A little tired today. I bet your daddy will push you on a swing or play on the slide with you though."

"Definitely," said Derek, his voice nervously eager.

Theo stood a moment, with furrowed brow. He walked to the swing and climbed on. Within minutes he was laughing, that out-loud laugh that still made Kali's flesh tingle. She couldn't see Derek's face, but Theo's was smiling. Happy. At ease. Derek must have suggested something, because Theo nodded and let the swing slow to a stop. Within moments, the two were off running to the slide.

Almost an hour later, after a couple of water breaks, Kali stood and waved them over. "It's time to go."

Theo shook his head vehemently.

"Yes. Time for lunch."

He stomped.

"Listen to your mother."

Kali glanced to Derek, not liking the intrusion, then back to Theo. "Take my hand."

Her hand wrapped around Theo's as she looked to Derek. "I should get your number so we can arrange another time."

"I can come by tomorrow after work. Take you two to dinner."

A wave of tension and uncertainty flowed through Kali. "How about I take your number. We don't want to rush things."

"Yeah. Okay. Of course. I'll walk you home, then."

"No need." Kali stiffened. She didn't want Lincoln seeing the three of them together. It was silly. Stupid. But ... she knew they'd look like a family. She felt it herself, to a degree. It was comfortable, standing here with Derek, seeing her son laugh and play with him, even with all the years passed, all the anger and hurt, the three of them together felt like family.

"Okay." Derek nodded, obviously hurt. "Hand me your

phone then. I'll put my number in."

Kali did. The number saved, Derek crouched down to Theo. "It was great playing with you today. I had so much fun."

Theo smiled.

"Maybe we can do it again sometime?"

A nod.

"Great." Derek rubbed his hand on Theo's shoulder then stood. "Thanks, Kal. Really. I know this couldn't have been easy for you."

Kali's jaw twitched. "It's not about me."

"I know. Still." His hand was on her shoulder now, the first time they'd touched in years, and all the previous touches seemed to flood her. "Thank you."

She nodded and stepped out of his reach. "I'll call you. Soon."

She turned, holding onto Theo with one hand, the cane with the other. It felt like cheating, the way her mind travelled so easily back to her life with Derek, the way, despite it all, she wanted to smile at him, erase the past. But the past couldn't be erased, and she had a future now ... or at least the chance of one, with a man who'd shown up time and again. A man who deserved her trust, her love. She was scared to give it, but she wanted to.

After her lies, Kali only hoped Lincoln would still want her. She walked faster, the cane tap, tapping in front of her with an efficiency she'd only gained in the past few weeks. If Lincoln was home, she wanted to be there with him, let him know she meant the words she'd said, that Derek being back didn't change anything—not between them. She wanted to step into his arms, apologize for her distance the past weeks, know he wasn't about to walk away.

CHAPTER ELEVEN

Lincoln stood outside the Brunswick Street apartment. He'd contemplated going back to the lot. It would have made sense. He didn't work tomorrow, which would mean he'd have all day to stop putting off the dream that had meant so much to him just months ago and work on the tree house. But he'd come back to the apartment. This was home. Because of Kali. If they'd never met, he'd be living in the tree house full time by now. He was sure of that. He would have done the necessary work to make it ready for winter. He wouldn't be working construction—not for anyone else at least. Life would be simple. And lonely.

At least he probably would have still had Romper. Without Kali, the dog was all he'd have. Lincoln started up the steps, hoping Kali and Theo would be there and hoping they wouldn't, hoping, most of all, that Derek wouldn't. His phone rang. He pulled it out and glanced at the unknown number. Probably a telemarketer. He debated cancelling the call, then pressed talk. "Hello."

"Lincoln."

Lincoln's body stiffened, his breath held.

"Lincoln, you there?"

He'd only given this number to four people. Kali, his mother, Rachel, and Andrew. Any of the final three could have passed it on.

"Lincoln, I know I'm probably the last person you expected to hear from today. Maybe the last person you'd want to hear from ever, but I need to talk to you."

Lincoln sucked in the cool fall air. He held the phone away, stared at it, then brought it back to his ear.

" ... and I know I don't deserve it, but just thirty minutes of your time. Twenty, even. A coffee shop. A public place." A pause, and Lincoln could almost see the uncertain grin his brother so rarely wore. "That way it'll be less likely you'll slug me."

"Not necessarily."

A relieved and rushed laugh. "So, you are there."

"I'm here."

"Will you meet me?"

"Why would I do that?"

"Like I said, I want to talk to you. I need to talk to you."

"So talk."

A sigh. "Not over the phone, okay? Twenty minutes. That's all."

Lincoln stared at his building's door. It'd be something else to think about. Something else to be angry about. If he could take that anger out on Joseph, maybe he'd have less for Kali. Admittedly, her lie wasn't as bad as Joseph's.

"Twenty minutes."

"Okay. Great. Good. The Brooklyn Warehouse? Tonight? Eight o'clock?"

"You're assuming I don't have plans?"

"Or the night after, or the next, but soon."

Lincoln sighed. It was an odd feeling, having Joseph ask him for something. Their whole life, it was always the other way around. "Tonight at eight."

LINCOLN STARED BACK up at the apartment. He'd almost wished Joseph had suggested they meet immediately. It would have been easier—rip off one band-aid and leave the other in tact a while longer.

He made his way up the steps and to his unit door. As he stepped into the living room, Kali stood from her seat on the couch. "Hi."

"Hello." Lincoln eased the door closed behind him, his whole body wary. He glanced around the room then looked to the shoe rack. At least Derek didn't seem to be here. One fear alleviated.

"Did you have a good time at the tree house?"

"It was peaceful."

"Peaceful." Kali smiled. "That's good."

Theo ran into the room and jumped in front of Lincoln. He couldn't help but smile. "Hey, buddy. How's it going?"

Theo motioned Lincoln down to his level and whispered. "I met my Daddy."

Lincoln glanced to Kali then back to Theo. "Oh yeah?"

"Yes."

"What's he like?"

"Mmm." Theo put a finger to his chin then spread his arms. "He's big. Like a monster. Or like a wrestler."

"Oh, wow. That's not scary, is it?"

"Mmm." Theo tilted his head. "He's funny. And nice. He tells jokes."

"That's good."

"He says he loves me. And he's my daddy now and always."

Lincoln glanced to Kali. "That's great. So you had fun. And you liked him?"

Theo nodded.

Lincoln stood and brought his gaze back to Kali. "You two figured everything out, then?"

She shook her head, arms wrapped around her middle. "Hardly. But we're working on it. He saw Theo today. We don't have another time set up yet."

Lincoln's brows raised. "No?"

"He wanted to, but I want to take things slow."

Lincoln nodded.

"Hungry?" Kali gestured to the kitchen. "I was thinking tuna melts."

"If you don't mind."

"Not at all."

Kali walked to the kitchen while Lincoln stayed behind. Usually he'd follow, help, make a salad, but he didn't know how to be around her. How to be normal. He'd started to think of her as his girlfriend. Maybe, as his future wife. But she was already married and she'd yet to mention the word divorce. He sank into the couch and propped a leg up on his knee.

He turned to Theo. "Tell me more about your day."

As Theo half told, half acted the day's events, the sounds of Kali's movements travelled through the room. When Theo's tale seemed over, Lincoln stood, suggested the boy go play in his room, and crossed to the kitchen. Kali, unaware of his presence, opened a can of tuna, drained it, and scooped it into a bowl. She turned to the fridge and jumped, a hand flying to her cheek.

"You're not supposed to sneak up on me."

Lincoln leaned against the wall. "Sorry."

Kali's smile twitched into focus. "It's okay." She stepped toward him. "How are you doing? With all of this?"

Lincoln shrugged as she stepped closer.

"I'm sorry."

He exhaled. "For what, exactly?"

Her shoulders rose then fell. "For not being honest about Derek, for keeping you in the dark. For keeping you at a distance all these weeks. I was nervous and scared and," another step and her hands were at his side, her long fingers caressing him, "I'm really sorry."

Lincoln stiffened. It was hard to remember the last time she'd touched him like this, the night before her doctor's appointment?

She pulled him so their torsos were touching. "I was scared and only thinking of the bad that could come if Derek was back. But there's good too."

Lincoln swallowed. "Good?"

"Theo will get to know his father. And you and me, we don't have this secret between us." Her hand reached behind his head as she rose on tiptoe and attempted to guide his face toward hers.

Lincoln stepped out of her grasp. "I can't. You're married, Kali."

She stepped away. "Only legally. And I was before too, so—"

"Only legally? What other kind of marriage is there?"

"A real marriage. Living together. Loving each other.

Actually—"

"You said you loved him."

"Yes," Kali opened the fridge and pulled out the mayonnaise, "as Theo's father. As a person I have a history with, but not ... not like ..." Her voice trailed off.

"Like what?"

She turned to the counter. "Not like a husband. Not like a person I'm in a relationship with."

"Does he know that?"

"We've barely seen each other in four years."

"Yes, but does he hope? Does he want—"

"I don't know." She turned, her voice rising, then settling again. "It doesn't matter what he wants."

"Today it doesn't."

"What?"

"He's back for good, right?"

Kali let out a little puff of air. "He says so."

"And you're not going to send Theo off with him alone."

"Not yet. Not until—"

"Until you trust him. Until you've spent enough time with him that you believe he's here to stay. You fell in love with him once, who's to say you won't again?"

"I'm to say."

"Why? How?"

"Because I'm here. With you."

"You're here because you needed a place to stay. And you're not *with* me, not in the way you're implying. Not in the way ..."

"But I can be."

"Suddenly? Just like that? Why not before, then? How does Derek being here change things?"

Kali's face crumpled. "I'm not ready to lose you."

Lincoln shook his head. "What does that mean? Not ready? So when you're ready, what, is it goodbye Lincoln, hello Derek?"

"No." She stepped toward him again.

"What then?" Lincoln tried to hold back his anger, his tone. Hurt filtered in.

"I don't know." Kali backed up to the counter and leaned against it. "I want us. Not Derek. That's over."

"You say that now."

"I'll say it a year from now. Even if you and I don't work out, Derek and I are over."

"He's your son's father. He's your husband."

Kali threw up her hands, her voice rising again. "Do you want me to get a divorce? Is that it? Fine. Now that Derek's back, now that someone else is there to sign for Marvin if need be, I'll file for divorce."

Lincoln stared. Is that what he wanted? Of course it was. But not to prove something. Not to stop a fight. "That's your choice. Don't do it on my account."

She stared back, her eyes moistening. "I don't want to lose you."

Lincoln stepped closer. "What if I wasn't here?"

Kali's brow furrowed. "What do you mean?"

"What if we'd never met, or even if after the first time you moved out that was it, if we hadn't seen each other in months and Derek came back. Do you think there's any chance you two would end up together?"

She opened her mouth, closed it, then opened it again.

"That's my answer." Lincoln turned.

"It's not." Kali's arm caught his, urging him back to her.

"How am I supposed to know what I'd say then? Think or feel then?"

"Are you still attracted to him? Do you still—"

"I want to keep seeing where things go with you."

"But you don't know if you want to be with me yet."

"I don't want to be with him."

"Yet."

"Lincoln." She shook her head. "I'm giving you all I can."

Lincoln's throat clenched. "Just answer as truthfully as you can. If I wasn't here, if you never even knew I existed, is there any chance you would get back together with Derek, try to make it work, be a family?"

Kali stayed silent, her eyes giving Lincoln all the answer he needed.

"Well, I guess that's that then."

"No. It's not. I don't know how I'd feel then, but I know how I feel now."

Lincoln backed out of the kitchen. "I changed my mind. I'm going out for dinner."

"But—"

"Then I'm meeting my brother ... I'm not sure how long I'll be."

"Your brother?" Kali moved toward him. "Really?"

"I may be late. I may just go to the lot after all."

"Lincoln." Kali took another step toward him. "I want you."

"For now." Lincoln's head shook. "For now you do."

Kali gestured to the kitchen. "Just stay. Eat with us. Just—"

Lincoln looked at, then past Kali. "I need time to think."

She stared at him. "Okay." Her throat convulsed. "I'll be here."

CHAPTER TWELVE

Lincoln raked his fingers through his hair as he stepped out into cool evening air. Still almost two hours before his meeting with Joseph. His stomach growled, but the idea of sitting somewhere to eat felt ludicrous. He walked aimlessly, pacing away the minutes until what, he didn't know. Not until the meeting with Joseph. He didn't want that to come. He could cancel, but that would mean calling him. He could not show, but that didn't seem right either—not that he cared about offending Joseph or leaving him sitting in the restaurant alone—that image was appealing. But he knew his brother. If Lincoln didn't show up tonight, tomorrow Joseph would be on his doorstep, demanding to be heard.

When Joseph wanted something, anything, he didn't back down until he got it.

Approaching the Common, Lincoln turned and made his way toward the downtown core instead. Running into Marvin, hearing his perspective on the prodigal son and husband returned, wasn't what he needed.

By the old library on Spring Garden Road, Lincoln sat on a bench, watching the pigeons lay their waste on the statue of

Winston Churchill. People passed, laughing, talking, hand in hand. Kids ran in front of their parents as mothers and fathers called out after them. A man, looking in an even sorrier state than Marvin did before moving in with them, shuffled along the street, a large blue bag stuffed to capacity slung over his shoulder.

"You're Lincoln, right?"

Lincoln shifted toward the deep voice and raised his gaze to the mass of man standing before him.

"And you're Derek."

The man gestured beside Lincoln. "Mind if I sit?"

Lincoln nodded his response. Derek sat on the opposite end of the bench, turned toward Lincoln.

"You're Kali's roommate? Or, rather, she's yours? It's your place, right?" He offered a smile.

"It's our place."

"That's really kind of you, the way you helped her out like that. My dad was telling me."

Lincoln narrowed his gaze.

"I appreciate it. I wanted you to know that."

"I didn't do it for you. I thought you were dead."

"Dead?" Derek leaned back, his face moving from shock to disappointment. "Did she tell you that?"

"She told me about the accident at Peggy's Cove. About your brother. I assumed and she didn't correct."

"Oh man, so yesterday—"

"Was a shock."

Derek let out a whoosh of air. "I can imagine that." He thumped his large hands on his thigh. "My wife knows how to keep secrets, that's for sure."

Lincoln assessed the man beside him. He seemed a casual

mix of confidence and uncertainty. But that comment, the way 'my wife,' rolled so easily off his tongue, Lincoln couldn't tell if it was calculated or natural. "It's odd, don't you think, that she's still your wife when you haven't seen each other in four years."

"We've seen each other."

Lincoln raised an eyebrow.

"Once, four years ago. After her mother died."

"For a few minutes?"

"Well, yeah."

"I'd hardly call that a reunion."

Derek's look of confidence gave way to uncertainty, and something else. "True. But we are still married, and that's part of what kept me going. If she was really done with me, if she'd moved on, found some other man to start a life with, I would have received divorce papers, don't you think?"

Lincoln's chest tightened. "You'd think, yes."

"But they never came."

"Because of Marvin."

"Hmm," Derek looked past Lincoln to the statue before them, "she say that?"

"She did."

Derek nodded. "Seems a weak reason to stay married to someone though. If that was the only reason."

"And you were never interested in divorcing her?"

"Never."

Lincoln started to stand but Derek held out his hand, motioning for him to sit. Lincoln stood, but didn't walk away.

"She said you two were figuring things out. I know you sleep in separate rooms."

"We do."

"So, what does that mean?"

"You'll have to ask Kali that."

Derek barely nodded. "She's my wife. We have a son together."

A son you abandoned, Lincoln wanted to say.

"I was going through a really difficult time. My brother ... it was my fault. And then losing my leg."

"Losing—"

Derek held up his pant leg. Lincoln exhaled.

"None of it's an excuse, but ... I mean if you two are together, if you're serious and pursuing a future ... I won't like it, but I'll respect it. I'm not going to step away from Theo's life, but ... are you two serious? Is it an established relationship? Is this—?" Derek's words stopped mid-question, as he waited for a response.

Yes. The words could come out easily. *Yes, it's serious. Yes, we're together. Yes, she's going to be my wife and not yours*. But it'd be a lie. He was serious. But Kali? Lincoln spoke through gritted teeth. "I don't think she'd say it was."

A smile of relief spread across Derek's large face, making the man seem soft, young. "Great. Wonderful. That's really great." He laughed. "So I only have four years of anger to contend with then."

The words squeezed out of Lincoln's throat. "Only, yeah."

"I love her. I've loved her since the first moment I saw her." He looked away, the smile on his face tender and thoughtful. "She was dancing salsa, not with a partner, just on her own. And her movements were like liquid. I'd never seen a woman so soft and so solid at the same time." He let out a little laugh. "Right then and there I knew she was the one for me, that she'd ruin me for all others. I told myself I was going to marry her." Another laugh as he rubbed his hands together.

"It wasn't easy. She resisted at first, but," his smile grew—so genuine, Lincoln almost started to like the guy, "it's like we were made for each other. We fit, you know? It didn't take her too long to see that."

"And yet you left."

Derek's face sobered. "As I said, I was in a bad place. And then I was scared—she can be harsh, cruel, and she said she didn't want me. I was weak after Jason died, and I kept getting weaker. I didn't have it in me to fight for us. I do now."

Lincoln stood a moment longer, wrestling with everything roiling inside him. Why was he standing here, listening to this? Why had he said he and Kali weren't serious. He was serious. He was pretty sure he loved her ... before he'd found out about Derek, about the lies, he would have said he was sure. Wouldn't he?

But the woman he'd found himself falling in love with wasn't married. And it wasn't his place to tell Derek the status of their relationship. If Kali told Derek there was no hope, no reason to fight, that would be her choice.

And if she didn't ...

Did Lincoln have it in him to contend with her husband, the father of her child? The husband she'd never divorced. Would it even be right to try? Lincoln shifted. "Well, I need to get going."

"Yeah, of course." Derek stood and offered his hand. "It was nice meeting you, Lincoln. I'm sure I'll see you around." He held Lincoln's grasp. "I know it's probably awkward for you, and a shock. Here you thought you were helping out this single mom, while all along she's had a husband, all the financial support she would have needed, if she hadn't been so," Derek hesitated, "proud, I guess."

Lincoln pulled his hand away. "Support?"

Derek's brow furrowed. "The money." He shook his head. "She never told you about it? Well, I guess she wouldn't if she let you think I was dead. I've put everything I didn't spend or need into our joint account for her. I've lived simply to do so. Not that I need much, anyway." Another smile. So guileless. Who was this guy? "There's over eighty thousand dollars in it now. She never touched it. That was actually part of what allowed me to stay away, to not step up and get my life back. I figured she was fine without me. Better than fine. If she hadn't been, you'd think with a child she would have used what she needed, right?"

Lincoln stepped back, the words making him sick. Kali, who seemed so desperate. Kali, who'd lived in that derelict apartment, who'd complained of rats and mold and claimed she'd do whatever she had to for her son. "Right." Lincoln hesitated. "You'd think she'd use it."

"But not Kali." Derek sighed. "I mean I don't know the details, I'm guessing she tells Dad the bare minimum, but I know she had to move out of her old place suddenly—that the building was being torn down or something?"

Lincoln nodded.

"And so Dad said that's why she moved in with you. But she could have had her own place. A nice place. And then she moved back in with you again after she got her own apartment, after she had to stop work because of the—?" Derek gestured to his head.

Lincoln nodded again.

"But she could have dipped into the account to cover the rent. To be honest, that's what made me really wonder about the two of you, if it wasn't just a friendly roommate situation."

"Because she didn't need a roommate."

"Exactly. And I hate to think of her using you because she was too proud to rely on money from me." Derek shook his head again. "I thought maybe she just wanted to be close to you. But that's Kali. Stubborn and prideful. Resistant to taking help from anyone." Derek's head tilted, the way Theo's so often did. It made Lincoln want to step away. "But she took it from you, didn't she?"

"Not without resistance." Lincoln pulled out his phone, his stomach twisting, bile rising in his throat. 6:57. Another hour before he needed to meet Joseph. "I really have to go."

"Sure. Yeah. Absolutely." Derek held up a hand in parting. "Like I said, See you around."

"See you."

CHAPTER THIRTEEN

Lincoln turned from Derek and headed to the harbour without looking back. The wind whipped at his shirt and ruffled his hair; he only walked faster. Once at the edge of the boardwalk, looking out into the rocking water, he stopped.

Kali had money. Kali had over eighty thousand dollars just sitting in an account. Lincoln had put his own dreams on hold because he believed she truly needed someone to help her, believed she'd be destitute. He had taken a job he didn't want to ensure he had enough to provide for her.

He knew about not wanting to touch family money ... he *needed* that job about as much as Kali needed his help. But her situation was different. If he'd had a child relying on him and the only way to keep that child safe and fed was to take what he felt was Joseph's money, he would have taken it.

But it wasn't the only way. Kali had him. Stupid, him. Lincoln relived her resistance, the way she'd acted like it was so hard for her to accept his generosity, how she'd skulked around the apartment those first days, as if he was the one putting her out, while all along she had another option.

She'd promised to pay him back for everything, and he'd believed she was genuine, but she'd hardly contributed to more than the cost of food this time around and hadn't fully paid him back for her half of the rent the first time she'd lived with him.

Not that he'd wanted the money. When she tried to give him small amounts here and there, he'd told her to wait till she was in a better financial situation. Never once had she said her financial situation was just fine.

Lincoln's shoulders rose and fell with deep breaths. Couples walked by and children laughed as he stood at the edge of the water, feeling the fool. Feeling duped.

Lies. All lies.

Lincoln stared across the water at what locals called the dark side but had been his home for years—a happy place, until his father's diagnosis destroyed all that. He'd been duped then, thinking the idyllic life he'd lived would last forever. He was duped by Lucy, by Joseph, now by Kali. Everyone he'd loved the most had lied to him. Even his father, telling him he'd always be there. Telling him things would work out fine.

Lincoln ran his hands through his hair and tried to calm his breathing. Was Joseph somewhere across that water right now, sitting in some lavish house he and Lucy only used on visits home from Montreal. Or perhaps they were at a restaurant, discussing whatever Joseph so desperately needed to talk to Lincoln about.

It'd be something regarding the business, most likely. Some papers Lincoln needed to sign, some portion of his shares Joseph wanted him to give up or move around. Joseph would know if he sent the papers by courier Lincoln would likely ignore them or send them back unopened.

A woman's laughter tinkled behind him—so joyous. Lincoln scanned the boardwalk. Where was a rock when you needed it? He wanted to hurl something into the black water, watch it break the surface and sink to the depths never to be seen again. But there was nothing to hurl. He could walk up the boardwalk. Four minutes away there'd be tons of rocks as big as a man's head ... and if he started hurling them, someone would probably call the cops.

Lincoln pulled out his phone again. 7:14. Plenty of time. He walked in the direction of The Brooklyn Warehouse. It was one of the things Joseph had taught him. When you want the upper hand in a meeting, be there first. It gives you a position of authority. You choose where you sit. You order the drinks, setting the mood. Joseph would be early tonight, he was sure of it, but Lincoln would be earlier.

KALI STARED AT THE CLOCK. She rubbed her arm, wanting and not wanting the minute hand to tick by. The creak of the apartment door startled her to a stand, and she turned toward the living room. Could she face him? She had to.

"Sweetness?"

Kali sighed and made her way to the entry. "Oh, hey, Marvin."

"Hiya, Sweetness." Marvin patted Kali's shoulder. "You have a nice day?"

"It was okay."

"Derek met the boy."

"He did."

"You'll have a nicer night."

Kali perched on the edge of the couch. "Why's that?"

"I'm moving out."

She stood. "What? You've been doing so well. Hasn't it been nice, knowing where you're sleeping each night. Having a—"

Marvin raised his hand, grinning. "It has been nice. Very nice. So nice I want my own room, not to be pushing you or Lincoln out of yours."

Kali's brow furrowed. "You got a—"

"Moving in with my boy."

"Oh," Kali sank back onto the arm of the couch, "that's good. Great. He has room?"

"He has three rooms." Marvin walked throughout the apartment, picking up his few belongings as Kali followed behind him. "Is the boy asleep?"

Kali nodded.

"Tip toe?"

Another nod. Kali waited in the hall until Marvin returned, his bag slung across his back. He patted Kali's shoulder again. "Thank you for taking such good care of me, Sweetness."

She smiled, relieved, exhausted, hesitant. Marvin needed stability if he was going to do well. If Derek took off again ...

"We'll see each other lots."

"Of course." Kali followed Marvin back to the main door. "Are you sure you want to leave? You don't have to."

"It's time to go." Marvin pushed open the door and waved. "I'll come say goodbye to the boy tomorrow."

"Yeah. Sure." Kali settled into the couch, the apartment seeming like a foreign place. She couldn't see the clock from here, which was probably a good thing. Just like it was good, technically, having Marvin gone.

The apartment had been crowded, and imposing on Lincoln the way they were, it wasn't right. Plus, Marvin being gone would give her and Lincoln time and space to figure things out.

Had Derek considered that when he invited Marvin to live with him? Or was he just thinking about his dad, about finally being there for him the way he hadn't been these past years?

Maybe she'd read too far into his 'fresh start' comment. Maybe he only meant to get along, to raise Theo together, while separate. That could work. That could be very good. And if she could make Lincoln believe that, maybe her breath would come easier.

CHAPTER FOURTEEN

Just like always, The Brooklyn Warehouse was so dark it'd be hard to read a menu. Lincoln had joked about it with Joseph the first time they'd been there. A way to keep the crowd young, said Joseph. The older generation wouldn't put up with it.

Lincoln sat at the table they'd sat in every time they'd come, in the seat Joseph usually occupied. It faced out, so no one could come upon him unawares. The power position.

A young woman with strawberry blonde hair and a black flower tattoo below her clavicle approached Lincoln and took his order. Ten minutes later and twenty minutes early, Joseph sauntered in, wearing a casual outfit of jeans and a collared shirt that probably cost at least two hundred and fifty dollars. His eyes flickered with annoyance and shock at the sight of Lincoln, then settled into an easy smile, his boardroom smile.

"Hey, there. Someone's early."

"Take a seat." Lincoln gestured to the chair across from him.

Joseph's chin twitched slightly as he sat. He leaned back. "How's your friend? Kali, is it? Her vision any better?"

"No."

"Ahh, too bad." Joseph cleared his throat. "You know, I didn't mention it last time, but I kind of like that hair style on you. It's rugged. Works with your current clothing choices, anyway."

Lincoln pressed his lips together and murmured something incomprehensible, even to himself.

"Well," Joseph's smile broadened then wavered, "seems like you want to get down to business. Should we order a drink?" He turned to signal a server just as the waitress with the flower tattoo laid a plate in front of Lincoln. "You ordered food?"

Lincoln picked up his knife and fork. "We weren't supposed to meet for twenty minutes. I'm hungry. And a twenty minute meeting doesn't exactly allow time for a meal."

"Can I get you anything?" The server asked Joseph.

He stared at Lincoln. "A Stella."

"Anything to—"

"Just the Stella." Joseph turned to the waitress. "Thank you."

Lincoln savoured his first bite. It was incredible. Pork chops with aged cheddar, a combination he never would have thought of. He took several more bites then swallowed. "So, what is this? Something with the shares?"

Joseph's brows raised. "The shares? No. Nothing like that."

"What, then?"

"I wanted to talk to my brother."

Lincoln pierced another piece of meat. "Do you still think that title is appropriate?"

"We'll always be brothers. Nothing can change that."

Lincoln added some cornbread to his fork and placed the combo in his mouth.

"You know Lucy's pregnant." Again. The word hung between them, unsaid. Pregnant *again.*

Lincoln nodded and swallowed.

"And you know we're getting married."

"Hmm."

Joseph rested an arm on the table. "The when has been a challenge. Lucy keeps going back and forth between whether she wants the wedding before or after the baby. Before, so we'll be married before the child's born. After, so she can look fabulous in a dress and pictures."

Lincoln took another bite.

"She's already showing quite a bit, so we've come to a decision. She wants the big wedding. Needs the big wedding. And it wouldn't be a bad idea for the company, either, invite a lot of the big wigs, make them feel special."

The waitress set Joseph's drink down in front of him as he nodded his thanks. "So we're going to have a small ceremony, just family, a handful of friends. Then maybe five or six months after the baby we'll have the big shindig."

Lincoln took another bite.

"And we want you to be there."

"For the big wigs? Don't most of them know I've been cast off?"

"What? No. I mean, yes, sure, we'd love to have you there. But for the real wedding. The small one. I always thought you'd stand with me. It's what brothers do."

"Not brothers who sleep with, then marry, their brother's girlfriend."

Joseph stared at Lincoln. "Okay. I deserve that." He took a

long draught of his Stella. "And I get that this probably sounds ludicrous to you, but there'll come a time when this will all be behind us. I think you'd regret not being there."

"Do you?"

"Lincoln."

"What?" Lincoln's leg bounced. He wanted to get up, leave—his fist clenched—but not before punching Joseph in the face. "Why are you even here? Why do you care if I'm in your wedding?"

"You're my brother."

"A fact you should have thought of before sleeping with my girlfriend."

"I know."

"Then why did it happen? How did it happen? I got a lot of it out of Lucy, but I want your side. That night. That first night, when you offered to drive her home, was it simply because you wanted to take her away from me? Too beautiful for your little brother? You needed a taste?"

"What?"

"And when you were so insistent on me moving to Montreal, how much of that was about her? You couldn't find your own woman? Though I know you could. You've never had any trouble getting whatever woman you wanted. So why her too?"

"Wait, wait." Joseph put his hands on the table. "Nothing started between Lucy and me until long after you were in Montreal. At least a year."

"Bullshit. The family dinner. The first family dinner, you knew how excited I was about bringing her home, showing her off, but I was sick and had to leave early, so you offered to drive her home, let her stay and get to know the family better."

"Yes, but—"

"She told me how you walked her to her door, told her how beautiful she was, joked that maybe she was with the wrong brother."

"Well, okay, but I was joking. Really. I never thought. I never—"

"Then you took her in your arms. Very romantic how she tells it. Very passionate, the way you kissed her, the way you tried to get her to open the door. But she stopped you."

"No."

"Are you saying you stopped it?"

"No." Joseph leaned forward. "I walked her to the door. I joked ... I can't remember quite what, maybe something like that. Then I left. We didn't kiss. I thought she was beautiful, yes. But—"

Lincoln put down his cutlery and leaned forward. "Why lie, now, when it doesn't even matter?"

Joseph shook his head. "Exactly. Why lie now?" He looked to the wall beside them, silent, then turned back to Lincoln. "She told you that? She told you it started then?"

Lincoln assessed Joseph, sitting there, from all appearances truly perplexed. He knew his brother. Or thought he'd known him, thought he could tell when he was lying or telling those half lies; he used to joke about them when Lincoln would catch him sneaking in late at night or find him in the woods behind the house with a joint. Half lies. Little lies, that Lincoln always saw through. But he'd never suspected Joseph and Lucy. Not once. So maybe he didn't know his brother as well as he thought.

Lincoln spoke slowly. "That's what she said."

"So you thought ..." Joseph shook his head again. "All those years." He rubbed a hand through his hair. "She said—"

"She said you two started writing after that. At first a text here or there, then an email. She said you suggested she start putting Montreal in my ear."

"No." Joseph held his hands up and shook them in front of him. "No. Absolutely not. I had no contact with Lucy between the night of the dinner and when you two moved to Montreal. None."

CHAPTER FIFTEEN

Lincoln stared across the table at Joseph, his thoughts zigzagging and rolling over. Either Joseph or Lucy was lying. Both, maybe. "That first weekend when I spent the whole time in the office and you were showing her the sights?"

Joseph leaned back. "I was showing her the sights. With the girl I was seeing at the time."

"Sherry?"

"Yeah. Sherry."

Lincoln shook his head. Sherry. One of the few women Joseph seemed like he might actually be serious about. The four of them had dinner that night. Was it that night? Had they talked about the sights? About spending the day together? Lincoln's head had been so full of trying to wrap his head around his new role, around the courses he was taking, so much from that time seemed a blur.

"Lucy and I didn't," Joseph hesitated, as if he were searching for the words, "get together until a month or so before she got pregnant. At least three years after you moved there."

"Get together. You mean that was when you established that you were actually in a relationship, that I was the odd man out."

"No. She was always forward. Touchy." Joseph paused. "Okay, we kissed once, maybe some time late in the second year. But it was just a kiss. Nothing more. We'd been drinking and were out at a club waiting for you. You were burning the oil at both ends back then. I was impressed, but everyone has to live a little. She was going on and on about how she never saw you, how she missed the touch of a man ... but it was one kiss. In the club. When I say get together I mean, you know," he made an unmistakable tone and expression, "get together."

"A month or two before she got pregnant."

"Yes."

"So you're saying you were together for what, three months before the ... accident."

"Probably less than that. And I wouldn't call it together. It wasn't a relationship. It was ... sex. A half a dozen times, maybe. Which kills me. It's worse, you know? It's not like I was head over heels in love with this girl. She was there and sexy and touching me and—"

A piercing pain shot through Lincoln's head. "You're saying this is her fault."

"No." Joseph waved his hands in front of him again. "Absolutely not. It takes two, obviously. I didn't have to ... respond."

The pain throbbed. "Just sex. Just sex you could have had with any woman."

"And I should have. Any woman but—"

"Then why are you marrying her? Why are you having

another kid?"

She assured me the first baby was mine. Told me before she told you. Said we needed to tell you, that she was going to break it off with you. I didn't want her to. I said she couldn't be sure, that we should end things right then and there, that you'd always wanted kids and I ... I did too, but I couldn't, not with your girlfriend. I told her it was a mistake, all of it."

Lincoln put his hands ups. "Just stop. None of this makes sense. Why would she tell me the opposite? That it was years, right from the start. That you loved each other. Why would she—?"

"I don't know." Joseph's face fell. He looked ... unravelled. Like the way he looked the day they learned about Dad.

Lincoln shook his head. "You didn't answer my question. If it was over, if it was all a mistake, how'd she get pregnant again? Why are you marrying her?"

Joseph shrugged, looking as miserable as Lincoln felt. "She assured me it was my kid, said you two always used protection. Always. A couple of times we didn't. She was broken over it, the baby being gone. It was hard for me too. I mean ... it wasn't planned, it never should have happened, but it's still a loss, you know?"

Lincoln knew. He still felt the loss, and the kid might not have been his. Probably wasn't his. He nodded.

"So you were gone—"

"Because you fired me."

"I didn't—" Joseph brushed another hand through his now unkempt hair. "Listen. You bombed a multi-million dollar meeting. This isn't some mom and pop company anymore. With each decision I have over two hundred and fifty employees to consider. I couldn't lose that contract. The company couldn't lose that contract. And I didn't fire you. I repositioned you. You're the one who chose not to take that position."

Lincoln kept silent. He reached for his drink and took a long swig.

"Anyway, you were gone and she was there and we had this shared loss. The shit had already hit the fan so ..."

"So you figured why not keep fucking her."

Joseph's face crumpled. "Essentially, yes. I'd like to think it wasn't as coarse as that. We built a connection then, the mutual pain—losing the baby. Losing you."

"She wanted to lose me."

Joseph shook his head. "I don't know. I don't think so, kid."

"Don't call me—"

"Sorry. Sorry." Joseph sat straighter. "Again, we didn't plan to get pregnant. I should be more careful. I know I should ... but it sometimes started up so fast, in places where—" Lincoln raised a hand and Joseph stopped mid-sentence. "That's my kid in her. She wants to be married. She'll make a good wife."

"A good corporate wife."

"That's true." Joseph seemed to search Lincoln. "But it's not a bad thing. She's beautiful. She's smart. She can be caring. She supports me."

Lincoln wasn't sure if he wanted an answer, but he spoke the words anyway. "Do you love her?"

Joseph took several breaths to answer. "I think so. I mean ... what's love, right? I'm not sure I've ever been in love before. Maybe this is it."

Lincoln had loved Lucy, had thought he loved Lucy, but in retrospect, had he? Or had he merely loved the way she'd saved him from his misery after Ginny, loved the fact that she gave him purpose, direction, the ability to stop making his own choices?

Lincoln stared at his plate. "You really never slept with her until a month or two before she got pregnant."

"I swear it."

"And before that?"

"We flirted, I guess. That one kiss. I'll admit, I found her sexy, but she was yours. She was off limits."

"Until she wasn't."

Joseph nodded, looking contrite. "Until she wasn't. I could blame it on the alcohol. I could blame it on the fact that I'd been working hard and so hadn't gotten laid in a while. I could blame it on her and that low cut, short-skirted dress she was wearing, or I could simply blame it on me." Joseph gave a sad shrug. "Once it happened once, it was easier."

"I still don't get why she said it'd been all those years."

"I don't know. It's—"

"Did she hate me that much?"

"She doesn't hate you. She's said so many times how bad she feels, the way it separated the family, the way it ... changed you. She regrets that it hurt you."

"But not enough."

"What?"

"Not enough to have walked away. Not enough to make sure I didn't have to see her again, be reminded. Not enough to not get pregnant with your child, marry you."

Joseph exhaled. "It's rotten. All of it. Especially that you thought ... all those years. That I could lie to you all that time. That she could. It makes more sense now."

"What?"

"You." Joseph let out a sigh. "This past year. The way you look at me like you want to kill me. I mean I'd deserve that no matter what, but a few times compared to—" He shook his head. "I'm so sorry, man. Every time I swore to myself it'd be the last. Every time. But we kept on seeing each other. And you were working such long hours. She'd call. She'd ... not that I'm blaming it on her. Not that I'm blaming it on you."

"Do you think she loves you?"

Joseph dropped his head into his hands and leaned forward on the table. "I hope so. It'd be pretty pathetic if both of us were entering into this marriage uncertain of love."

"Do you think she planned it?"

Joseph sat back. "What?"

"You two. The pregnancy. Everything."

"Planned?"

"From the beginning. She met you. You were the better brother. The more successful brother. The one destined for success. I was a crap-shoot."

"Lincoln."

"It's possible, though. Don't you think? Lucy always wants the best. You're the best."

"No, I—" Joseph hesitated. "No. That's ridiculous. It just happened. We were weak and selfish and it happened. These things happen."

They stared at each other. Lincoln pushed his half-eaten plate away. "I can't go to the wedding."

Joseph made a sound of understanding. "I had to ask. If you change your mind, you're wanted. It's in two weeks, at Christ Church. Two o'clock. Mom and Rachel would have any other details you need."

Joseph placed a fifty on the table and stood. "My treat.

And thanks, anyway, for meeting me. I'm impressed you gave me even that."

Lincoln's jaw twitched. He watched Joseph as he turned away. "Hey."

"Yeah?" Joseph turned back.

"It's, uh ... better ... or at least less bad."

"What?"

"Knowing you only lied to me for months, not years, that our whole life in Montreal wasn't a lie."

"No, man. No. It wasn't." Joseph's lips pressed together. "Those were good times. Closest we've ever been. Proudest I've ever been of you—seeing the way you worked so hard. You deserved it all, you know—the promotions, raises, success. Family or no." Joseph rubbed a hand across his eyes and banged his fist gently on the table. "You shouldn't be working construction sites."

"Don't."

"Mom says you built a tree house, though? On a lot toward Musquodoboit?"

Lincoln nodded.

"Just like you always wanted to. I bet it's no typical tree house."

Lincoln shook his head. He couldn't do this. Chat. Share tidbits about their lives.

Joseph thumped the table once more. "Okay. I'm going. You might not want to hear this. You might not believe it, but I love you and I'm sorry. If I could turn back the clock I would. And I hope one day ... I hope one day won't be like today. I miss you. And I want my kid to know his uncle."

Lincoln's throat tightened. He looked away.

A final thump and Joseph was gone. Lincoln sat until the

waitress came over to him, asking if there was anything else she could do. He pushed the fifty toward her.

He sat after she brought back the change, not touching it. Eventually he stood, his limbs feeling numb, his mind reeling. It changed everything and nothing, knowing the truth ... if it was the truth. It was. He was sure of it—Joseph's bafflement. And Lucy, as she told the story, she'd been angry, vindictive. She'd revelled in the details, in the way they'd twisted and torn at him. It was his fault, she'd said, that her child was dead. The lie, obviously, was her payback.

CHAPTER SIXTEEN

Lincoln stepped onto the street, startled by the darkness around him. The sun had started to set long before he'd entered the restaurant, but somehow he'd expected day, needed day. He turned toward home then stopped. Exhaustion poured over him. Home meant Kali, meant more lies and betrayal. She was married. She had money. Enough money that she'd never needed him. She certainly didn't need him now. So why was she there, in his apartment, waiting for him?

Simply because she didn't want to take anything from Derek, just like he didn't want to take anything from Joseph? He could understand that, to an extent.

Still, he couldn't go home. Couldn't confront her. Not yet. He didn't even want to risk getting his truck. Kali spent a lot of time at the window lately ... though perhaps she'd just been looking for Derek.

He wouldn't risk it. A cab drove by. Lincoln flagged it down and stepped inside.

AT TEN O'CLOCK KALI still sat in the living room, waiting. A gentle ache grew in her head. When had she taken her last painkiller? She thought through the day. She'd missed her morning dose, her afternoon dose. Both?

Kali thought again. She'd missed both, and yet the pain in her head was hardly worse than she was used to even with the meds. Had she taken any yesterday? She thought back. The morning dose only.

She smiled and took a deep breath, willing this not to be a fluke, willing it to mean the swelling was finally subsiding, willing it to mean she had cause to hope. Kali closed her laptop and snuggled into the couch, stretching her legs long. There was no point thinking about Lincoln, worrying about Lincoln; he'd either stay or he wouldn't, trust her or not. Just like there was no point worrying about what the tumour would or wouldn't do. Ultimately, they were both out of her control.

Still, she couldn't help worrying and wondering. Just as she willed her barely aching head to be a sign of the tumour's shrinkage, she willed Lincoln to come home. Willed her life to become something resembling happy.

"BUDDY." ANDREW OPENED the door, his expression a mix of surprise and interest. "What is it this time?"

Lincoln rubbed a hand along the back of his neck. "Can I

come in?"

"You can. I've got company though."

"Right." Lincoln rubbed his neck again. "Sorry, I should have called. I'll go."

Andrew looked past Lincoln. "You take a cab?"

"Yeah."

"Stay. You look like you could use a distraction."

Lincoln let out a short laugh and followed Andrew into his living room.

"This is Sandy, Sarah, Josh, Jody, and Pete."

Lincoln tilted his chin in greeting.

"This is my cousin, Lincoln."

"Another heir to the Fraser fortune?" asked Jody as he rose from an armchair and squeezed in beside one of the women on the love seat—Sarah, Lincoln thought.

"That's right." Lincoln sat in the open seat and took the beer Andrew handed him. "Though I'd rather carve my own path."

"Oh yeah?" The other woman, Sandy, leaned forward. "And what path will that be?"

Lincoln pressed his lips, not wanting to get into it. "Top secret."

"Only millionaires have the means to have top-secret endeavours," said Sarah. "Which means you're not really carving your own path, are you? If you're building it on your family's fortune."

"Geez." Andrew kicked up his recliner. "Is this how you guys talk about me when I'm not around? If you don't like the free drinks and food, you know where the door is."

"We're just joking with him." Sarah gave Andrew a smile.

"Well, trust me." Andrew gestured his beer toward

Lincoln. "This guy's not taking any free handouts."

"Speaking of millionaires," said Josh, gesturing around the room, "when are you going to upgrade? Let us hang out in style. You should have a pool, a hot tub—"

"Pool table," said Jody with a laugh.

"Yeah," continued Josh, "and a place about three times as big. Aren't you rolling in it, Mr. Manager?"

"I do all right." Andrew took a swig of his drink. "But my focus is live smart. Enjoy the now, of course, but I'm aiming for Freedom Forty-Five. I'll probably hit up some business meetings from time to time after that, help out with my expertise, but it's about being smart." Andrew tilted his bottle toward his head while glancing between Josh and Jody. If I go big now, I'll be working till I'm sixty. He pointed his bottle toward his friends. "Contrary to what you lot seem to think, the money doesn't come from nowhere."

"Anyway," said Sandy, reaching forward for a handful of chips, "I'm sure there are better things to talk about."

"Like how we're going to beat Team Know-It-All in the next trivia match?" asked Jody.

"Exactly!" said Sandy, pointing at him. "They creamed us tonight. We need to come up with a way to regain our title."

The conversation flowed easily after that, and Lincoln spoke only when needed—enough to seem sociable, but no more. It was nice though, sitting with a group of people, no hidden agenda, no lies. He couldn't remember the last time he'd hung with a group of friends. The closest thing would be the night's out in Montreal with Joseph, Lucy, and Joseph's friends—mostly corporate connections, so even on casual nights, it was never truly casual.

Before that? Undergrad. Years ago. It seemed foreign, to

think of that life—weekends drinking with buddies, trivia nights, like this group had apparently come from. Concerts. Hikes. Summer evenings at the beach with bonfires and winter kitchen parties. It'd been good, better than good. He'd almost forgotten he hadn't always been such a recluse.

THEY LAUGHED THROUGH the evening, and after the last of Andrew's friends filtered out of the door, Andrew came and sat across from Lincoln. He settled in then stared at Lincoln a moment before speaking. "So, what's on the go this time?"

Lincoln sighed. "Her dead husband's not dead."

"Kali's?"

Lincoln nodded. "And she's still married."

"Shit."

"Yep." Lincoln took a drink. "Oh, and I saw Joseph tonight. He wants me to go to his wedding."

"Are—?"

Lincoln shook his head. "I learned, though, that they weren't going behind my back for four years, just a couple of months. Just."

"What?" Andrew leaned forward.

"Lucy lied. For some reason. Maybe hate? They didn't have this secret relationship. According to Joseph, they slept together maybe half a dozen times and not until a month or two before she got pregnant."

"The first time."

"Yeah."

"Well," Andrew sat back, "I guess that warrants your little pop in."

"I couldn't go back to her."

"To Kali?"

"Yeah. Oh, and get this, that destitute mother I thought I was helping, she's not so destitute. She has over eighty thousand dollars in a joint account with her husband—money he gave her."

"She told you this?"

"He did. He tracked me down tonight, wanted to see what our status was."

"Whoa. Whoa. Whoa." Andrew held out his hands. "He's here? You met him?"

"He's here and wants back in their lives."

"And that leaves you?"

Lincoln shrugged.

"Do you think they're going to get back together? Or ... what's the deal?"

"They're separated, says Kali. "And she says no, they're not getting back together. But he wants it."

"Where does that leave you two?"

Lincoln set his drink on the side table and leaned back. "Things were progressing. Slowly. They halted a couple of weeks ago. I guess when she first figured out he may be in town." Lincoln looked to the floor before lifting his gaze back to Andrew. "I was an idiot, thinking it could be different."

"What?"

"Love. Believing. Trusting. She still loves him."

"She told you that?"

"Yeah. Said she always would, but it didn't have to change anything between us."

Andrew rested his elbows on his knees. "Well, maybe it doesn't."

Lincoln raised an eyebrow.

"He's obviously not her husband anymore, not in the way

it matters. But he's always going to be her kid's dad, right? Lot's of people though, with that kind of connection, that love, they're no good for each other." Andrew hesitated. "She's definitely been good for you. And it seems like maybe you've been good for her."

"Used by her."

Andrew clasped his hands together over his lap. "Do you really think that's how she saw it? Or do you think maybe there's some other explanation? She doesn't seem like the type to just—" Andrew hesitated. "Have you asked her about it?"

"No."

"Then maybe you shouldn't jump to conclusions."

"When did you become such a sage?"

"Sage?" Andrew laughed. "Nah, man. Just from what I can tell, you really like this woman. A kid. A tumour. And yet you stuck around, getting almost nothing in return." Andrew grinned. "What's a husband and hidden cash?"

"A lot."

"Maybe. But maybe nothing much. Who knows, maybe this guy re-entering the picture will make things easier for you two. They establish shared custody, you and Kali have the chance to explore whatever you've got going on, without the kid in the way all the time."

"He's not in the way."

"You know what I mean. I bet it's hard for romance to bloom with a five-year-old cuddled up between you."

"He's four."

"Not the point, Lincoln. Not the point."

Lincoln's brow furrowed. He stared at Andrew. "You don't think I should walk?"

"After all you've already been through with this woman?" Andrew shook his head. "Not yet, anyway, not until you've figured things out, given her a chance to explain."

"And if I stick around and she decides she's still in love with her husband, that she wants to put her family back together?"

Andrew contemplated a moment. "Then I guess you'll be no worse off then than if you walked now." He tapped his drink on the arm of his chair then took a swig. "And at least you'll know you gave it a shot."

"What would you think if you were a kid and some guy got in the way of your mom and dad?"

Andrew tilted his head back and forth. "If she were happier with that guy, if I still got to see my dad? I hope I'd be okay with it."

Lincoln let out a puff of air.

"The kid loves you. He doesn't even know this guy."

"Yeah." Lincoln took a deep breath. "Also, I quit."

Andrew laughed. "You mean your job? The job you came begging me for?"

"Yeah." Lincoln grinned. "Carving my own path and all. I'm going to finish the tree house, establish it as a model, see if I can get a business going."

Andrew grinned back. "Sounds like a plan, though is this two-weeks-notice or are you walking out on me?"

"Do you need two-weeks-notice?"

"Nope."

"Then I'm walking out."

Andrew laughed again as he set his drink on a side table and stood. "Well, unlike you, I have to get up and go to work tomorrow. You want to crash?"

"Nah. I'll call a cab."

"Suit yourself." Andrew stretched, then walked over to Lincoln and clamped a hand on his shoulder. "Whatever happens, you're going to be fine."

Lincoln let out a little guffaw.

"Seriously." Andrew squeezed Lincoln's shoulder. "You'll be fine. Life is fresh. For us, anyway. You've got years to figure it out."

"You got it figured out?"

Andrew stepped back, a laugh bursting out of him. "Hell, no. But I'm trying. Enjoying the ride as much as I can in the meantime."

"You still seeing that girl? Katelyn, was it?"

Andrew let out a sigh and began collecting bottles and glasses and plates from the room. "I am not. And probably better off for it."

Lincoln stood and helped Andrew bring the dishes and bottles into the kitchen. "Sorry. I should have—"

"It's all right. Your shit's been much more intense than mine of late. Seriously though, call that cab. I want you out of here." Andrew winked. "Got to get my beauty sleep."

Lincoln reached for his phone. "Thanks."

Andrew closed the dishwasher and turned it on. "That's what I'm here for."

CHAPTER SEVENTEEN

Kali stayed motionless as the door quietly opened. She wasn't sure if she'd slept ... but sensed she must have. Lincoln wouldn't enter so quietly if it was still early. She breathed softly, hoping he'd step toward her, pull up the blanket or whisper her name, checking to see if she was awake.

His footsteps crossed past her and to his room. Several minutes later his door opened again and steps padded down the hall to the bathroom. When his door opened once more, Kali stared into the semi-darkness.

After several minutes she rose, her heart pounding in her chest, and tiptoed to his room. She pushed open the door slowly then stood in the shadows, listening for movement. "Lincoln?"

"I'm here."

Kali walked to the edge of his bed and perched. Not once had she done that–sat on his bed, been in his room with the lights off, the only other person in the apartment asleep.

"I'm so sorry."

Silence.

Kali pursed her lips and closed her eyes in the darkness. "How are you?"

Lincoln shifted to his side—away from her. "I don't know."

"I get that. It's a lot to take in."

"Lies always are." His voice was soft, unaccusing, but still the words cut.

Kali nodded in the darkness. "Can you understand how at first, when you were a stranger, when I felt so embarrassed to even be here, it would have been hard to explain a husband who left, who I had no communication with?" She stopped, waiting for a reply. When it was clear none was coming, Kali continued. "For all I knew he'd never come back."

Lincoln took several breaths in the silence. "Was the possibility of us a lie too?"

"No," Kali breathed. "No."

"What if I'd wanted to marry you? What then?"

She ran her hand along the sheet. "If I said yes I would have applied for a divorce."

"Would you have told me, or done it in secret?"

"I—"

"And what about Marvin? I thought staying married was to help take care of him."

"I don't know." Kali shifted toward Lincoln. "Can I lie down?"

Lincoln's voice caught. "I don't know."

Kali closed her eyes and let her chest expand. "Well, I'm going to." She eased onto the bed and under the covers, facing him. Her hand found his and grasped it. "Believe me, please. I want this."

"What's this, Kali?"

"You. Me. Wherever life takes us."

Lincoln released a soft sigh. "Maybe it should take us apart."

"Maybe. But I don't think so."

"Kali, why are you here?"

"To talk to you."

"No. Here. Living with me. Was I just the easier option, easier to bruise your pride taking my charity than taking his ... though I hardly think you could call it charity. Theo's his son. You're his wife. It's his responsibility to provide for you."

Kali propped herself up. "What are you talking about?"

"The money, Kali. You don't need to be here. You didn't need my help."

"I ..." Her voice faltered.

"All your talk about losing your job, applying for EI and disability. You didn't need any of it, not really. And before that, the rats and mold. You didn't need to be living in that apartment." Lincoln's voice shifted. "What kind of mother would do that? Expose her son to such danger over pride, or stubbornness?"

Kali turned on the bedside lamp and sat up. "What the hell are you talking about?"

Lincoln propped himself up. "The money."

"What money?"

"The eighty thousand dollars."

Kali stared at him blankly.

"In your joint account."

"Our? What?" Queasiness slid through her. "I don't know anything about any money."

Confusion and uncertainty settled over Lincoln's expression. "The money Derek's been putting in your joint account since he left. He said there's over eighty thousand now."

"The ..." Kali's hands shook. She remembered it now: the day before the accident at Peggy's Cove they'd gone to the bank and set up that account. It was ridiculous, Derek had said, that they hadn't done it yet. They were husband and wife, not roommates. They should share an account. They'd set it up with his bank. The plan was to transfer her payroll to the account, their bill payments too. But then they'd gone to Peggy's Cove and none of that happened.

Kali crossed the room, yanked open the door, and settled on the couch in front of her lap top.

She reached for her satchel, grabbed her wallet, and pulled out card after card. "It's got to be here," she muffled under her breath. At last she held it in her hands, the bank card she'd only used once, to set up her account. It had sat, untouched, in her overstuffed wallet ever since.

Kali typed in the numbers then tried passwords. Invalid. Invalid.

"Damn." She lifted her head and stared at the wall ahead of her, sensing Lincoln's presence yet unable to see him in her non-existent peripheral vision. And then it hit her, the memory of Derek elbowing her in the side, saying if his and Jason's new auto shop went belly up, the account would mean he'd have access to all she had. You'll be my *sugarmommy*, he'd laughed. Sugarmommy. She typed it in and the screen opened. Kali sat back as the breath streamed out of her. Eighty four thousand, three hundred and sixty-five dollars and fourteen cents.

She stared at the figure then turned to Lincoln. "I didn't know. I swear, I didn't know."

Lincoln sat and listened as she explained. She squeezed

her eyes shut as all the years of struggle and stress and worry passed over her. So much of it. All of it, almost, didn't need to be. The rats, the nights she'd lain awake, listening for their scurrying, fearing they'd bite Theo in his sleep.

She shook her head and let out a sob. "I didn't know."

Lincoln wrapped his arms around her, drawing her against him. "All those shitty apartments. All those awful, inconsistent shifts because I couldn't afford a quality daycare." She let out a harsh laugh. "And poor Mrs. Martin. The amount she charges me, I'm practically robbing her."

Kali pulled away from Lincoln. "How did you know about this?"

"I ran into Derek this evening."

Kali shook her head again.

"He thought you didn't take it because you didn't need it. He thought you were fine. When he found out from Marvin that you weren't, he thought you were too proud."

"How could he?" Kali rubbed a hand across the side of her face. "And all this time I thought he ... the things I thought." She took a deep breath. "I'll pay you back right away. All of it."

Lincoln put up a hand. "That's not what this is about."

"I know." She laughed. "But I will. Too proud to take his money? No. Like you said, Theo's his son. His responsibility. We're due his support. I would never be too proud to do something to help my son. I moved in with you."

Lincoln's face tensed.

Kali put her hand on his leg. "Who you were ... or at least who I thought you were, how you presented yourself; you have to admit you can see how hard that would have been for me. How scary. With a three-year-old."

Lincoln gave a tight nod.

Kali turned her head to the screen again. "It's so much. How could he have saved so much?"

"It's the army, I guess. Maybe he lived on base. Maybe a lot of his food was provided."

"I suppose." Kali kept her gaze on the screen as she sensed Lincoln shifting away from her. Kali let out a laugh and turned back to the computer screen. "This changes everything."

"Everything?"

"Well," another laugh, "a lot. It changes a lot. I no longer have to rely on you or EI or disability cheques. If I'm not able to get a job for a while, it'll be okay. We'll be okay."

"That's not what I meant."

Kali turned at the sound of Lincoln's voice.

"Does it change things with you and me, you and Derek?"

CHAPTER EIGHTEEN

Kali narrowed her gaze as she stared at the computer screen. The money changed a lot. She no longer needed Lincoln. And Derek hadn't abandoned them ... not completely, anyway. Not the way she'd thought.

As if he was pulling the words from her mind, Lincoln continued. "He didn't leave you to struggle. He probably scrimped himself to give you all he could."

Kali bit her lip.

"He was thinking of you the whole time. Despite you pushing him away, he never stopped trying to do right by you, in the way he knew how."

Kali kept her eyes on the screen, the number and all it represented—eighty four thousand, three hundred and sixty-five dollars and fourteen cents. Lincoln's words sank in, rubbing away the bitterness. So many times she'd thought of Derek in the early days, telling her he'd always be there for her, convincing her she wanted marriage, a family, a combined future, convincing her it wouldn't be like it'd been for her mother. So many times after he left she'd hated him for letting the dream fall apart, breaking every promise he'd ever made, having her believe in a lie.

When she'd had to move back in with her mother, an infant in her arms, she'd wished they'd never met. When her mother died and she moved into that shitty first apartment, not even able to pay the rent on the aging house her mother had managed all those years, she'd hated Derek more. Hated him for the extra two years of school she had to take while balancing studies and being a single mom. Hated him for the inadequate daycares that couldn't see the potential in Theo. All that hate. All that anger. And he hadn't abandoned them, not in one of the ways it mattered most.

"He was, wasn't he?" Amazement flooded over Kali as she kept her gaze on the numbers on the screen. "I'd told him to stay away, so, listening, he supported us in the only way he knew how. Or tried to."

Lincoln's voice was barely audible. "So what does it change?"

She turned to him. "I don't know."

"It would probably make it easier to love him again."

"Lincoln."

"Do you love me, Kali?"

Kali leaned away from him. "You can't just ask—"

"I know you care for me. I know you're thankful for the way I've helped you and Theo. But what are we doing here? Playing house? I want more than that, and I don't know that I can wait around to see if I'm second choice."

"You're not—"

"He's your husband. He's Theo's dad."

Kali edged toward Lincoln. "And he still abandoned me. Us."

"He must have been depressed. He lost his brother. He

said you pushed him away. You said it."

She raised a hand to Lincoln's face, fear and confusion making it hard to breathe. She wanted Lincoln. She needed Lincoln. But the money did change things, a lot of things. When it came down to it, when she thought of what Derek must have gone through, losing a limb, dealing with the loss of Jason, and still scrounging away all he could for his wife and son ...

Had she been the one to abandon Derek? Should she have been more understanding? She'd made vows—in sickness and in health. The state Derek was in after Jason's death, it had been a type of sickness. No denying that.

Kali let her hand fall from Lincoln's face. Did she love him? She cared for him, loved him, sure. She was thankful. He'd been there for her when no one else was. But was she *in* love with him? She'd hardly allowed herself to think of it, to let herself open up to him in that way.

She'd thought she had time. In four years no man had shown Lincoln's persistence. In four years, no man had made her even consider trying again. Derek had ruined her ... or so she'd thought. And now Derek was back, the sight of him making her insides come alive, the scent of him, his smile, igniting memories she'd hardly allowed herself to hold onto. And he hadn't abandoned her as completely as she'd thought. He'd sacrificed for her. Even when he saw she wasn't taking his offering, he'd persevered.

But Lincoln ignited her insides too. How many nights had she lain in bed, knowing he was just steps down the hall, knowing how easy it would be to tiptoe out of her room and into his, crawl in beside him, let her passion explode—kissing, touching, knowing. But she knew it wouldn't just be sex. Not with Lincoln. It'd be a promise. It'd be her telling him she was ready for something serious. It'd be commitment. And she couldn't be committed. She was married.

Kali kissed Lincoln, the touch gentle. She didn't want to lose him, that she knew. He kept his lips closed, unresponsive. She wasn't married. Not really. Not in the way it mattered. She straddled his legs and kissed him again—his lips, his neck, above his eyes—releasing the passion she'd held pent up for so long, wanting his touch to erase the memory of Derek's.

No amount of money erased the fact that Derek had walked out of her life. He may have sacrificed, but he didn't fight. Lincoln had fought to stay in her life. Lincoln showed up, again and again, even when she'd pushed him away.

"Kali." Lincoln held her wrists in his hands. "No."

Kali caught his gaze in the dim light. "What if I told you I was ready?"

"Kali." He shook his head.

"I know I was scared before. But I'm not anymore. I'm certain this is what I want."

"But not certain I'm the one you want. The one you'll choose."

Kali sat back. "It's not about a choice between you and him. It's ... it's ..."

"What?"

"I don't know." Kali's throat tightened. Her stomach twisted as she shifted back onto the couch. "It's hard to trust again. To trust in a future. But I can trust in now. You and me. Right now."

Lincoln's expression tightened. "I've waited this long. I want more than right now. It's not easy for me either, to trust, to hope. Learning you're married ... learning this whole time

I've been the other man. The cheater."

"No." Kali shook her head. "I know it hurts, but it's not like with your brother. I haven't been with Derek in over four years."

Lincoln inhaled. "But it's still a lie. A betrayal."

Lincoln started to stand but Kali grasped his arm. "You saw Joseph today. What was that about? How did it go?"

Lincoln stood. "He wanted me to come to his wedding."

Kali's eyes widened.

"We also discovered Lucy was more of a liar than either of us thought. It wasn't a relationship. It hadn't been going on years. A month or two. Just sex, says Joseph."

"But—"

"Not that it makes a huge difference. It just means that he, that they, hadn't been lying to me all those years. That not all of it was a farce. That's something."

Kali stared at Lincoln, not knowing what to say. She'd been lying to him longer than Joseph had. "Will you go?"

Lincoln laughed. "No." He turned from her.

"Where does this leave us?"

He didn't turn back. "I'm not sure. I guess where we were before. Figuring things out." He stepped into his room and shut the door.

THE NEXT MORNING LINCOLN woke to the sound of an alarm he hadn't needed to set. Thoughts from the night before ran through his mind. Pushing them out, he tried to think of all he needed to do to get the tree house finished in time for winter. Not that he'd necessarily live there. But he may. And having it done would help progress other things—figuring out a business plan, determining the best way to proceed. Excitement tingled through him. It may never be a big business, but it could be something. It could be enough.

Months ago, after Kali first suggested he tap into the niche market of luxury tree houses and mini homes, he'd researched it. A market existed, and not many people had tapped into it, especially not here, in a cold climate. Having his tree house fully functional for the winter would give him an edge against the competition.

Competition.

All of yesterday's pain and confusion surged through Lincoln, followed by the sensation of that final kiss. Despite the lies, the uncertainty, he wanted Kali. It wasn't easy, not any of it, but still he wanted her, felt he'd be lost without her. And Theo, it made him sick, the thought of walking—or being pushed—away, the thought of not seeing that firecracker smile ever again. He needed them.

But what about them? Did they need him? Would they be better off with him or without?

Lincoln could be a father to Theo, he believed that. But Theo already had a father, who, despite the past four years, seemed like a decent, genuine guy.

If Lincoln truly believed he'd be better for them, he'd fight. But what if he wasn't and through staying, fighting, he screwed up Kali and Theo's lives?

The even bigger problem: Kali wasn't sure. And if she wasn't now, after all they'd gone through, would she ever be?

Lincoln inhaled deeply. Not that it had actually been much time; less than six months had passed since he jumped in front of that car to save Theo. Six months that felt like a lifetime.

Lincoln startled at the sound of his ringing phone.

"Mom. Hi."

"Lincoln." His mother's voice shook. "Are you busy today? Could you come by sometime?"

"Are you okay?"

"I'm fine, I just ... can you come by? Today?"

Lincoln glanced to the clock. Eight o'clock. Too early to request a casual visit. "I'm coming now."

"You don't have—" Marilyn paused. "Okay. Come by now. Have you eaten? I'll make you breakfast."

"You don't have—"

Her voice was firm. "I'm making you breakfast. See you soon."

Lincoln ended the call, knowing there was no point arguing. His mother used food as comfort and a way to spread love when all was fine. When it wasn't, busying her hands in the kitchen seemed her salvation. He remembered clearly the year they found out about his father having Alzheimer's; they'd eaten like kings.

Lincoln changed quickly and entered the hall. Kali's head popped out from around the kitchen. "Morning. Breakfast is ready."

"Oh." Lincoln stepped toward the table where Theo sat, stuffing bite after bite of pancake into his mouth. He squeezed the boy's shoulder in greeting. "Sorry. I'm going to my mother's for breakfast."

"Your—?" Kali's brow furrowed. "Don't you have work

today?"

"No." Lincoln exhaled a puff of air. "I quit."

Kali's expression remained questioning. "When?"

"Last night."

He could see the why on her face. She opened her mouth then closed it. "Okay. Enjoy visiting your mom. Tell her I say hello."

Lincoln smiled his parting. Two weeks ago he would have taken her in his arms, given her a quick kiss on the lips if Theo wasn't in the room, on the cheek if he was. "Thanks. And I will."

"Will you be home for dinner? I thought maybe a pasta salad. I've been looking up recipes. Trying to expand my repertoire." Her grin shook.

Lincoln hesitated by the door. "I'm not sure. I thought I'd head back to the tree house, get some work done."

The grin fell.

"I'll call you though, if I won't be here. K?"

"Okay. Yeah. Sure."

Theo bounced around the corner, holding his plate up with both hands. Kali smiled down at him. "More?"

He nodded as she put a hand on his head with pure affection. "That's my big boy."

Lincoln watched them disappear into the kitchen. Could he do it? Walk away, leave her to figure out if she could have a future with Derek? It may break him.

CHAPTER NINETEEN

Lincoln used his old key to enter his mother's house and was instantly greeted with the smell of sausage, onions, and garlic. He suspected eggs were on the menu too.

Turning the corner to the kitchen, a smile spread across his face. His mother stood, humming to herself as she worked.

"Smells good."

Marilyn turned with a smile, much of the stress he'd heard in her voice earlier gone. "You got here quickly."

Lincoln stepped into the kitchen. "What's going on?"

He'd thought about it on the drive, the most likely scenario being something to do with Joseph and the wedding. She'd want Lincoln there even more than Joseph would.

Marilyn turned back to the stove. "Why don't we wait until we've finished eating. Talks like these are always better on a full stomach."

Lincoln nodded and pulled out a stool at the breakfast nook.

Several minutes later, Marilyn turned back to him with two plates in her hand.

"This looks amazing. Thanks, Mom."

Marilyn's eyes crinkled with pleasure. "Orange juice?"

"Apple?"

"Coming up." She returned with a glass of juice for Lincoln and a cup of coffee for herself. "You have the day off?"

Lincoln repeated the news he'd given Kali last night, this time including his decision to start his own business.

Marilyn laid a hand on Lincoln's. "I've said it before and I'll say it again. That sounds like exactly the type of thing you're meant to do." Marilyn squeezed his hand before releasing. "I think you'll do wonderfully. Plus," she smiled, "you'll get to make use of that Masters in Business."

Marilyn laughed gently. "Do you remember following your father around? Spending hours in his workshop?"

Lincoln shifted in his seat. "Some."

"Whatever he built, you'd want to build in miniature. Well," a louder laugh, "you probably wanted to build it full size, but he convinced you miniature was the way to go. Rachel's doll houses and play room were the most customized on the block."

"I remember you telling me that."

"You know, your father regretted letting the business get so big. So corporate. He was proud of Joseph, of course, but—"

"Proud of Joseph? Wasn't Dad long gone by the time Joseph took over."

"He's not gone now." Marilyn's voice softened. "But even years after the diagnosis there were days, hours, where he'd be the same man he always was. Completely lucid. They grew fewer and further in between, but whenever they came he wanted to know all about you kids. Everything about you."

Marilyn's eyes moistened. "He said even in his final years running the company, during those first small expansions, he often regretted not keeping it small. He missed the beauty and simplicity of what he started out with—a small business more about connection and customization than profit.

"He loved sitting with an owner and designing their perfect dream house from scratch rather than letting them pick and choose features from cookie-cutter templates." Marilyn paused. "He's proud of Joseph, he is, but what you're about to do, it would light him up."

Lincoln swallowed a bite of food and set down his fork. "Can you tell me what this is about now?"

Marilyn gestured to their plates. "We're almost done." She took a sip of her coffee. "How's Kali doing? Is her sight any better? And Theo? Such a sweet boy."

Lincoln pushed the final bites around on his plate. Part of him wanted to tell her it all—that Kali was married, that her husband was here and wanted her back, that Lincoln had no idea what to do about any of it. "They're good." He looked up with a slight smile. "The tumour didn't look like it had shrunk on the last scan, nor had her vision improved, but the doctors think it's likely just swelling from the treatment and that in another few weeks the swelling will subside and they'll see how effective the treatment was."

"And she's managing? It must be so hard."

"She's managing."

"She's lucky to have you."

Lincoln nodded.

"Not every man would have stuck around. Theo's lucky too. It's important for a boy to have a solid male figure in his life."

Lincoln let out a short laugh. "I don't know how solid I am."

"You're there, which is important for a boy without a father."

Not anymore, Lincoln thought but didn't say.

Marilyn inhaled. "I know how hard it was for you. You lost him so much earlier than the others."

"Mom."

Marilyn gestured to their plates again. "You're done?"

"I'm done."

She folded her arms in front of her. "I know it's hard for you. But he's still your father."

Lincoln leaned back and looked to the other side of the room. "Please, we've been through this before. I know you think he's still there. He's not. He's just this shell, he—"

"He's not a shell." Marilyn snapped. "He is your father. Even if he can't always find a way to express that, he's your father. He's the man who rocked you to sleep, who told you stories, who carried you on his back for hours. He is and will always be your father. If you visited, you'd know that." She exhaled, her nostrils flaring. "You'd see it. There's glimpses still. Moments of clarity. Not always in words, but in a touch, a glance. He's *in* there."

Marilyn wiped her eyes. "He still whittles, you know. Little figures. They're all over his room. Some are a little rough and disfigured, when he forgets his ... destination. But some are beautiful."

Lincoln's throat went tight at the look of love in his mother's eyes.

She let out a puff of air. "At least he used to whittle, up until a few weeks ago."

Lincoln's brow furrowed, waiting for more. His chest tightened at the expression that crossed Marilyn's face.

"That's why I called you over. I know you think he's not there. I know you think he's not your dad. But his soul's still there; you might not realize that now, but one day you will."

"Mom."

"No. Listen." Marilyn pursed her lips. "It's bad. He has weeks at the most. More likely days. And if you don't go visit him, if you don't give him a proper goodbye, you're going to regret it."

Lincoln's jaw clenched as he watched the way his mother's lip trembled. "Days?"

Marilyn nodded. "Days."

"They're sure?"

"Yes. They're pretty sure."

Lincoln looked at the leftover scraps of food on his plate. Images came back to him—his father strong, healthy, his energy taking up the whole room as he marched into this kitchen for breakfast or dinner, wrapping his arms around his wife, rubbing a hand on Lincoln's head. Or the times he did bicep curls with Lincoln on one arm and Rachel on the other, sending them into peals of laughter. How thoughtful he was, always imparting wisdom.

And then the last time Lincoln saw him flooded his vision—his father, words slurring, eyes unfocused, a stranger, the way, even then, his motor skills had started to decline. "Can he speak? Can he move on his own?"

"Not words usually. Sounds." Marilyn smiled gently. "I can understand some of them, the meaning at least. He has very limited movement."

Lincoln, his gaze still on the plate, nodded. "He won't

know if I come or if I don't."

"Maybe. Maybe not." Marilyn paused. "But you'll know." She waited until he looked up. "Your father is a fighter. He's fought through this whole process. Most people with early-onset don't live past ten years. It's been over fifteen."

Lincoln kept his gaze down. "Seventeen. It's been seventeen."

"Yes." Marilyn nodded. "It's been seventeen."

She laid her hand out, palm up on the table. When Lincoln didn't move she gestured with it. He placed his hand in hers. "I can't tell you what to do. But I can tell you that it's more likely you're going to regret not going than going." Her voice caught as she struggled with the words. "I know it's going to be hard for you, baby, he's not going to look like the father you knew, not the one you remember. But he's *in* there, I promise you. And you need to say goodbye."

Lincoln's throat burned. He wanted to say yes. If not for him, for her, to make her tears stop. To make her proud of him. "I'm not sure if I can."

"You can." She squeezed his hand and nodded. "You can." Marilyn stood. "I can't make you. If you don't go, I'm still going to love you as much as always." She cleared the plates and stared at him. "Go somewhere alone, or talk to someone, whatever's needed. But think long and hard before you decide you can't do this, because this is your last chance." She turned to the counter.

Lincoln stared at her back as she rinsed the plates and opened the dishwasher. He walked toward her. Marilyn turned and wrapped her arms around him. She didn't speak as she stepped back and gave his shoulders a squeeze. Lincoln shifted. "I'm sorry, Mom."

Her smile was so light it baffled him. "It's time. Time he's freed of this body that's been such a prison. It's you I'm worried about. Your brother and sisters will be fine too. It's you who concerns me."

She patted his arms once more. "Promise you'll think about it? Really dig deep."

Lincoln nodded.

"Say it."

His mouth twisted; his voice gruff. "I'll think about it."

"All right." Marilyn stepped back. "You go off to your day."

Lincoln hesitated, all the unspoken words he wanted to speak—of Kali, of Joseph, even of Lucy, the lies—lingered on his tongue. He wrapped his arms around his mother again and held tight, shaking.

"Oh, my baby," Marilyn crooned in his ear. "It's all going to be all right."

CHAPTER TWENTY

Kali hung up the phone with Derek for the second time that day, their plans for tomorrow now cemented. The absurdity of it made her feel off, like she was living a fantasy life. To be talking to him casually, scheduling plans ... after resigning herself to the fact that she may never see him again.

But life was about change, about rolling with that change: accepting, reshaping, or working through the bad and searching out all the good possible. It's what the last discussion at the CNIB support group she'd been going to had focused on. And a lot of good came from Derek being back in town.

A smile crossed her face as she remembered the way Theo's nervousness, excitement, and expectation had flitted across his face when she'd told him they'd be seeing his Daddy again the next evening. Later, on their morning walk, he'd run up to Mrs. Martin as she worked in her garden. He tugged on her skirt, his body practically thrumming with eagerness. It was the first time Kali had heard him speak in front of Mrs. Martin.

"I have a Daddy now."

Mrs. Martin had glanced to Kali, a question of surprise on her face. "Is that so?"

Theo nodded. "He's come home. And he loves me. And he's staying forever."

"Oh!" Mrs. Martin looked to Kali again before returning her gaze to Theo. "Well, that's wonderful."

Theo gave a little skip as he rejoined Kali on the sidewalk.

"We're separated and he was in the army. He's not anymore."

Mrs. Martin hadn't asked any questions. Just nodded with understanding. People left, and then they came back. It wasn't so unusual.

IN ADDITION TO THEO'S excitement, Derek being back meant support, and, maybe not yet, but hopefully one day, when she finally trusted this was real and he wouldn't disappear again, shared custody. One day a week, perhaps, maybe two. A few weeks in the summer. She'd miss, Theo, of course, but she could also use the break.

It wasn't only Theo Derek's return affected. Marvin seemed to have a new lease on life. And if Lincoln could forgive her, Derek taking Theo for an evening or weekend could mean more opportunity for her and Lincoln's relationship to grow.

Kali turned to the sound of the door. Warmth seeped through her at the sight of Lincoln. "How was breakfast with your mom?" Noting his face and the slump to his shoulders, she stepped forward. "What is it? What's wrong?"

Lincoln rubbed a hand over the side of his face and sank to the couch. "This has been the week from hell." He let out a short laugh. "It hasn't even been a week. Three days. This has been the three days from hell."

Kali sat beside him. "What is it?"

"My father, who has basically been dead to me for years anyway, is actually dying. Has days." He stared toward the other side of the room. "But why should I care, right? I mean, not heartlessly, like 'I don't care,' but really, I haven't seen him in eleven years. The Dad I knew has been gone for that long ... longer, really."

Kali put a hand to his leg. "It isn't the same thing."

Lincoln turned to her, his eyes moist. "My mother wants me to go visit him. Say goodbye. But how do you say goodbye to someone who isn't even there?"

Kali gave his leg a squeeze. "You say the words, maybe hold his hand."

"You make it sound so simple."

Kali let out a soft sigh. "It can be. I've seen this many times before." She bit her lip. "People can sense presence, love, especially when they're close to death. It goes beyond brain power, conversational skills, sometimes even beyond consciousness. The brain waves, heart rate, of patients in comas have been known to shift, settle when a loved one is in the room, speaking to or touching them. All you need to do is say the words."

Lincoln closed his eyes, his head shaking. "I've been such a wretched son."

"You've done what you needed to do for self-preservation. That's understandable."

Another sad laugh. "To who?"

"Well," Kali shifted, "to me. I get it."

"My family doesn't. They think I'm weak and selfish."

"Have they said that?"

"Linda has, basically, the others ... I see it."

"You were a child; they were almost grown. It's different."

"I'm not a child anymore."

Kali lifted her hand and set it in her own lap. "No. You're not."

"I'm angry, you know? At him. He's the one who's suffered all these years, lost everything he once was, and I'm angry at him."

"That's fairly normal."

Lincoln raised an eyebrow.

"Trust me. It is."

He nodded and turned his gaze back to something on the other side of the room. "He promised he'd always be there for me. Swore it. What a lie. No one is always there for anyone, ever. But I didn't know that then. I believed him."

Kali's throat clenched. She resisted the urge to take him in her arms, sensing it wasn't what he needed. Not now. "That's probably what you needed to believe at the time. At the time, maybe it was the right thing for him to say."

"I can't see him. Not like—"

"Of course you can."

"All wasted away. Barely even human?"

Kali sat straighter, annoyance edging into her sympathy. "He's human. Nothing can change that."

"Yeah, but."

"No." Kali fought the sharpness in her voice. "He's human and he's your father. You know where he is. I can see how you feel he left you, but it wasn't his choice. You had eleven wonderful years with him and, what, four or five partial ones?" She looked away. "I understand you not visiting him, but that was your choice. He was there. He was the one suffering from one of the cruelest diseases out there. If I—" Kali shook her head, her voice cutting off.

Lincoln stared at her. "If you what?"

Kali closed her eyes and took a deep breath. "If I'd had the chance to know my father, if he'd stayed around long enough to give me memories, advice, to know he gave a shit about me—" She stopped and put a hand on his thigh. "Look, I know it's different, and I know it's been hard, but you had a father. You still have a father. Maybe he doesn't know it, but you do. And you have no idea what he may know. Maybe he remembers you, somewhere at the core of him, but can't express it. Maybe in his lucid moments he's missed you, wondered where you were, felt abandoned." Kali's voice trembled. "I know what it is to feel abandoned and have no way to tell the person how hurt you are."

Lincoln's eyes narrowed; he reached for her hand. "I'm sorry, I—"

"Listen, you don't know what he knows or doesn't know, what he feels or doesn't feel, and as much as I think you should go for you, if going for him would give him even the slightest amount of comfort, if sitting by his bed would let him feel some of the love he may have been missing from you all these years, then yes, you'd be a selfish bastard not to go."

Lincoln stared at Kali, his eyes wide. "Okay."

"What?"

"I'll go."

Kali rubbed a hand across her face. She let out a puff of air and pushed her hands along her thighs. "I'm sorry, I shouldn't have, this is about you and your dad, not me and mine ... I just started thinking and—"

"No, you're right. I've been selfish. I don't know what he knows or feels. It's too late now ... to erase all the years I stayed away. But I can stop being selfish for an hour."

Kali closed her eyes, shame flowing over her again. She'd had her father stolen from her, and yet she'd been robbing Theo of his ...

"You're right. I was lucky to have him for as long as I did. Not everybody gets even that. So thank you." Lincoln gave a small smile. "For calling me out."

Kali smiled. This was about Lincoln. Not her. Not Theo. "Any time."

Lincoln took Kali's hand, his touch strong and gentle, and gave it a squeeze. Kali squeezed back just as Theo bounded into the room.

CHAPTER TWENTY-ONE

Lincoln pulled up in front of Westwood. He maneuvered his truck into a spot far from the entrance and turned off the ignition.

Three days. It'd taken him that long. Three days, and each one a gamble, lowering the chance that he'd need to show up at all. He'd spent two of those days trying to work off his insecurities at the lot. The first day, while picking stuff up at the apartment, he'd seen Theo, laughing and smiling in Derek's arms. It hadn't been easy.

Kali didn't bring Derek into the apartment, which Lincoln appreciated, but he'd happened to be walking by the window when he heard Theo's laughter below and caught sight of the scene. It intensified his need to have a backup plan, a place this winter to call his own if Kali chose Derek. Though if she chose him, she may not be needing Lincoln's apartment after all. He shook his head, trying not to think of it—Kali moving in with Derek. Theo moving in with Derek. Lincoln saying goodbye for good.

Either way, Kali no longer needed Lincoln's apartment. She'd made that especially clear as she handed him the cheque—all the money she'd owed him since they met. Even her share of the room in New York. He'd tried to say no, but she wasn't having it. It felt like farewell, taking that small piece of paper, but she was still in his apartment—their apartment—with no sign of leaving.

Either way, all of it was an excuse, a way to justify his cowardice, a way to delay walking across this parking lot, down the hall, and to his father's room. One fear had nothing to do with the other.

Lincoln grabbed hold of the truck's door handle and pushed it open. He crossed the lot—one foot in front of the other. That's all it took. Lift one foot, set it down, lift the other, repeat. The automatic doors slid open and Lincoln stepped inside, turning in a direction he hadn't turned in over a decade.

At the reception, he listened to the simple instructions then gave a nod of thanks. He heard Linda's voice before he saw her—tense, strained, attempting to whisper, something she'd never been good at.

"We don't know what he'd want now. We can't know."

Rachel. "He signed a DNR. He didn't want feeding tubes or IV. He wanted to be allowed to die. That's what we know."

"That was years ago." Linda's hiss. "He had no idea of the developments. They're discovering new things all the time. Next week or next month there could be something that—"

"Or years." Aunt Gertie now, her voice soft. "Would you really want him to suffer for years?"

"No, but—"

Lincoln turned the corner to see Aunt Gertie, one hand on Linda's shoulder, the other reaching to hold her opposite hand. "Let's hope and pray those developments are in time for you, okay? And if they're not, we'll do whatever it is you want when the time comes."

"Lincoln." Rachel stepped toward him, her face lighting up then softening into a smile.

Linda spun, her expression immediately turning from fear and sadness to what he could only call disgust. "It's about time."

"Linda." Aunt Gertie chastised. She turned to him. "Lincoln, sweetie. We're so glad you came."

Lincoln's throat closed. He couldn't get a word out if he wanted, not that he knew what to say. Gertie wrapped Lincoln in his arms. After stepping away she gestured to a room up the hall from them. "Your mother's in there now but I'm sure she wouldn't mind you joining or taking a turn."

Lincoln nodded and stepped past the women, wishing he had something in his hand. A hat, a sweater, a bag ... something to twist, or at least hold on to. The room smelled of antiseptic and flowers. Standing at the door, he saw his mother's back, her hands, and the raised mounds of legs under a sheet. He entered the room and Marilyn turned.

She turned away again and leaned forward, kissing or whispering words to his father, Lincoln presumed, though a cupboard of some sort prevented him from seeing past the middle of the bed. Marilyn turned back to Lincoln and waved him toward her. Step by step, he managed to move his feet forward, his father slowly coming into view.

But this wasn't his father. The body in the bed wasn't even reminiscent of the man he remembered from over a decade ago. The body on the bed looked like the shell of a man. Thin to the bone, shrivelled, and ancient. The man's eyes stared vacantly at something on the far wall.

Marilyn put a hand on Lincoln's shoulder. "It's okay. It's him. I know it doesn't look it, but it's him."

Lincoln gave a slight nod to his mother then turned his gaze back to the man in the bed.

"Sweetie," his mother's voice was dulcet, the way she'd talk to a young child, "this is Lincoln. He's come for a visit."

Lincoln swallowed. "Does he understand?"

Marilyn tilted her head. "He might. Either way, we still talk to him." She patted Lincoln's shoulder. "I'm going to go out for a bit. Just sit, talk ... or not. Let him know you're here."

"But what do I—?"

Marilyn squeezed his shoulder. "You'll figure it out."

Lincoln watched his mother leave the room than turned back to this man who was supposed to be his father. Again he wanted something in his hands to hold, twist, clench. He pulled out the chair his mother had sat in and cleared his throat. "Hi."

No response. No flicker of his father's eyes or acknowledgement that Lincoln was here beside him. Lincoln glanced around the room, looking for a clock. No luck. How long would he need to stay here to satisfy a visit? Five minutes? Ten? Fifteen? He could pull out his phone to start timing but didn't want one of his family to walk in the moment he was looking at the screen.

Lincoln took a deep breath and leaned against the chair back, his shoulders drooping as he stared at his father, who stared past him. It seemed impossible that this was the same human who'd held Lincoln on his shoulders, built houses, laughed such a booming laugh it reverberated off the walls.

Anger coursed through him. Which was ludicrous. This disease wasn't his father's fault. He'd have kept his promise if he could. But still, staring at this stranger, the anger took over: for all the years of watching his father deteriorate, for all the years it happened out of his view.

A sound at the door and Lincoln twisted in his seat.

"Don't mind me." A middle aged woman breezed in and went to the other side of the room. She shifted his father, moving pillows and rearranging Alexander Fraser's limbs. A stranger rearranging his limbs ... because he couldn't do it himself.

Lincoln stood. "I'm sorry. Do you need to—?"

"Don't get up on my account." The woman waved a hand at Lincoln.

"Oh." Lincoln sat. "What are you doing?"

"Adjusting his position. Every two hours." She stopped her maneuvering and stared at Lincoln. "You've not been here before, have you?"

"Not, uh, not for a long time."

"Hmm. Family?"

"His son."

"Oh." The woman put her hands on her hips. "You're the one who was away."

Lincoln swallowed. "Yeah."

"Well," the woman smiled and made a few more adjustments to his father before standing straight again. "Good you're here now."

She came around to the cupboard behind Lincoln and pulled out a bottle of lotion. "It's about time he gets his hands rubbed. Usually whoever is visiting does it." She passed Lincoln the bottle.

"Oh, I ... uh ..."

"It's fine, sweetie. His hands get cold. Not enough

circulation. All you need to do is apply a little lotion and gently rub. His wrists, hands, each finger. You can't do it wrong." She grinned. "And he likes it."

Lincoln took the bottle and turned back to his father as the woman vanished as quickly as she'd appeared. He stared at the bottle, then at the frail hands before him. Undoing the cap, he poured some lotion in his hand. He stared at that too. It felt odd, the idea of reaching for his father's hand without permission, taking it in his own.

"Dad?" Lincoln's voice came out quieter than he expected. "The nurse said you need your hands rubbed now. So, I'm going to do that. Okay?"

He waited for some kind of response, knowing it wouldn't come, then reached for his father's closest hand. It was lighter than he imagined, the skin feeling more like paper than flesh. He started at the wrist, as the nurse said, then slowly, as gently as he could, worked his way across the hand and each finger. When he raised his head to reach for the other hand he startled. His father's gaze was on him, clearly focused on him, and his expression had shifted. Lincoln couldn't call it a smile, not on his father's lips, not quite. But in his eyes ... maybe.

"Hey, Dad." Lincoln kept his grasp on the hand he'd massaged and wrapped his other hand around it. "I'm sorry it took me so long to come. I thought about it. A lot." Lincoln looked away and blew out a stream of air before returning his gaze to his father. "I guess I was scared. Really scared. I didn't want to see ... this." Lincoln caressed his thumb over the top of the frail hand. "I thought it didn't matter either, not to you. I hope it didn't. I'm sorry if it did. I'm sorry if I hurt you." Lincoln's breath faltered and he wiped a hand across his face.

"A lot's happened in the past decade. I bet Mom's told you

most of it ... what she knows anyway. I graduated university and grad school too. I went to work for Joseph for a while and I fell in love—maybe twice. Maybe not at all. Neither worked out." Lincoln bit his lips, his gaze still on his father's, on that unchanging almost-smile.

"I think I'm in love again, but I'm not sure if that's going to work out either. She has a kid. A boy. And he's amazing. I'm definitely in love with him. Without a doubt. He's got a dad though, and I don't know if it's right, me being in the way, or if I'm just scared or jealous. Scared she won't pick me, you know?"

Lincoln gazed at their hands. He sat silent.

"I wish I knew if you knew me. If you knew these words even. It's so hard not to get angry." His voice tensed. "You should have been here." He shook his head, his throat raw. "So many times I wanted to talk to you, get your advice. I'd try to think about what you would have told me each time, but I could never quite figure it out. I wanted to make you proud, but never felt like I was."

Lincoln closed his eyes, his father's words coming back to him when he'd lost his temper as a child. *Breathe it out. Just breathe—slow and deep, and your anger will go away, or at least become less intense.* He'd wink then. *It'll allow you to think.*

Lincoln took a deep breath, opened his eyes, and gave a little shrug. "Maybe you'd be proud now. I'm going to start my own business. Building. Tree houses, actually." Lincoln gave a little laugh. "Do you remember that vacation house we went to one summer? I was probably eight, maybe nine. The one with the tree house in the backyard? That's where the fascination started. Just you and me, away from the girls, away from Joseph. It was our special place. You taught me to whittle that summer, taught me about building in general, that each part was equally important, even the ones no one would see. Especially those."

Lincoln inhaled softly. "Even if you don't remember, I'm sure you would if it wasn't for … for," Lincoln's voice faltered, "this.

"Anyway, that's what I'm going to do. I've already built one. Out on a lot toward Musquodoboit. It's really great. Beautiful and sturdy. Safe. I'm working on winterizing it." Lincoln stopped, his shoulders shaking. "I really missed you." He closed his eyes. "And I love you. And I'm sorry. You deserved better from me. I should have been stronger." Lincoln leaned forward and reached his arm across his father, careful to let the weight of his head rest on the bed, rather than that frail chest.

"I wish I could change things. I wish—"

A noise emerged from his father, shocking Lincoln to an upright position. His eyes were still smiling, though sadder now. His Dad's hand moved in Lincoln's, the slightest squeeze.

Lincoln wiped his arm across his face, squirted more lotion into his palm, then reached for his father's other hand and started massaging.

We tell ourselves a story:
We matter. This matters.

CHAPTER TWENTY-TWO

Theo laughed, his face lighting up. He clapped his hands then ran around to the start of the track Lincoln had built for him months ago. He set his and Kali's car up again.

Kali grinned and caught Lincoln's eye. Lincoln smiled at her, at them, and how far they'd both come—Theo overcoming his fear of speech, Kali triumphing through the pain and loss of her vision. He'd played a roll in all of it. He'd helped. But they didn't need that help anymore.

"Okay, last run," said Kali. "Then you need to get yourself changed for bed."

"And stories."

"And stories." Kali laughed.

Theo stood and pointed his arm at Lincoln. "You."

"What? Race?"

Theo's eyes brightened. "Yes, race. And stories!"

"You want me to read to you tonight?"

Theo nodded as he waved Lincoln over to the track. Lincoln picked up a car and crouched down between Theo and Kali. After two more races, Kali insisted enough was enough.

Lincoln situated himself on the bed as Theo, in his race car pyjamas, sidled up beside him. He dropped five books into Lincoln's lap. "Oh, I don't know about that." Lincoln gave Theo a sideways grin. "I think just two. You already had some extra races."

Theo crossed his arms and shook his head.

"Yup. Just three." Lincoln winked. "You pick which ones."

Theo sorted through the books, pulling out the thickest three, and Lincoln started to read. After the third, Theo held up the fourth book.

"Nope."

Theo tilted his head and grabbed the fifth.

"Not happening."

With a little sigh, Theo gathered all five books and set them on the bedside table. He lifted his arms to Lincoln. Lincoln closed his eyes as the little arms reached around him. He stood and tucked Theo in, then walked to the door, his hand hovering over the light switch. "Sleep well, buddy."

Theo smiled and snuggled into the pillow.

Back in the living room, Kali shifted over on the couch at the sight of Lincoln. She patted the cushion. Lincoln crossed the room and eased himself down beside her, shifting his body so that he could see her clearly.

"He go down all right?" Kali asked as she shut down her lap top.

"Yeah, no problems."

Kali leaned into the couch. "You feeling okay? You've been really quiet tonight. The last few days, really."

"Saw my dad a couple of days ago."

"Oh." Kali's brows raised. "That must have been ..."

"Hard. It was very hard."

"And are you glad? That you went?"

Lincoln looked to the seat cushions. "I wish I'd gone sooner. I wish I could bring myself to go again." He looked back at Kali. "I think we should take some time apart."

"What?" Kali sat up. "What do you mean?"

"I didn't have my dad growing up ... for most of it anyway, not in the way I should have. And I know this is a different situation, but I, I don't want to stand in the way of Theo having his father."

"You're not."

"But I could be."

"No."

Lincoln raised a hand. "Look, if I'm not here, if you're able to spend time with Derek, get to know each other again without thoughts of me, who knows? You said yourself ..."

"I didn't say anything."

"You implied."

Kali's expression tightened. "Listen, if you want to walk, you can walk, but don't use Theo having a father as an excuse. Theo having his father is all about whether Derek stays or leaves, and that has nothing to do with you and me. If you want to leave because you're afraid I won't choose you, then say that. But I've told you, if I don't, it's not going to be because of Derek."

"But maybe it would be if I wasn't here. And yeah, maybe you're right. Maybe I'm afraid. Maybe I'm using Theo as an excuse. Ginny left. Lucy left. My dad left. If you two left—"

"I've known you for less than six months!" Kali gasped. "I can't promise you forever."

"And I'm not asking you to."

"But you are. That's what this is—"

"It's not. Really." Lincoln motioned to stand.

"Sit down."

Kali nearly glared at him. "So what, are you kicking us out?"

"No. Absolutely not." Lincoln settled back into the couch and leaned forward, his arms resting on his knees. "The tree house is livable for now. I should be able to make it winter safe in time if I keep working."

"Winter safe." Kali laughed. "And what about the road in? What about food?"

"This was my plan all along. And now, because of your idea, it's improved. I'll work on my business—"

"From a tree house in the middle of nowhere? How are you going to do that without phone lines and electricity and internet?"

Lincoln lowered his head. He hadn't thought about that. "I have a generator. And maybe satellite internet. I can buy a computer. If that doesn't work, both Cole Harbour and Musquodoboit have libraries."

Kali rubbed a hand on her chest. "So this is it? We're done? You're breaking up with me?"

Lincoln shook his head. "We can't break up. We were never really together. Right?"

Kali's eyes narrowed.

"No, though. Not unless you want this to be the end. I don't. I'm not ready to lose you. I just think maybe it would be good for both of us to have some time apart. To think."

"Don't you think we could think better together? Figure it out to—"

"I need time. You. Derek. Joseph. My father. I just need

time."

"Isn't that the point of being with someone? So during the hard times you're not alone. So when you have some burden you can share it, make it—"

"The way you shared with me when you thought Derek was back?"

Kali's throat convulsed.

"You didn't share. Maybe if you had."

Kali pulled her lap top to her chest, her arms wrapped around it. "Fine. If you need time to think, take it. But I'm not ready to give up on us. Yet, anyway. So don't take too long." She stood. "And Derek and me, we're not happening. So that part of your plan, it's pointless."

Lincoln smiled. "I hope that's true, but if it's not, it's okay."

Kali shifted in place. "So when are you taking off to the woods?"

"I thought tomorrow after breakfast. So I could say goodbye to Theo."

"And how long do you propose this break will be?"

Lincoln shrugged. "I'm not sure."

"Will we still talk?"

"I don't know."

"Well, you've thought everything out."

"If there's an emergency or—"

"Fine. I get it." Kali backed toward the hall. "Good night."

CHAPTER TWENTY-THREE

The next morning, Kali stood at the window watching Lincoln's truck pull away from the curb. He'd forgotten today was her meeting at CNIB. Not that he would have been taking care of Theo anyway, he'd have been at work. But still, he wasn't at work, and several weeks ago he would have been insulted if she didn't assume he'd want to watch Theo for her.

A break. Time apart. It made sense. She hadn't trusted him. She'd lied to him ... a lie of omission, which was still a lie. In some small way, in his eyes at least, she'd made him a cheater.

And what about in her eyes? She'd been telling herself the past few months her resistance to taking their relationship further had to do with her fear of committing, of trusting someone again ... but had it been more? She didn't feel married. She'd been willing, eager to sleep with Lincoln in New York, but that hadn't even been about sex, or intimacy. It'd merely been about a last chance.

Kali inhaled, taking time during the exhale to assess her body. A mild headache, discomfort really, almost no nausea.

The fatigue was lessening everyday, as if she was slowly climbing out of a rut and could finally see a glimpse of the sun.

She was getting better, or at least her symptoms were. Her vision may not return, but what she had, if it stayed this way, was manageable. And her eyes were opened now, to the opportunities she still had.

Allison, her supervisor at Westwood, had called last week about setting up an assessment to judge Kali's ability to return to work with assistive technology. She told Kali to call back as soon as her doctors felt confident the swelling from treatment had reduced.

And Kali had other options too, counselling, training ... Alika and the others she'd met at the CNIB were opening doors Kali never imagined existed.

"When you leave?"

Kali turned to Theo, who stood at the entry to the hall in a red t-shirt and dinosaur briefs. "Where are your pants?"

Theo grinned. "Today I wear no pants."

"Ha." Kali shook her head, trying to suppress a grin. "I don't think so."

"I do think so." Theo swayed his hips. "No one sees the dinosaurs. I want them to see the dinosaurs."

"The dinosaurs are for you." Kali crossed the room and scooped Theo up in her arms, tickling him. "No one else needs to see them."

Theo pointed to Kali.

Kali smiled down at him. "Okay. For you and for me. No one else needs to see them."

Theo tilted his head, a smile so sweet Kali found it hard not to give in. "But maybe other people need to see them too.

Maybe they like them."

"They might." Kali gave Theo a squeeze and set him down. "But we're not going to find out. Pants or shorts go on outside the house. Always."

"Please." Theo turned and thrust out his bottom, pointing to the triceratops on his rump. "Look, he's nice."

"He's very nice." Kali laughed. "And he'll be nicer underneath your jeans." Kali gave Theo's bottom a soft smack. "Go change. We've got to get you to Mrs. Martin's, and trust me, she does not want to see you walking around in your dinosaur undies!"

Theo shifted into his thinking pose, elbow in one hand and chin in the opposite. "Maybe I can go to Daddy's."

"Hmm?"

"Maybe Daddy can daycare me."

"Oh." Kali swallowed. "I don't think so."

Theo raised his arm in the air, his smile flashing. "I think yes!"

"We don't know Daddy very well yet."

"He's nice. And fun!"

"I know but—" Kali's voice trailed off.

Theo's brow furrowed. "But he's my daddy, right?"

"Yes."

"Cherie says daddies live with you. And when they don't then you go to their house when you're not at Mommy's and ..." he paused, thinking, "two Christmases and two birthdays."

Kali pressed her lips into a half-grimace, half-smile. "Sometimes that's true, but not always."

"I get two Christmases?"

Kali rubbed a hand along her neck. "Maybe." She hadn't thought about that, hadn't thought about a lot of things. "We could probably all spend Christmas together."

Could they? If Lincoln's 'break' really was just that, could the five of them all celebrate Christmas? Would Lincoln want to join his family—it'd be a big Christmas dinner, most likely, with cousins and aunts and uncles, maybe a secret Santa. Kali and Theo would be invited, for sure. But Derek? Marvin? Theo stared at her, his head tilted, waiting for a better answer.

"Go put on your pants." Kali's voice came out firmer than she intended. She softened it. "We need to get you to Mrs. Martin's or I'll be late."

Theo turned and took exaggerated stomps down the hall. For the briefest moment, Kali missed the days before Theo asked questions and before she needed to give answers.

Lincoln was right. They had a lot to think about. Kali wanted Lincoln. She was sure of it. Or, at least sure she didn't want him walking out of their lives. But if he did walk? And if Derek stayed and wanted to give it another try?

She'd convinced herself she could be alone, that Theo would be enough, but after these past months with Lincoln—having someone to rely on, talk to, curl up on the couch with, kiss ... she wasn't sure she wanted to be alone anymore.

If only she could turn back the clock, tell Lincoln the truth. She didn't want to be alone. And if Lincoln left and Derek stayed ... maybe she still wouldn't have to be.

"Ready." Theo's arrival snapped Kali to attention.

"Good. Great." She motioned to the door. "Put on your shoes and lets go."

ALL THROUGH THE CNIB meeting, Kali's thoughts travelled from the discussion at hand to the questions Theo had raised.

Two Christmases. Two birthdays. It wouldn't be so bad. But she also didn't want Theo to think his parents couldn't be in the same room together. They could. She could. Should she try again with Derek? Should she? Could they make it work?

That'd been her childhood dream for years—for her father to come back, to be a father, a dad. For her parents to make it work. To be a family. A real family. Kali inhaled. Not that there was any such thing as a 'real' family. Family was family. It was what you made it—blood or no. Still.

Still.

It felt like a betrayal: considering Derek, imagining a life with Derek. But it's what Lincoln wanted her to do, why they were on this break, and not once had she made a commitment to Lincoln. It was to Derek she'd made the commitments.

A BURST OF LAUGHTER erupted from the group. Kali glanced around the room, chuckling, though she had no idea at what.

Focus, Kali. Focus.

She nodded at something Alika was saying, though the words didn't take on meaning. Her mind reeled with possibilities, the past and the future. She'd shut herself off to Derek in every way imaginable when he'd stood on their porch then turned away, choosing a life without her. She'd justified keeping Theo from him, never replying to a letter or card by telling herself he'd been the one to abandon them first. Absolutely. Only it hadn't been absolute. The money proved that. The trip back for her mother's funeral proved that. If she was honest with herself, the cards and letters and occasional phone calls early on proved that too. Phone calls she'd never answered. Letters she hadn't read.

She had to acknowledge her own role in their relationship

falling apart—instead of blaming it all on him, choosing to be the martyr.

He'd left, but she'd pushed him away, again and again. She'd resented the phone calls, letters, birthday and Christmas cards. What was a twenty-five dollar gift when she had real bills to pay? A slap in the face, that's what.

But what would a returned card or letter have meant to Derek as he lay in a hospital bed, recovering from the loss of a limb? As he dealt with the guilt of his brother's death, the pain of comrades lost? She could have written back, easily. She wouldn't have even had to write anything. She could have sent pictures of Theo in his favourite cowboy hat. She could have sent artwork, hand prints. She could have not been so bitter and selfish.

"Kali?"

"Huh?" Kali returned her attention to the room. All eyes were in her general direction. How many times had her name been called? Kali focused her gaze on Heather. "I mean, yes?"

Heather clapped her hands together. "Oh that's great. So, you're my partner for planning Dining in the Dark?"

Dining in the Dark? Kali tried to filter through the bits and pieces of conversation that had floated around her while she was lost in her own thoughts. They'd been talking about fundraisers earlier, and outings they could go on. "What exactly will it entail?"

Heather gave her an odd little smile. "Well, as I was saying, I can handle most of the legalese required, but I'd love to have someone come with me to pick a restaurant, set everything up with the owner, help coordinate the distribution of flyers, coordinate social media and media outlet notifications."

"Oh," Kali put a hand to her throat. "I don't know if I—"

"You'd be great," insisted Casey, the Independent Living Skills coordinator, who was sitting in on today's meeting. "And you were saying in last week's session that you wanted to get more involved."

Kali glanced between the two women. "I thought maybe I'd help out here at CNIB, not—"

"We'll get a free meal out of it," grinned Heather, "a really good meal. For us and one guest each."

"Well—"

"Please." Heather's smile increased. "Plus, it'll give us a chance to get to know each other better."

Kali's chest thumped. Taking something else on right now ... maybe it was exactly what she needed. A distraction. "Sure." Kali smiled back, hoping she wasn't getting herself into something she'd regret."I'd be happy to."

CHAPTER TWENTY-FOUR

Lincoln sank to the floor of his little cabin in the sky and pulled out his phone. He'd been putting in twelve hour days and sat amazed at how much progress he'd made. It was only lunch time and already he'd put in five hours. Another week like this and the cabin would be fully livable for the winter.

He flipped open his phone without looking at the caller ID. "Hello?"

"Lincoln?"

"Rachel?" Lincoln hesitated at the tone of her voice.

"Did ...?"

"Yeah." Rachel sighed, the sound so sad Lincoln wanted to reach through the phone and hold her. "A part of me is relieved. Think I'll go to hell?"

"No. You? No."

The line went silent for several breaths. "It's so wretched."

"I know."

"Do you?"

Lincoln bristled at the accusation in her voice.

"I'm sorry. I know it was different for you, I know—"

Lincoln straightened. "No. I deserve that. You were there. You saw it all. For years."

"You don't deserve anything." Rachel sighed. "None of it matters now. He's gone. He's not suffering. Hopefully, wherever he is he remembers ... everything. Everything he'd lost. Hopefully he's him again."

"Yeah." Lincoln's eyes misted; his father, the man he'd seen just days ago, the man who'd barrelled into the kitchen on Saturday mornings, Lincoln hanging off of one arm, Rachel off of the other. A man so strong nothing could stop him ... except his own brain. It didn't seem possible they were one and the same. "How's Mom?"

More silence. "I don't know. She's Mom. Strong. Taking care of all of us. But there's this emptiness in her eyes. It's like she's wilted." Another soft sigh. "Dad was her life."

"But not for years. Not really."

"She went four to five times a week, Lincoln. At least. Sometimes more."

"That much?"

"That much. She had her life outside of that. She was good at compartmentalizing. But all that time, all that energy." Silence. "Do you think anyone will ever love us like that?"

"Mom does."

"You know what I mean."

He did know and couldn't imagine it, at least not for him. "Someone will love you like that."

Rachel's voice tightened more. "I'd have to let them first."

"What?"

Emptiness flooded her words. "I'm too scared to test, but until I do I push every man away who shows interest. How could I do that to someone? Knowingly put them through what we've all been through? How could I condemn someone, someone who loves me but doesn't have to, to watch that?"

Lincoln stood and paced the small room. "You can't think like that."

"Why not? You don't?"

Silence.

"Does Kali know?"

Lincoln hesitated. "She does. But we're not ..."

Rachel let out a short laugh. "Oh, you are. But I guess she has her own ticking time bomb. It's the possibility of mutual destruction."

"Rachel." Lincoln kept pacing. Rachel was supposed to be the optimistic one. The family Pollyanna. The peacemaker. He'd never heard such bitterness come out of her mouth.

"I'm sorry. I just ... it's hard."

"It is."

"Anyway," Rachel sighed, "all of the family are getting together tonight at Mom's. You'll come."

To a place where his abandonment of his father would be more evident than ever, where every person present would have visited the man more in the past week than Lincoln had in the past decade? Where Joseph would be, and Lucy too. Their unborn child. "When's the funeral? I'll be there for—"

"It wasn't a question." Rachel's voice hardened. "You'll come tonight. And you'll be there tomorrow and the next day and the one after that, for the funeral."

"Rach—"

"Mom needs her children right now." Another sigh. "I'll see you tonight."

The line clicked.

Lincoln stared at the phone. His father was dead. Really dead. Truly dead. Not just lost. Not just missing all of the things that made him him.

Lincoln pushed out a long breath of air as a hollow tension radiated through his chest. Needing air, he made his way to the porch.

His father was dead. And Lincoln hadn't been there. He'd said his goodbye, yes, but he hadn't been there. He'd told himself he was going to go back. Each of the days that had passed he'd told himself that. Now it was too late.

Had Joseph been there at the last moment? Linda? Rachel? His mother could have missed it, but Lincoln doubted that. As the time came closer she wouldn't have left his side, she would have held his hand. If not his mother, Lincoln hoped someone had held his father's hand. He hoped, in that last moment, his father had known he was loved.

A drop of moisture landed on Lincoln's collar bone. He looked to the sky before realizing this rain had come from his own eyes.

He rubbed both hands over his face, wiping the liquid away.

His father was dead.

LINCOLN WORKED ON the tree house for another four hours then returned to the Brunswick Street apartment to shower and change. Plumbing was one of the things that still needed work at the tree house and he didn't think a dip in the lake would suffice for tonight's gathering.

Walking up the steps to his unit, Lincoln debated whether he should have called Kali before returning, but it was still his apartment. The only reason, really, would be to avoid an encounter with Derek.

He unlocked the door to an empty living room. A peek into the kitchen revealed it was vacant as well. Lincoln grabbed a change of clothes from his room and made his way down the hall, the sound of voices increasing with each step he took. He rapped deftly on Kali and Theo's bedroom door, not wanting to startle her with the loud groan of the shower starting up.

"Hello?"

"Hi." Lincoln pushed the ajar door open all the way.

"Lincoln!" Theo scrambled over Kali's bed, where he'd sat, half dressed, and flung himself into Lincoln's arms.

Lincoln lifted the boy, a thick emotion filled lump pushing away the hollowness he'd felt since Rachel's phone call. "Hey, buddy." Lincoln squeezed Theo tight.

"What is it?" Kali stepped toward them. "Is your dad?"

Lincoln gave a slight nod as he set Theo down. "He's passed."

"Passed what?" asked Theo.

"Oh," Kali put a hand to Theo's head, "passed away. Lincoln's daddy isn't here anymore. He's died."

"Lincoln has a daddy?" Theo's eyes widened. "Why don't we know him? Is he Mrs. Marilyn's husband?"

"He is ... was ... yes. But he was very sick, so he didn't live with her."

"Where'd he live then?"

Kali looked from Lincoln to Theo, seeming like she didn't know where to give her attention. Her gaze landed on Theo. "He lived in a home for sick people. Where Mommy worked, actually. So nurses could help take care of him."

"In the hop-ital?"

"Not quite. Kind of." Kali took a breath, her gaze on Lincoln now. "Theo, finish getting dressed, okay? Lincoln and I are going to talk."

"I spilled ketchup on my shirt," said Theo.

Lincoln nodded at Theo as Kali ushered him out to the hall. She put a hand on Lincoln's arm. "How are you?"

Lincoln turned from her. "I need to shower. To change."

"Okay." Kali kept her hand on his arm. "But how are you?"

Lincoln shrugged while trying to rub away an encroaching headache. "I don't know. My dad's dead. But I haven't spoken to him, not really, in over a decade. So ..."

Kali's brow furrowed. "Are you going somewhere?"

"To Mom's. They're gathering. All the family ... I think all the family. Maybe. I don't know. Maybe just my family."

"I can come. I'll call Mrs. Martin or see if Marvin will come over, or bring Theo or—"

Lincoln shook his head. "No. That's not a good idea."

"What? Why? The break? I don't think that really—"

Lincoln looked away. "I need to shower." He stepped past Kali and into the bathroom. With the door closed, he peeled off his clothes, his body feeling not his own, nothing feeling right. He wanted Kali to come, wanted her hand on his arm, wanted her next to him as he was hugged and silently chastised by his relations. Wanted her so bad it ached. But seeing her, knowing if Derek had his way he may never see her again, made him ache more.

Lincoln stepped into the shower, twisted the nozzle to as hot as he could stand, and let the water pour over him for several minutes before reaching for his shampoo. He'd come so far, from a hermit wanting to distance himself from the world, to yearning to be part of it again. He feared this gathering of family, but yearned for it too—to see the glimpses of the father he used to know in Rachel's laugh, in Linda's nose, in Joseph's strong presence, and in his Uncle's entire being.

CHAPTER TWENTY-FIVE

"This place is so lovely." Heather laughed. "It's kind of a shame no one will actually see it."

Kali nodded then answered, remembering a moment too late that even though she was looking right at her, Heather probably wouldn't see the slight movement. "Yeah. It's really nice."

"At least they won't need to see the food to appreciate it."

"Mmhmm."

"Kali." Heather nudged Kali's shoulder. "You doing all right?"

"Yeah." Kali turned to Heather with a smile. "Sorry, kind of a rough night."

"Headaches bothering you?"

They weren't. Amazingly. "Mmhmm." Kali ran her hand over the linen. Had she ever eaten in a restaurant this fancy? "The manager's taking a long time, don't you think?"

"It's probably intentional. He wants to give us time to discuss, come up with any questions we may have. I'm pretty sold, though."

Kali turned her head to take in the space once more. "It's

spacious. The ceilings are high, the walls uncluttered. It's very accessible from outside. The seating isn't too close together and the manager seems more than willing to accommodate. I'm with you—this is the one."

Heather gave a satisfied smile. "Every year it's getting easier. The first year we held it we went to ten restaurants before we found one that was on board."

"Well, I guess as the word gets out they realize it's good marketing for them too."

Heather turned so she was facing Kali directly. "Have you decided who you're bringing?"

She had. She thought she had. Only now they were supposed to be giving each other space. Serious space, not invited to his father's funeral space. "Not sure yet."

"I've brought my husband every other year but this year I decided to give my sister the free pass. She's come before, of course, buying a ticket. But my eldest has a soccer game so my husband's going to that." Heather paused. "Theo's father isn't in the picture anymore, is he?"

"Actually, he is." Kali wrapped her arms around her middle. "Just recently."

"But you're not ..."

"No. We're not." Kali turned, pretending to take in the room again. "I think he'd like to be, but the past is the past."

"I understand that. Though as life passes, you do realize things can be forgiven that you never thought possible, and the bonds of family are strong." Heather hesitated. "You and the father, it's amiable?"

Kali swallowed and stepped to the wall, letting her fingers graze over the raised wallpaper.

Heather let out a short sigh. "I'm sorry if I press too much,

Kali. When I get excited, my filters don't always work as they should."

"It's okay. I just—"

"Ladies." The manager walked back into the room. "My apologies for the delay. As you know, we're opening for the day shortly and there was a halibut issue in the kitchen." He gave a slight laugh, "Halibut issue," and shook his head. "But that's the life."

"No problem." Heather shifted her head, and Kali could tell from her gaze she was searching for the source of the voice through her pinhole of vision.

"So, what are your thoughts?" the manager asked.

Heather grinned as she zeroed in on his face. "If you're game, we are."

MARILYN STOOD IN FRONT of her children, her eyes red, her face puffy, her shoulders held back—strong and tall. "Tonight it's just the five of us." She looked to Linda. "Though you could have brought Steven and the boys."

Linda waved an arm. "You said you wanted your children tonight. They'll manage on their own."

Marilyn nodded a smile as Lincoln looked to Joseph, who didn't have Lucy by his side. Marilyn made no mention that he could have brought her.

"The rest of the family wanted to come but I've thought about this. I've had a lot of time to think about this." Marilyn's lips pressed into a little heart before she continued. "Tonight is for us, the family your father and I built. Tomorrow the relatives can come by, some close friends. The next day will be the wake. A closed casket, with a huge blow up picture he chose in the early days, so everyone will remember him as he was." A pause. "Then the funeral."

Marilyn placed her hands on her hips. "Until then, as much as we can, I want us to focus on the joy. Not on what we've lost, but what we had for too short a time. Focus on the amazing man your father was and all he did.

"At the funeral we can focus on the loss. Bawl as much as we want. Lament. Rage. Curse the heavens." She paused. "For everything else, the focus will be on what he gave us. How full of life he was in the short years we had him as him."

Lincoln shifted in his spot between Linda and Rachel. Linda had walked into the room with stooped shoulders, a trembling chin, and a hand full of tissues. Rachel had already been sitting, staring distantly at nothing but the wall, it seemed. She'd barely acknowledged Lincoln when he sat down beside her. Lincoln looked now to Joseph, who stared at their mother, his expression solemn, his jaw clenched and quivering. For the first time in almost a year, Lincoln felt no hate. All he saw was his brother, who he missed. Who he loved.

Lincoln brought his attention back to their mother.

"After the funeral, there'll be a gathering here. A party. With whiskey and food and music. I've ordered your father's favourite local band to set up out back."

Marilyn let her gaze travel over her children. "Don't think I'm saying you can't be sad now, or mourn or grieve. But as I said, I've thought about this a lot. I've read about this a lot. We've been grieving your father since you were children.

And you'll be grieving him in one way or another for the rest of your lives. For these few days, as we're surrounded by each other and all the people who loved him, all the people whose lives he touched, let's be joyful—as best we can. Let's remember. Let's have his presence in it all and maybe, for just these few days, it won't feel so much like he's gone."

Marilyn took a seat on the loveseat across from her children. Again her gaze travelled over the four of them. "Can we do that?"

Lincoln looked to his sisters then turned to Joseph, who leaned forward, his arms on his knees. "We'll do our best, Mom." His smile was tight but genuine. "I think it's a nice idea. To think of Dad as he was." Joseph blinked, his voice deep and rough. "It's been a while since I've done that to be honest."

Marilyn shifted and reached for Joseph's hand. He leaned forward and grasped it as she squeezed. "I think it's been that way for a lot of people. Myself sometimes too." She released his hand and leaned against the arm of the chair, her shoulders slumping. "He's been someone to pity, to avoid, to fear. But that's not who he was, not at all. That was the disease. Your father, though," she let out a soft laugh, "he was a man among men. Someone to trust, to follow, to respect. Someone who was loved and loved back."

An ache spread through Lincoln's throat as Marilyn looked to her lap before raising her gaze to her children. "That man knew how to love. I want to celebrate that. Remind people of that. Remind you of that." Again her smile seemed lit from somewhere deep within. "I know you have your differences, your hurts, but for these next few days, for me, please put them aside. They're real. And they're hard. I know that. But they're also less than the love you share beneath it all, than the blood that courses through your veins. So put it aside. Four days." She looked to the ceiling. "Not even. Today's almost done." This time she looked at each child before continuing. "Okay?"

They nodded. Rachel quickly. Linda and Joseph more hesitantly. Lincoln last, though he wasn't sure why. His mother's request wasn't unreasonable. If anything, it felt like a get-out-of-jail-free card. Like a burden lifting.

"Good." Marilyn slapped her hands on her knees. "Your Aunt Mev brought over one of her favourite stews."

"I thought I smelled that," said Rachel, finally perking up the slightest bit. "The stew beef one, right?"

"I think so," said Marilyn. "I was thinking dinner then family movies? See you all learning to walk and talk and ride your bikes." She stood and they all followed.

Linda's voice came out softer than Lincoln had remembered hearing since her boys were babies. "How about your wedding video? That'd be a good place to start, don't you think? The day that started it all—for our family, anyway?"

Marilyn's eyes crinkled as she laid her arm across Linda's shoulders. "The day that cemented it all, at least. It started long before that. Did I ever tell you about the first time I saw your father?"

"You told me." Joseph took his place at the table as Rachel brought over the stew. "It was on Natal Day, and you and Aunt Mev were there to meet two men Mev had met at a church picnic."

"Two older men," added Rachel as she set the stew in the centre of the table.

"And you met those men. Aunt Mev liked the one for her,

you were not so keen on the one for you," continued Linda.

"You all started dancing," grinned Joseph, "your man gave you a spin, your sandal broke—"

"And you literally fell into Dad's arms," finished Rachel.

"So you do know the story," laughed Marilyn. "And what happened next?"

As Lincoln's siblings continued the tale he soaked in this piece of history he'd never heard. They laughed, ate, and recounted stories—just the five of them, almost six. It felt like Dad was there, almost. It felt like home. Home in a way he hadn't felt, not this fully, since the day his father couldn't find the way back to their house, since everything changed.

It felt good.

Late in the night, after family movies, a look through his parents' wedding album, and a game of Monopoly, Lincoln climbed into his childhood bed, the familiar yet foreign sounds of his siblings getting ready for bed filtering through the closed doors. A smile crossed his face as he drifted to sleep. It was good to be home.

THE NEXT TWO DAYS FILLED with more stories, more family, more friends. Uncle Albert told the story of the first ladder his father had built, and how it collapsed beneath him when he was on the second to top rung. He'd been cleaning their mother's gutters and pulled the whole front portion off as he grasped it, trying to save himself.

Joseph recounted the way their father had always made time to tuck each of them in at night and read a story. 'Bedtime stories weren't just for mothers,' he used to say. And when Joseph was eight and declared he was too big for stories, their father had nodded. But the next week, when Joseph came down with the flu and changed his mind, their father was back in his room, every night, and kept the routine up till he was eleven.

Lincoln was more silent than the rest. He had less years of memories. And when tales of his father came up after diagnosis, even after being admitted to the home—tales of when, despite what should have been, Alexander returned to them for brief moments, just as he was, Lincoln had nothing to say. Rachel talked of the way he used to tease the nurses. Marilyn spoke of the days he'd lean forward, eager to know all the details of his children's lives. Linda's smile glistened as she told everyone of the days he remembered his grandchildren, who had been born long after he was deemed lost.

Laughter flowed through the room and into tears. Expressions of anger over the cruelty and uselessness of such a disease erupted. Tensions between Lincoln and his siblings, his siblings and their significant others, trickled in as well—he caught Joseph and Lucy arguing twice and Linda and Steven maybe three times as much.

But mostly the days were defined by love and shared memories. It was good. More healing than Lincoln could have imagined. Still, he missed Kali, missed Theo's smile and still surprising bursts of laughter.

CHAPTER TWENTY-SIX

A white wooden church with green trim. It looked like it should be on some country lane, not in the middle of the city. Kali adjusted her skirt as she assessed the steps. Probably when it was built, this was country.

Kali took a long breath of the crisp fall air, her gaze on the people milling on the steps, the walkway, and filing in through the doors. She gripped the railing with one hand and proceeded up the steps. Inside, she took a program from an usher—had she seen him before? At Rachel's birthday party?—and followed the mourners in front of her toward the aisle.

The family was at the front. She could make them out even from the back of their heads. Marilyn, Linda, Linda's husband, she supposed, the boys, Rachel, and Lincoln. No Joseph or Lucy, at least that she could see.

Kali slipped into a seat near the back of the church. Crashing a funeral. Was that even a thing? It's not like anyone really received an invitation, did they?

She'd called Lincoln three times. He'd answered the third, apologized for the missed calls. He was busy. Family and friends surrounded him constantly. It wasn't a good time to talk. Which she could understand. Of course she could understand. But she wanted to be part of the family surrounding him.

Kali pulled her gaze from the back of Lincoln's head and let it travel around the church, taking in the antique looking stained glass depictions of stories she could only wonder about. She'd been in one church, once, with a friend from school, but it was nothing like this. It looked more like a convention hall; not something sacred.

Her mother's funeral service had been held in a small hall, referred to as a chapel, at the funeral home, but she knew it wasn't a church. Just a space for people to sit and mourn.

Kali noted the back of a head that must be Joseph's, a blond woman with a baby bump a step behind him. At the front he leaned over to kiss Marilyn on the forehead then slid into the seat across the aisle, his shoulders tall and rigid.

Kali continued her scan of the space. The church was almost full, yet people still streamed in. Many more and it would be standing room only.

A man in a long white dress walked to the front of the church and the low murmur of voices quieted. He spoke words of love and remembrance. Some of the references he used and concepts he talked about seemed foreign to Kali, but overall, his words spoke of comfort.

Rachel sang, her voice reverberating through the small hall as tears streamed down her face. Kali took in the large photo of the man this was all for, Alexander Joseph Fraser. It was disconcerting—associating the image of this robust, healthy person with the frail man she'd seen at Westwood. Even more disconcerting was seeing so much of Lincoln in him. A crystal ball into the future couldn't be much more accurate. Lincoln, in fifteen years. She could see in Alexander the way Lincoln's shoulders would broaden farther, the way his laugh lines would deepen. She could see the wisdom and love that, if life went the way it should, would grow in him as it had grown in the gaze of his father.

But there was another possibility too, that, if he lost the genetic lottery, Lincoln's resemblance to his father would continue, making him unrecognizable, stripping him, day by day, of everything that made him him. The thought made her shudder, but not want to run away.

Kali's eyes closed as more images passed through her mind—the first sight of Lincoln, flinging himself onto the pavement over Theo, cradling his body around her son. She'd been furious in her fear. She'd hardly wanted to look at him—dirty, dishevelled ... though he wasn't dirty, not really. He just gave the appearance of it with his long shaggy hair and worn out clothes.

Even then a spark of attraction had flared, disgusting her. She'd already had one homeless man in her life to take care of. She didn't need another one.

But that had never been Lincoln. He'd been the one to take care of her, ease her problems, shelter her—in more ways than one.

More images came to her—the dance lesson on Canada Day, the shiver as she guided his hands around her, as he attempted the steps, shy and unsure, but trying. And then he'd leaned forward, and despite a longing deep inside for his lips to meet hers, the fear that flooded her—complications, betrayal, abandonment—was stronger. She'd pushed him away. Violently.

Yet he'd stayed. He'd allowed her to stay. He'd made her son fall in love with him. He'd made her fall in love in with him. Kali's breath caught. Had he? What she felt, it was more than caring.

She didn't want to lose him. She ached for his pain. She loved him, certainly. But was she in love?

It didn't feel the way it had felt with Derek—fast and furious, like she was falling, like she had no control. Not at all.

And she still loved Derek, that much was certain. These past weeks, seeing him with Theo, seeing hints of the man she'd fallen in love with and the new man he'd become, she couldn't deny love existed. But nothing like before. She didn't want him. She wanted Lincoln. Lincoln. Kali's attention drew back to the front of the church as Joseph stepped to the microphone.

Like Lincoln, Joseph was tall and broad, but unlike Lincoln's subtle confidence, Joseph's exuded from him. He commanded the room with his presence and a focused attention seemed to emanate toward him.

"It's not easy to stand here." His voice travelled through the room, so sure and strong the microphone was superfluous. "But it's comforting to know that despite the cruelty of my father's disease, the way it stripped away so much of what we loved about him, what he loved about himself, the man he truly was never faded in the minds and hearts of the people who knew him." He gestured his arm to the crowd. "Standing room only."

Kali turned. It was true. The back of the church was packed, leading into the foyer. People crowded in shoulder to shoulder.

"I can only imagine that in some way, big or small, my

father touched each of your lives, the way he touched ours." And here his voice faltered slightly as his face twitched then returned to its stoic expression. "My father was a strong man—not just physically, but mentally, spiritually. He was tough and firm growing up. He had goals. Passions. He was also fun. He knew how to relax. He knew how to tell a story that could have the whole room grasping their bellies in laughter. He knew how to love too." Joseph's eyes crinkled. "I remember once I'd come home two hours past curfew, sixteen-years-old, three sheets to the wind and stumbling up the front steps, hoping beyond hope that Mom and Dad were sleeping in their beds, because if they weren't, I knew I was in for it."

A small chuckle sounded through the crowd.

"Now, I'd done stupid things before, and I'd been punished for them. But this, this was the worst." Joseph gave a dramatic pause. "The door opened before I'd managed to maneuver my keys from my pocket and there was Dad, towering over me, his head shaking. My body tensed. I was ready for it. A lecture. A grounding. My car privileges revoked forever. He stepped toward me, wrapped his arms around my shoulders, and helped me into the house." Joseph paused again, his lips pursed tightly this time. "He set me down on the bench by the door and, without a word, untied my boots and gently removed them. He walked me to the kitchen, gestured for me to take a seat, and brought a tall glass of water. He sat in silence as I drank it all.

"'Did you puke?' he asked. I nodded. He nodded back at me. 'You're going to have a wretched day tomorrow. I'll help you through it and we'll discuss your punishment when you feel better. Remember the punishment you brought on yourself though. I'm not going to tell you not to drink again, 'cause I know you will. But moderation, in just about all areas in life, will serve you well.'"

Joseph smiled, his eyes glistening. "He walked me to my room, directed me to lie down in what I later learned was the recovery position, set a bucket beside me, tucked me in, and kissed my brow. The next morning he brought me eggs, bacon, toast, and orange juice. That afternoon he took me on a run, to sweat the toxins out, he said. Not once did he speak a harsh word.

"The day after that he sat me down and grounded me from car privileges for two months. He told me he was proud of me, though, for leaving the car at a friend's. Again, he reminded me, moderation."

Joseph wiped the back of his hand across his eyes and gave a chuckle. "Not saying I've never had a bit too much to drink again, but I've never been three sheets, and that love, that kindness, the wisdom in his words, is something I'll never forget."

Joseph took a long breath as his gaze travelled the room.

"These past few days I've heard new stories of my father and been reminded of old ones I'd near forgotten. Dad wasn't perfect. No one is. But he was a good man. A kind man. The disease sometimes made him angry, aggressive, but that wasn't him, and in these past days I've been reminded of that. Reminded of the man he was and the man I'd like to be in honour of him. A man who puts his family first. Who doesn't just think about the bottom line or what's practical, who puts people first, who has real vision."

He looked to the floor, silent for several breaths. "I'm going to miss him. I've been missing him for years, wishing he was here to guide me, but too proud to admit it." He raised his gaze to the crowd. "Life is short. Health, our minds, they're not guaranteed. If there's one thing Dad would want us to take from his life, I think it would be to make the best of it, focusing on the things that matter, the things that will last. We have no guarantees." He looked toward his family, and Kali wished she could know whose gaze he caught. Linda, who knew a similar fate was coming for her? Marilyn, whose pain was probably worse than anyone's—pain for herself, but also for her babies. Lincoln, who Joseph had failed, betrayed, near destroyed.

Joseph's gaze left his family's aisle and scanned the crowd. "I'm not sure what else I meant to say." His voice wavered, the confidence nearly gone. "Thank you for coming. Thank you for helping us remember the good, when so much of the past seventeen years has been focused around the bad." He glanced to his family again. "It means a lot to us."

The room remained hushed as Joseph stepped down from the podium and made his way back to his seat beside Lucy. Over the next ten to fifteen minutes, one of Linda's sons read a poem, the minister read scripture, and then Marilyn walked to the front, saying they'd appreciate it if only close family and friends joined them at the grave site, but everyone was welcome to her place for food, laughter, the sharing of memories, and Alexander's favourite band. "It'll be a rip-roaring good time," she said with a brave smile. "I want it to be a party Alex would have loved."

CHAPTER TWENTY-SEVEN

Kali stood with the rest of the seated crowd, her hands clasped in front of her, as the family made their way down the aisle. First Marilyn, then a couple Kali remembered as Mr. Fraser's sister and brother-in-law. Next came Joseph and Lucy, Linda and her crew, Rachel, Lincoln, and a stream of cousins, aunts and uncles Kali vaguely remembered from Rachel's birthday party.

Marilyn stopped for hugs and handshakes and kind words along the way, slowing the procession. Her eyes brightened as she caught sight of Kali. She took both of Kali's hands in her own. "I was hoping we'd see you." Her voice came out soft, loving, and again Kali wondered what life would have been like to grow up with a mother like Marilyn. She let one hand fall but squeezed Kali's with the other. "You're welcome to the grave site. You should have been sitting up front."

Kali made a noise of uncertainty.

"Either way," another squeeze, "we'll be seeing you at the house, won't we?"

Kali opened her mouth as her gaze flitted to Lincoln, who looked back, something in his eyes she couldn't read. She turned her head back to Marilyn, who was holding up the line, and nodded.

Lincoln's gaze flitted back and forth as people addressed him, but it always returned to Kali. At her row, he stepped out of the procession and slipped in beside her, his mouth by her ear before she even had a chance to breathe.

"What are you doing here?"

"I ... I thought."

He looked to the procession.

"Your mom said I should come to the grave site."

His expression seemed torn. Uncertain.

"I don't have to, I mean—"

"Perhaps that's best." Lincoln looked to the aisle again. "Thanks for coming. It was thoughtful of you." He stopped, words he didn't speak swimming behind his eyes. "I should go."

Kali's breath pulled as he stepped away. Her arm reached out, as if to draw him back, tell him how stupid she'd been, that six months was enough, enough to build a future on, but she let the hand fall. What if it wasn't enough?

THE CHURCH CONTINUED to empty in organized rows, so by the time Kali stepped into the aisle the family and friends on their way to the grave site had long gone. How long would it take? Twenty minutes, thirty, an hour?

She scanned the crowd, looking for a familiar face, but of course everyone close enough to be invited to Rachel's birthday party was close enough that they'd be en route to the grave site by now. Her phone in hand, Kali punched the Fraser's address into Google Maps. Two buses and two eight and ten minute walks would get her there in an hour and fifteen minutes. Not bad. It would at least ensure she wasn't at the house before the family. Slipping her phone away, Kali turned toward the street as a hand fell on her shoulder. She spun.

"Kali, hi."

"Cynthia." Kali took a step back. "What are you doing here?"

"Oh," Cynthia let out a slightly offended laugh, "Alex was on my rotation the past couple of months. The family asked me to come."

"Okay." Kali nodded. That made sense. Families often became close to the Westwood staff. In her short time working there Kali had received two funeral invites.

"Did you know Lincoln was his son? He never came to visit, so—"

"I knew. Yes. I mean I've known for a while."

They stared at each other. Cynthia gestured to Kali's purse. "Sorry to snoop, but I noticed the map. You need a drive to the Fraser's?"

"Oh," Kali gestured to the corner, "I was going to take the bus."

"Nonsense." Cynthia nodded her head toward the parking lot. "You'll come with me."

"Won't we be early?"

"I think someone was sent to open the house. It's fine."

Kali's chest felt tight, stupidly so. Cynthia was kind. Sweet. Lovely. And very obviously interested in Lincoln. Or at least she'd seemed so at Theo's birthday party.

Cynthia turned back to Kali as she walked to the parking lot. "I should have known Lincoln was his son. He looks so much like Joseph. Give him a hair cut and they could almost be twins." She laughed, "Good genes, I guess," then hesitated. "Or, well ..."

"Some of the genes are good, yes." Kali fell into step beside her.

"Joseph's safe. Did you know?"

Kali nodded.

"Hopefully that means Lincoln is too." Cynthia twirled her keys on her fingers. "I'm surprised you're not with them now, that you were sitting in the back. Are you two still ..."

"How's the gang?" Kali pulled open the door to Cynthia's blue Kia. "Dianne still running the place?"

CARS LINED THE STREET in front of the Fraser's house and people streamed in, just the way they had streamed out of the church minutes before.

"Wow." Cynthia pulled in to a space only a car as small as her Kia would fit. "So that's Casa Fraser." She tilted her head to Kali. "Nice, but no mansion."

"Mr. Fraser built it," said Kali as she unbuckled her seat belt. "Marilyn doesn't want to leave it."

"That makes sense." Cynthia stepped out of the car and waited until Kali was out to continue. "And it's sweet too."

Kali flipped out her cane and fell into step beside Cynthia.

"Do you have much left?"

Kali kept her focus on the sidewalk ahead, though she could feel Cynthia's gaze on her. "Vision, you mean?"

Cynthia remained silent. Another laugh erupted—embarrassed this time. "Yes, that's what I mean. You couldn't see my nod, could you?"

"That's okay." Kali glanced to Cynthia with a smile. "It's hard to remember. I have enough. Enough to manage, anyway. The cane is more a safety measure at this point. I could get by without it if I needed to."

Silence. Kali shifted her head again to see if Cynthia was making another motion she couldn't see. Cynthia caught her gaze. "We're all rooting for you. Hoping the treatment worked well, hoping you'll be back to work again soon."

Kali brought her focus back to the pavement. Tap, tap, tap. Cynthia was kind. Nice. She didn't want to be aggravated by her. "I'll know in a couple of weeks, or at least have a better idea." Kali kept her gaze on the sidewalk. "I may not go back to Westwood even if I can."

"It's pretty much the best job a nurse can get."

"That's true." Kali held back the rest: it would be difficult, no matter how much technology could help. It'd be different. And if she messed up on account of her lack of vision to disastrous consequences, she wasn't sure if she could ever forgive herself.

They turned up the drive, and once inside the house, Kali excused herself from Cynthia, claiming a trip to the restroom. When out of view, she made her way up the stairs, hoping no one would notice and think she was being a snoop. The party was clearly getting started on the main floor, but she was here for Lincoln, not anyone down there. And crowds still made her skittish—all the noise, the moving bodies, the voices coming from various directions at once.

Inside his room, she crossed to the bed. The top bunk was hastily made. She rubbed her hand on the sheets. Had he been staying here? The thought made her smile, that rather than spending his days and nights alone in the tree house like she'd feared, he'd been here, among family. She knew that already, though, the call yesterday when he'd told her as much—at least that he'd been spending his days among family. She was glad he was spending his nights among them too.

Kali settled on the lower bunk and took in the room once more. The band paraphernalia, the desk, the shelf of books. It didn't feel like the room of the Lincoln she knew, but then she supposed it wasn't his room, not really, not anymore. Her teenage room would have hardly represented who she was today either.

Kali shifted farther onto the bed, grabbed a pillow and leaned it against the wall, her head settling into the downy softness. When the family returned she'd go down, brave the crowd. Until then, this was the perfect place to be.

CHAPTER TWENTY-EIGHT

"Kali?"

Kali snapped awake with a jolt, her eyes scanning the room until they found Lincoln, standing with his suit jacket over his arm, eyes wide and mouth partially open.

"What are you doing here?"

"The crowd." Kali shrugged. "Figured I'd get away from it, at least until you arrived." She stretched. "I must have fallen asleep. I'm sorry. I didn't mean—"

Lincoln's brow furrowed. "That explains why you're in my room, but what are you doing here?"

His words weren't accusatory, but they cut through Kali. She offered a slight smile. "For you."

"But I said. I mean ..." He shook his head. "We're supposed to be taking some time, to think, to—"

"We've had time."

"With all that's been going on I've barely—"

"Come here." Kali patted the bed beside her.

Lincoln started a step, hesitated, then crossed the room and sat beside her. She took his hand in both of hers. "How are you?"

He turned his gaze to the floor. "I don't really know. Mom wanted us to focus on the joy these past days."

"I got that impression."

"And it's been good. Great, really. I feel closer to Dad than I have in years ... over a decade. More, maybe."

Kali gave his hand a squeeze.

"But at the same time it makes it hurt all the more. All I missed, from him being gone, from me staying away ... The others, they have these memories, moments where he came back to them, if only for a few minutes. And even when he wasn't quite Dad, they talk of his kindness, of his consideration.

"Rachel told a story of this day he thought she was an Avon lady. He spent an hour talking to her. Telling her about life, and listening to her problems. She said she wasn't sure she'd ever had someone speak to her with such attention, such focus, and he gave that to a woman he didn't know. A stranger, as far as he was concerned.

"The others all had similar stories, similar moments. I missed all of that."

Kali inhaled and let the air out slowly. "I'm sure you missed a lot of wretched moments too, moments they wish they could wipe from their minds."

"Yeah." Lincoln turned his face to her. "But I don't think I should have missed those. I think maybe they were important too."

Kali rubbed her thumb along the back of his hand. "There's no right way to do any of this. No perfect answer. You did what you needed to do for you. Wherever your dad is right now, I'm sure he understands that."

Lincoln let his head fall. "I'm not."

"You were there in the end. You had your moment with him, right?"

"Not the end. But close."

"Close enough. I think that's what matters." Kali leaned in and rubbed a hand along Lincoln's thigh. "I know all about beating yourself up for things you can't change. It's not worth it."

Lincoln's barely there smile grew before it faded again. "I've missed you."

"I've missed you too."

Lincoln finally reciprocated her touches, his hand resting gently on her neck. The touch tingled, and Kali closed her eyes, savouring it. Her lips parted.

"I don't want to miss you. It feels like shit."

A laugh bubbled out of Kali as she opened her eyes and met his gaze.

Lincoln's hand dropped. "Have you spent much time with Derek?"

A vice seemed to tighten around Kali, cutting off the laughter. "Some. Not much."

I love you, she could almost say. *I want you*. And she did. She wanted him. She shifted closer, so their thighs almost touched. Her fingers tingled with the desire to run her hands through his hair, draw him close. The sweet possibility flashed through her mind: it would only take a moment, to step to the door, close and lock it, then return to the bed, indulge herself in touch. And if she said it, would he? *I love you*. But those words had power. They were a promise she wasn't sure she could make, no matter how much she wanted to in this moment. A release for her. A comfort for him. Kali pressed her lips together, pushing the thoughts away. "We don't need to talk about Derek."

Lincoln looked to the door. "I should probably head back down."

No. Kali reached for him, drawing him to her, letting their lips touch. He was hesitant at first, but then his arms wrapped around her, his mouth opened as their tongues explored. He leaned forward, gently lowering Kali's back to the bed. This was it. This was what she wanted. Passion and urgency flowed through Kali as her heart pounded, as his hands explored her body. She reached for his shirt, grappling with the buttons. Lincoln stiffened. Kali swallowed, her hands releasing the soft fabric.

He pushed himself off of her and to his feet. "What are we doing?"

"We're—"

"Nothing's changed, Kali." He gestured to the door. "And anyone could walk in. This is ... it's ..." He shook his head. "My dad just died."

"I know. I thought." Kali sighed. "I don't know what I thought. I just—"

"Look." Lincoln gestured again to the door. "I don't want to be rude. But maybe it's best if you go."

Her breath held.

"I want you here, but if we don't work out ... Already people have asked about you. If you're here now and then disappear ... there'll be more questions. Questions I don't know how to answer." He paused. "And what we almost did ... that's not going to solve anything."

Kali stepped toward him. "And if we do work out?"

Lincoln shrugged and looked away. "Then hopefully

you'll be at the next family funeral."

Trying to mask the way his words cut, Kali pushed out a smile. "Are they all such shin-digs?"

"No." He shook his head. "But I guess they all try to focus on the good."

AFTER A SHORT DEBATE on who would exit the room first, Lincoln left Kali still sitting on the bed and made his way down the hall. He stopped, turned back to the half open door, and took a step. One part of him said to go back, take her in his arms, tell her he'd been an idiot, tell her he wanted her, needed her, and everything else be damned. He stepped to the bathroom, throbbing, and braced his hands against the counter, reliving the feel of her body under him, the touch of her tongue ... and he'd pulled himself away. He was an idiot.

But then Derek flashed in his mind. Her husband. No matter what she said, no matter how she tried to dismiss it, Derek was still her husband and Lincoln wasn't going to be the one to break up a family. Derek, with his quiet confidence. Was the only thing standing between Kali, Derek, and wedded bliss her own anger and hurt?

Lincoln had seen that anger—if Kali could get past it, who knew how she'd feel about Derek? Who knew if they could be a family again ... and wouldn't that be the best thing, for all of them? All of them except Lincoln.

He wanted her here, not just in his bed, but by his side as he went downstairs, as he got through this night. But he didn't want the false hope, the family and friends labelling them a couple, drawing her into stories and referencing future plans only for her to drop him days or weeks later, leaving Lincoln a joke once again—unable to keep a woman.

Not that he had reason to think that's what his family thought ... but with Lucy walking around with her little baby bump—Lucy, who'd been at past family events on Lincoln's arm—how could they not?

Lincoln turned from the counter and took a deep breath. Maybe he was weak. Maybe he was foolish. Maybe he was insecure. He continued down the hall.

At the bottom of the stairs, he turned toward the kitchen and its bursts of raucous laughter. He glanced back to the stairwell. No sign of Kali. The house was full. Boisterous. Most people wouldn't have even noticed her, connected her to Lincoln—but the people who mattered would, the people who already knew her. He should have told her to stay, enjoy the party. Enjoy the food. He was weak. Cowardly. Shameful.

Lincoln turned again to see a glimpse of Kali's afro as the front door closed. He gazed at the door. After what had just happened, it would be ridiculous to chase her. Still, he had to hold himself back.

THREE HOURS LATER, Lincoln found himself in his mother's sewing room, away from the crowd. They'd been a good three hours—drinking, dancing, laughing, stories. He'd smiled and joined in the fun, forgetting for brief moments the way he ached. But after isolating himself the past year, he could only handle so much.

He stood beside his mother's glider, picked up a delicate

piece of fabric from the side table, and turned it over, taking in the intricately embroidered flowers—a baby's gown. He let it fall.

It had been odd, to say the least, being around Joseph and Lucy these past days, though Lucy actually hadn't been around that much ... work, said Joseph in explanation of her absence. Which Lincoln found suspect. Lucy's job was mostly a pick your own hours type of deal.

She was cordial when with Lincoln. If ever they had to speak—a rare occurrence—she kept the conversation light. Whenever she was around, he did his best to avert his eyes from her bump, but his gaze kept drawing to it, causing a twitch in the pit of his stomach. His niece or nephew was in that perfectly round belly.

The baby they'd lost probably wasn't even his, but it could have been. He'd believed it was. As he chased after Lucy, desperate to tell her he was wrong, stupid, that he wanted their child, hopes had flared, images of all to come—cuddles, tickling, laughter, love.

He picked up the gown again and fingered the flowers his mother had so carefully stitched. Did this mean the baby was a girl, or was his mother being hopeful, eager for her first granddaughter after two grandsons?

"It's pretty, isn't it?"

Lincoln spun at the sound of the familiar voice, softer than he was used to. He dropped the gown. "Yes."

CHAPTER TWENTY-NINE

Lucy crossed the sewing room to Lincoln, her hand on the belly that seemed to grow each time he saw her. "I think it's going to be a girl. Joseph doesn't want to find out. I guess your mom thinks so too."

Lincoln's body tensed. Even after all these months, over a year, he still had to fight not to imagine it—her and Joseph's bodies entwined, slick, all while Lincoln sat obliviously by, like a dupe.

But it hadn't been years of deceit, he reminded himself. Months. A handful of times. He stepped away as Lucy reached for the gown. "I'm sorry, you know. For all of it." She stared at the gown, fingered it as Lincoln had. "Not just for the affair. But for the lies." She turned, her gaze soft and beautiful. He hated it, how beautiful she was. The fact that he couldn't deny it. Is that what had made him so blind? An inability to believe that someone this beautiful, this angelic looking, could be so cruel?

He'd seen her callousness at times throughout their relationship: her desire to control, her apathy, but it had seemed nothing compared to the privilege of being able to hold her in her arms, kiss her, call her his own. Lincoln swallowed; the anger and distaste that usually boiled within him wasn't there. In its place was an emptiness that felt far worse.

"I was angry and bitter. About the baby. About you, for not wanting it right away. It felt like a betrayal, you suggesting I abort it, even though I was the one who'd betrayed." Lucy exhaled a small breath of air. "Still, I was angry. And after," she hesitated, "it felt like your words cursed it in some way, that I lost it because of you, your lack of elation. Which was completely unfair." She paused. "It wasn't an accident."

Lincoln's gaze narrowed. "What wasn't?"

"Getting pregnant."

Lincoln stared.

"I loved you. In a way. At the start. But there was something about Joseph ... I don't know if I meant to ... to seduce him, you know? I don't know if it was a conscious choice or if it just happened. But when we first met, you were a bit of a mess. Lack of focus, unsure what you wanted out of your life, and then I met Joseph and he was all the things I wanted in a man, all the things I wanted you to become." Another pause. "This sounds awful, doesn't it? I sound awful."

Lincoln backed away from her until he was almost against the wall on the far side of the room.

"If he'd given in that first night, maybe it wouldn't have been so bad. We'd only been dating, what, three or four months then? It could have been a simple switch." Lucy looked to the gown again. "Well, not simple, but not so disastrous." She turned her gaze to Lincoln. "Anyway, he didn't. And I cared about you. I did. I decided I was being ridiculous. I decided I wanted you. And so I focused on you, and I saw you turning into exactly the man I knew you could be. The man both of us knew you could be."

"You and Joseph?"

Lucy nodded. "It became almost a plan between us, pushing you in the right direction, helping you fulfil your potential.

"And I tried to be happy. Satisfied. I was for a while. But I couldn't get Joseph out of my system. I'm not used to men being blind to my advances." She rubbed her belly in what seemed an unconscious motion. "Not blind, exactly. But resistant."

Lincoln continued to stare, his throat tight, his breath hollow.

"And with you, it's like we created a monster." She let out a little laugh. "I pushed you so much to be the man I thought I wanted you to be, to climb the corporate ladder. And you did. You were amazing. But the more you did, the more you stopped seeing me, talking to me, touching me."

Lincoln swallowed. So she'd seen it too. The monster. The one they'd both ended up hating.

"It's not an excuse, I know."

Was it? Or at least an explanation? He had stopped noticing her, all his focus on becoming the type of man, a businessman, Joseph could be proud of, that she could be proud of.

"But I allowed myself to be pushed toward my attraction for Joseph because of it. He was focused, driven, yes. But he still made time for the people who mattered. He still had a life outside of work."

Again, she caressed her belly. "It was of my own creation, I know, the way you'd become, but I started to feel like nothing more than a pretty face to have on your arm at corporate events. It was always the future, the future. With Joseph, at times, we could live in the present."

Lincoln shook his head, exhaling the breath he hadn't even realized he'd held. "I thought you wanted the future. I thought—"

"I know." Lucy perched on the sewing table. "I did. I just didn't realize that getting it would take over our lives. That I'd feel like ... an accessory." She glanced to the floor. "Do you remember how many times in that last year I asked to go for a walk in the park or out to dinner or a play? It was always later, soon, next week." She let out a short laugh. "You had to work or prepare for work or go to some networking event that I could join you for if I wanted—your lovely accessory.

"Eventually you even stopped making Sunday brunch." Lucy shrugged and smiled. "You used to love that. I loved it." She shook her head. "If that's what life was going to be, alone except for when I made you look good, what was the point? Yeah, we'd be rich, esteemed ... but that isn't everything."

And yet she'd picked Joseph. Richer, more esteemed, but who, apparently, made time for her. Lincoln held a hand to his head, amazed he was listening to this, amazed he hadn't stormed out, amazed he could understand what Lucy was saying, see the truth in it. It wasn't an excuse for her cheating. Definitely not. But it was an explanation.

Lincoln's head throbbed. He rubbed it, wishing he could back right into the wall, disappear into it, turn back time.

"I'm not saying this to defend myself, really." Lucy stepped closer to him. "Just to explain. I started to get angry. I started spending more time with Joseph, who was funny, who listened to me, who tried to defend you, to assure me it wouldn't always be like this. He was so kind and supportive. Those feelings I had when I first met him, they all came back. That's when I started wondering in earnest what it would be like to be with him, and when he resisted ... well, I already explained that. I tried harder. Eventually I wore him down." She held the gown in both hands, sliding it between her fingers. "But still, after every time, he resisted. He hated it, hated himself for what we were doing. Each time he said never again, that he couldn't do that to you." She gave a sad shrug. "But he was already doing it, and by that time I was so angry with you for letting this happen, for not seeing that it was happening, not even suspecting ..."

Lucy's voice intensified. "I wanted him. I *think* I wanted to hurt you. You became an obstacle. And a baby, his baby, became the solution."

Bile rose in Lincoln's throat. He held his hand up; he wasn't sure why, to stop Lucy, or direct her away from the vomit he feared was about to spew.

A choked laugh escaped her throat. "I sound like a bitch, don't I? I am." She held out her hands, as if in supplication. "But I'm also human. And when I woke up in that hospital bed and learned the baby was gone, all that sorrow turned to rage. I loved the baby. I did. And I really wanted to hurt you then, for being the reason it was gone."

Lincoln could see it again—Lucy in the hospital bed, so small, so frail. Joy had surged through him as her eyes opened, as he grasped her hand. Fear and sorrow flooded right after, knowing he'd have to tell her the child was gone. He'd said the words and her eyes clouded over.

We can have another, he'd whispered.

We? she spouted, her face and voice defined by rage. *It wasn't even your baby.*

The room had spun. Wasn't his baby?

"And that's when the lies came to me." Lucy's voice was soft, regretful, barely audible. "I hurt so much. I felt as if an essential part of me had been torn out. I wanted you to suffer like I was suffering."

Lincoln's chest rose then fell. She'd wanted to make him hurt, wanted him to suffer. So she'd fabricated not a casual affair, but a relationship that lasted years, lies that lasted years. She'd turned his whole life, everything that mattered to him, everything he believed about two of the people he'd loved most in the world, into a lie.

Lincoln's words came out in a whisper. "I still wanted you. Even then. Even when I knew the baby might not be mine."

"But not when you knew I'd been cheating with Joseph. Not when you thought it'd been going on for years."

"No. Not then."

"The problem was," she whispered back, "you didn't want me before. Not really."

"I did."

She shook her head, back to caressing the white gown. "We both made mistakes." The blonde waves of her hair swished against her face, even now, so beautiful. "Mine were worse. Mine were unforgivable."

Were they? Lincoln stared at her, at the blue eyes he'd once seen his future in. He couldn't deny it, he'd taken her for granted. He'd put work first. If he was honest, and it hurt to be honest, at times he had treated her like an accessory, just as she said. He'd betrayed her too. He could see it now—flashes of Lucy, glammed up and smiling as she presented him with

Cirque du Soleil tickets for the anniversary date he'd forgotten about due to an important meeting. Lucy sidling up to him on the couch as he sat, laptop in front of him, her hand on his thigh, moving higher, higher, and him pushing it away. *Not now, Darling, I have to work.* Lucy, time and again, suggesting a walk, a dinner, a play, and him saying no. He'd told himself he'd been doing it for them, for her, and he'd believed it.

Lincoln's throat tightened. *I'm sorry,* he tried to say, but the words wouldn't come.

"Anyway," Lucy let out the slightest smile, "looks like I'm getting my just rewards."

Lincoln's eyebrows raised.

"Joseph is furious."

They furrowed.

Lucy circled her belly once more, the gown trailing from her fingers. "He says he'll be there for the baby. Support it. Support me, even if I don't want to work. Even if I want to stay home with the child. But he called off the wedding."

Lincoln stepped forward. "What?"

"Maybe not forever. But for now, I guess. Your Dad dying, that's taken its toll on him, I could see that. I think it's reminded him how important family is. How important you are. He couldn't believe I lied. Said he couldn't even look at me the same. He didn't accept my explanation that, in a way, you cheated on me first."

She shook her head. "He said everything we have is based on a lie. And at this point in his life, he can't have that. He needs something true. Real. He needs family."

She bit her lip, and an image of Kali flashed through Lincoln's mind.

"But this baby's family too. And me now, kind of." She shook her head once more. "Anyway, I just ... I've been wanting to say I'm sorry. For it all." Her eyes glazed over; she blinked rapidly and held a finger under one eye.

Lincoln stepped toward her, confused and disturbed at the urge to take her in his arms, offer comfort.

She wasn't a monster. Neither was he. "I'm sorry too."

"What?" Her eyes widened.

"For not seeing you. For letting you feel alone. Unwanted."

"No." She waved a hand between them. "No. That's not why ... that's not what ..."

"I'm sorry, Lucy." He rested a hand on her shoulder, the touch shocking them both. "I hold fault too."

A tiny sob escaped as she looked up at him.

"We all lie sometimes. I think I was lying to myself."

Her perfect brows furrowed.

"Blaming it all on you. Feeling like a victim." Lincoln took a deep breath. "I'm not sure I can say I hope you and Joseph figure it out, but I want to be able to say that." Lincoln hesitated. "Do you love him?"

She nodded.

Lincoln nodded back. "I should go."

Lucy's mouth opened and hung there, no sound coming out. Lincoln left the room and made his way to the noise of the crowd, feeling as if his world had inverted.

If he could forgive Lucy that, and he could. If he could forgive himself, how could he not forgive Kali?

CHAPTER THIRTY

The next day, after Lincoln's siblings dispersed to their various jobs and lives, Lincoln stayed behind to clean. The party had gone late into the night and the evidence lay strewn throughout the house and yard.

Marilyn stood on the back patio, a shawl wrapped around her shoulders and a cup of coffee in her hands. "You don't have to do that, hun."

Lincoln smiled up at her from the yard, a half filled garbage bag in his hand. "I know."

"I was going to hire someone to come take care of it."

"Save your money."

Lincoln picked up several more plastic cups, then set the bag aside to start folding tables and chairs.

"Crazy how messy people get after a few, isn't it?"

"Yeah." Lincoln felt his mother's gaze on him as he worked.

"How are you? After these past days?"

Lincoln turned to her. He let out a tired smile. "It was good, I think. Focusing on Dad when he was Dad—fully, I mean. The stories, the memories. A good way to do it."

"And now? That it's over?"

"I feel I got some of him back." Lincoln piled a group of chairs and brought them to the back porch. "Besides, we can always remember, right?"

"That we can." Marilyn stepped toward him and ran a hand through her hair. "I"m proud of you, you know."

Lincoln cocked his head.

"For being in the same room as Joseph and Lucy. For standing tall. For the business you're about to start. All of it."

Lincoln looked to the ground before returning his mother's gaze. "Yeah. Well, I learned some things. And realized some things. Joseph and Lucy weren't the only ones to blame. I played my part."

Marilyn let out a soft murmur of understanding. "We always do."

"Did you know they're not getting married? Or at least not next week. Maybe never."

"Joseph told me last night. He didn't go into detail. Just said he didn't know her as well as he thought, and that he was no longer sure a child was enough reason to tie them together forever." Marilyn took a sip of her coffee. "He was really nervous. I think he thought I'd disapprove. There's a lot I've disapproved of ... but you're my kids. He said especially after all the stories about me and your dad, he wanted to find someone he was sure of, not just someone he felt obligated to be with." Marilyn paused. "I want that for him. For all of you."

Lincoln moved back into the yard for another set of chairs.

"How do you feel about that?"

Lincoln collapsed and piled several chairs. He inhaled the crisp morning air, heavy with the scent of fallen leaves. "I want him to be happy, I guess." Lincoln let out a slight grin. "When I don't want to smash his face in, that is."

"And you, are you happy?"

Lincoln hesitated. "I'm all right."

"I didn't see Kali much these past days. A moment at the funeral. I thought she'd come back here."

Lincoln focused his gaze on the chairs. "She did."

Silence.

"I asked her to leave."

He piled his arms full and returned to the back porch, avoiding Marilyn's gaze.

"Love's complicated, sweetie. It's not always easy. Even when it's right."

Lincoln looked at his mother. "You think it's right? Me and her?"

"I think it could be."

Lincoln set the chairs down. "Me too. I'm just not sure."

"We never can be. Not one hundred percent."

"You weren't sure of Dad?"

"Sometimes I was. Sometimes I was terrified. Even after we were married. Even after Joseph and Linda. Days passed sometimes, weeks, when I wondered. Not always about him specifically, but what the life being with him meant. He wanted a wife at home, someone to be with the kids."

Marilyn pressed her lips together and looked past Lincoln before returning her gaze to him. "I wanted that too, but not always. And when he was diagnosed, I wondered at times if I'd made the wrong decision, tying myself so irrevocably to one person."

"You could have left."

"No."

"People do. They get divorced. They move on."

"No. I couldn't have left. I didn't want to. I wanted him to not be sick. I wanted to reverse so much. But even when parts of me doubted, the core of me knew, no matter what it cost, he was my husband, for better or worse, in sickness and in health. Those vows, they mean something. They're a promise" She stopped, staring not at Lincoln, but at the yard. "He was the man for me."

The man for her. Lincoln got that. He thought he got that. And she'd made vows, a promise. Just as Kali had, with Derek.

Lincoln leaned against the porch. "You don't regret it? Not having your own life? All the years you gave up taking care of him?"

"I have my own life." Marilyn let out a soft smile. "I just didn't have my own career. And no, I don't regret a minute of it."

Lincoln nodded. To not regret a minute, a minute of seventeen years of watching the man you loved, the man you planned to grow old with, deteriorate into the faintest shadow of his former self. He opened his mouth, wanting to ask her if it was true, really, or just something she told herself to make it easier. "Dad was lucky."

"So was I."

Lincoln winced.

"For a time, unbelievably so." Marilyn smiled softly. "Even in the end, there were moments when despite what the doctors said, he was there, my Alex." Marilyn took another sip of her coffee. "You may have said," she hesitated, "this old mind isn't quite what it used to be, but does Kali know? The possibility?"

"Well, yeah."

"She's a nurse. I know she'd know. But does she know you haven't tested?"

"Yes."

The two stared at each other. "What are you doing, Lincoln? I've seen the way you look at her. The way she looks at you. That doesn't come along every day."

"She doesn't ... she's not sure. She—"

"She will be. If you give her time."

Lincoln's chest tightened. "It's not that simple."

"Nothing ever is. But that doesn't mean you—"

"I should get going." Lincoln stepped back from his mother.

Marilyn nodded. "Thanks for cleaning." She crossed to him and cupped his chin. "My sweet boy."

Lincoln's bottom lip trembled. He wanted to step into her arms, feel them wrap around her the way they had when he was a young child—so safe and sure. He wanted to apologize for all the years he wasn't there when he should have been, holding her hand, holding his father's hand. He wanted to tell her everything about Kali and Derek—how she'd lied, how maybe it didn't matter, but that Derek did, and if he had really changed, if he could be there for Kali and Theo, then Lincoln probably shouldn't. They'd taken vows. Made a promise.

He wanted her to tell him if stepping away was admirable or stupid.

"You're going to be okay, you know that?"

"What?" Lincoln swallowed.

"In general. You're going to be okay."

Lincoln's brow furrowed. "You will too, Mom."

Marilyn stepped back, one arm wrapped around her middle. "I know."

Lincoln walked past her toward the house.

"Sweetie."

He turned.

"If you want her, tell her. Be there, no matter the complications. If you aren't, you won't have a chance."

Lincoln gave a half nod then turned. He walked through the house, grabbed his bag by the front door, then passed through the front, up the drive, and to his truck. He sat in the cab for several minutes before turning the ignition and driving home.

CHAPTER THIRTY-ONE

I don't want to get in the way. So if you need time to figure things out, that's okay. Would that come across right? Or like he was giving her permission? She didn't need his permission. His blessing, maybe? No. Besides, she'd already told him she didn't need time. She'd figured it out ... at least where Derek was concerned.

Lincoln slowed the truck to pass through the toll booth on the bridge then brought his vehicle up to speed again.

They should put a hold on the physical, probably, until things were figured out ... though the physical could help it get figured out ... maybe.

I'm not going anywhere. Not until you tell me to.

That may be better. It put the 'ball' in her court. But was it too passive? Would it imply he wouldn't fight for her? He would. He could. He wanted to ... but not against Theo's father. Not if Derek would be best for the boy. And if he was, but not best for Kali? She'd said they could work it out. That having Derek back could be great for her and Lincoln. Shared custody would give her and Lincoln the time they needed to grow. Which was saying something. Something big. Kali loved Theo, lived for Theo, but rather than seeing the negatives—her son away from her—she saw the positives—time for her and Lincoln.

Lincoln pulled in front of the Brunswick Street apartment and stepped out of the cab. His head spun. In just moments he'd be standing in front of Kali, telling her ... what? He wanted her. He just didn't want to mess up Theo's life. Lincoln's foot hit the porch's first step as the building door opened.

"Hey."

"Hi." Lincoln stepped backward off the step.

"I was hoping I'd run into you sometime soon."

Lincoln stared. It wasn't like he could return the sentiment. He glanced past Derek to the building's main door.

"She's up there. They both are."

Lincoln brought his gaze back to a grinning Derek.

"Theo and I had our first alone outing today. Kali was nervous. And I get that. But at least she trusts me."

Lincoln took a long breath. "That's great."

"Wasn't anything super big. A couple hours. We went to the Common park then had brunch. He's such a great kid, isn't he? So smart and funny and observant."

"He's special. Yeah."

"Yeah." Derek's grin broadened, then slackened slightly. "Can we talk?"

"Oh, I—" Lincoln looked to the door again.

"Not long, just—" Derek gestured down the street. A short walk, maybe?"

"I—"

"Please."

Lincoln shrugged and nodded down the street as Derek

fell into step beside him.

"I think I misread the situation before." Derek gave Lincoln a side glance before looking forward again. "I thought you two were just roommates. Friends. When I think on it, Kali implied more. She definitely did. But I just ... I thought ... maybe I was eager. Excited. Maybe you're just not who I would have pictured her with." Derek pasted on a smile. "I must have sounded like an ass."

Lincoln walked on.

"I'll take your silence as confirmation." Derek gave a short laugh. "But you've stayed away. So it makes me think maybe she's more serious about whatever's going on between you two than you are."

"I wouldn't say that." Lincoln spoke carefully. He straightened. "I wouldn't say that at all."

"Then—"

"I didn't want to get in the way. I know what it is to grow up without a Dad."

Derek nodded. "Didn't, or don't?"

Lincoln swallowed, letting several strides pass before he answered. "Didn't. I was trying to make the choice for her. Or at least let her make it without me being a factor. I don't feel that way anymore."

Now Derek let several strides pass. "I messed up. Big time. I know that. And Kali knows that. I think she also knows I was going through a really dark time." Derek looked to Lincoln again, his words hastening. "Not that it's an excuse, but it is an explanation."

They reached the corner of Brunswick and Uniacke. Lincoln gestured for them to continue straight.

"I've got my life back together now though. I'm here. For

good. Whether Kali wants me or not, I'm here for Theo. And not that I think she would, but if she has a problem with that, I'd fight for him. Go to court. Whatever. I've missed too many years. I'm not missing any more."

Lincoln nodded.

"But I'm here for her too. I want her too. I'll fight for her, in a different way, obviously. But I'll fight."

"Listen, I don't—"

"You being gone. It'd make things easier."

Lincoln kept his gaze ahead, frustration and uncertainty seeping through him. Kali had chosen him ... except she hadn't. She'd merely said she wanted to keep trying, see if he'd be the one she chose. But he'd chosen her, was willing to risk hurt and pain, for her.

"You don't have kids, do you Lincoln?"

"No."

"And you've never been married?"

Lincoln shook his head.

Derek stopped walking and turned to Lincoln. "Those two things, they bond people in ways you can't even fathom. I was a mess. But I'm not anymore. I can be the man Kali needs. I am the man Kali needs. I know it. She just doesn't. Not yet. She thinks she owes you something."

Lincoln winced.

"Maybe that came across wrong, but I'm not sure how else to say it. I asked her if she loved you and she couldn't answer. If she had, if she'd said it without thinking, maybe I'd step back, but she didn't. She told me some of what you two have been through, how you were there for her, for both of them. If she doesn't love you after that—" Derek's voice softened. "I'm sorry man, I don't mean to be harsh, but I don't think she ever will. Not really. Not the way a decent guy like you deserves to be loved."

Again, they walked in silence, Lincoln's shoulders tensing, his throat constricting.

"I know she still loves me." Derek's voice came out low but firm. "If only with a flicker of what we had before. But it's there. I can see it. I can feel it. And I love her. I never stopped. Not for a moment. Not a day passed when I didn't think about them. All I'm asking is for you to give me a shot."

"I have. I did!" The words exploded out of Lincoln. She couldn't answer. She didn't love him. Or not enough to say it. Lincoln's arms tingled. His legs felt heavy. He had driven over here to tell Kali he was staying. To say he would fight. And here Derek—her husband, her child's father—was demanding the opposite.

"Not enough." Derek spoke gently, as if speaking to a child. "Not in a permanent way. That's all I'm asking."

All?

"You love Theo too, right? I know it can work—shared custody, that whole deal. But having parents who love each other, live together, as a family. If you ..." Derek stopped, "walk away. Really walk away. And make it clear, not this wishy washy figuring things out thing you've got going on. Do that, and I think Kali would give me a shot. I think she wants to."

No! The word yelled inside Lincoln. Screamed. Who was this guy, to think he had a right to tell Lincoln what to do, to ask him to give up the two people who meant more to him than anyone else?

Their family. Derek, not Lincoln, was their family. Theo's father. Kali's husband. He'd abandoned them, but still, his request wasn't ridiculous. Inappropriate, maybe. Maybe. But Lincoln knew what it was, to be in such pain, to need to get away, to search and grasp at any solution to the pain that seemed possible. And all Lincoln had lost was a woman he'd maybe never even loved, a child who probably wasn't his, and a brother. But his brother didn't have to be lost forever. Maybe he wouldn't be. Derek's was.

He turned to Derek—his face full of hope, pleading. This man was legit. He wanted Kali. He wanted Theo. If Lincoln stood in the way ...

"Tell her it's over? That's what you want?"

"I can't give you the words, man."

Lincoln shook his head. "We live together."

"She said you have another place. Some cabin? Isn't it where you've been staying?"

Lincoln looked past Derek, his jaw tensed, his fists clenched.

"Wasn't that your dream or something?" Derek took a loud breath. "I get it though. The apartment's yours, right? I'm not saying kick her out. But maybe give her notice, you know? She has the money. We talked about that. The misunderstanding. She knows about it now. She'll use it. She can get her own place. Eventually, hopefully, she can move in with me or we'll get a new place. It's not like you'd be kicking her out on the street."

Lincoln scanned Derek. He was huge. Massive. With about three and a half inches on Lincoln, and probably one and a half times his girth. Yet his expression was hopeful, hesitant, frightened. He looked so vulnerable.

"Okay."

"Okay?" Derek's grin erupted. He grabbed Lincoln's arm

and shook it. "Thank you. This is ... oh! I feel like I have a shot, you know? A real shot. I just—"

Derek's arms wrapped around Lincoln with such speed he stumbled and would have lost his balance if not for Derek holding him up. He let go just as quickly.

"Sorry." Derek laughed. "I thought there was no way. I thought you'd fight for her or ... just, I don't know. Make it difficult. And she's so confused, you know? This will just ..." Derek's voice trailed off. He looked at his watch. "I have to get to work." He clapped a hand on Lincoln's shoulder. "You've made my day."

Lincoln watched Derek walk away, such a spring to his step the limp was hardly noticeable. I thought you'd fight for her. Lincoln had thought that too. He opened his mouth to call out to Derek, tell him he wasn't backing down, he was walking into that apartment to tell Kali he loved her, he'd be there for her, he wasn't going anywhere unless she was the one to tell him to get lost. No sound came out. I thought you'd fight for her. And the fact that he hadn't? Maybe it meant stepping away really was the right thing. Maybe it meant he wasn't the man she needed.

CHAPTER THIRTY-TWO

Kali straightened at the sound of familiar footsteps on the stairs outside the door. It'd been less than a day since he'd asked her to leave his mother's home. She glanced to the hall, hearing no sound from Theo playing quietly in their room. As the key turned in the latch and the knob twisted, Kali shifted toward the door. "Hey."

"Hey." Lincoln locked the door, bent to untie his boots, then turned toward her. "How's it going?"

"All right. Good, I guess."

Lincoln nodded, his arms awkwardly at his side.

"How are you?"

He shrugged. "All right, I guess." He crossed to the couch and sat at the opposite end. "I ran into Derek on the way out."

"Derek?" Kali's brow furrowed. "He left hours ago."

"After we talked I went for a walk."

"Okay." Kali swallowed. She didn't like it, Derek in Lincoln's apartment. Lincoln intercepting Derek for a talk. Derek and Lincoln interacting at all. At first she'd tried to prevent their paths crossing. But Lincoln hadn't been here, and it was impractical, always meeting Derek somewhere else. "What'd you talk about?"

"You."

Of course her.

"And Theo."

"Okay." Kali pulled her legs up under her. "Care to—"

"He wants you three to be a family."

"We are a family." Kali leaned forward. "I mean, we're Theo's parents. Theo's family. No matter what."

"You know what I mean."

"And is that what you want?"

Lincoln gave a slight shrug. "The question is what you want."

Kali leaned back. She couldn't do this again, talk about this again. These past days, the uncertainty, wondering if Lincoln would come up those steps. Wondering how he was. She missed him. Wanted him here. But to say it, when she couldn't say more, say what he wanted to hear ... or at least what she thought he wanted to hear.

"Derek loves you. He screwed up. Hugely. Massively. But people screw up." Lincoln looked to the floor." I know what it is to be your own villain."

"What?" Kali's eyes widened.

"To take your life and shit all over it. To have the pain be so intense ... or the confusion, uncertainty, that making things worse is all you seem capable of." Lincoln gave a slow shrug. "He's not like that anymore. Or, at least, he doesn't seem to be."

Kali stared at Lincoln. "What are you? His advocate?"

A long sigh flowed from him. "I don't know. Maybe. I guess."

"You guess?" Kali stood.

"It's like," Lincoln hesitated, "we're each responsible for our own misery. We make choices. Right choices. Wrong choices. Bad choices. We're our own villains and heroes. Derek's been the villain in his life for a long time. He's trying to be the hero now." Another pause. "I can respect that. I do respect it. And if he wants to make it right ..."

"You're going to walk away?" Kali's voice tightened. "Just like I thought you would."

"It's not like that."

"He can be the hero for Theo. It doesn't mean—"

"But what if it could work? What if I wasn't here? If you'd never met me, do you think you two would have a chance?"

Kali pushed away from him on the couch. How many times did she have to tell him the same thing? "I think we had this conversation already."

"I know." Lincoln nodded. He looked like he wanted to leave, like he wanted to be anywhere but here. "I keep thinking about my dad, those early years ... having him there all the time. All the good memories. The amazing memories and moments and lessons that got taken from me too soon. Theo hasn't had it up to this point, but he could from now on."

"And if Derek wants to be there for Theo, he will be, regardless of you and me, regardless of—"

"But not in the same way. And if you two could make it work I don't want to be the reason you don't."

Kali could hear the edge to her voice. Her shoulders tensed. "So, as I said, you're walking away. Like he did."

"It's not the same."

"The same end result, though."

Lincoln gave a short nod, his gaze back on the floor. "I've

been thinking about Lucy a lot the last few days, too. We even talked. For a bit. It makes sense she wanted something else, something more. She may have pushed me to it, but I lived and breathed work. It was my mistress and I loved that mistress more than her. She should have left me, not cheated on me with my brother, but it doesn't erase my part in her unhappiness, which led to the affair. And all that misery afterward..." Lincoln's eyes closed as he shook his head, "that wasn't because of Lucy, wasn't because of Joseph or the baby. It was just me."

Kali's eyes narrowed. "What does this have to do with us?"

"I don't want to keep making wrong choices. Maybe you'll end up with Derek. Maybe you won't. But it feels wrong, to stand in the way of that possibility, if I'm even standing in the way. Maybe you truly have no interest in him, but maybe I'm an excuse, one you don't even realize, a way to avoid him hurting you again. If it was more than that, if I was more than that." He stopped, his gaze on her.

You're more. She could say it. Blurt the words. Yes, she might be afraid of Derek failing her, yes, a part of her was still angry. But Lincoln was more than a buffer. More than safe. Her mind flashed to the feel of his lips on her, his hands. To the way he laughed with Theo, listened to him, saw his potential, believed in it, maybe even more than she had.

"If I was more," he continued, "I don't think we'd be having this conversation." Lincoln stood, his usually firm shoulders slumped. "I'm going to move out."

"This is your place."

He smiled and gestured around the room. "I did all this for you and Theo. Not me."

Kali stood facing him. "Where will you go?"

"The cabin for now. If it's not winter ready in time, I have options."

Kali crossed her arms. "I'll move out. I can now. It's no problem."

"If you want." Another smile. "The business would probably go better with easier internet access. Then again, it'd make more sense for me to rent a place closer to the lot. It's quite the drive there and back. You really don't need to leave."

Kali's chest tightened. "I don't want Derek."

Lincoln gave an unreadable smile as he stood before her, silent. Was he waiting for the words that would make him stay? *I want you.* If she said it, would it be enough? But she'd said it already, hadn't she? Why did it have to be a promise? Why should it mean forever?

Because she'd added 'now' to the end of it. *I want you now.* He wanted commitment. She craved freedom ... or at least didn't want chains.

He wanted a relationship. An acknowledged relationship, a real chance, not this non-committal experiment she'd initiated. Not a test.

She could throw her arms around him. Kiss him. Make him forget every word he'd just said. But what if he pushed her away? What if he didn't, yet once they lay beside each other, the passion faded, they were left in the same position they were in now?

"I'm going to go say goodbye to Theo."

Lincoln stepped past her. Kali turned. "So what, goodbye forever? You just won't see him anymore?"

Lincoln turned back, his face drawn. "I don't know. We'll have to figure that out. Maybe a slow fading of visits or time together. Whatever you think is best."

"WHAT I THINK IS BEST?" Kali's face was unreadable. A mix of anger, hurt, and something Lincoln couldn't decipher.

Moments earlier he'd almost taken her in his arms, told her he was being a fool. That whatever was best for her was best for Theo and that he was best for her. He knew it. He felt it.

Only he didn't. All he knew was she was best for him. All he knew was how much he wanted her to want him, need him, the way he needed her.

"I'm not just going to walk out of Theo's life. But I don't want to confuse him, either."

Her arms crossed over her middle. "I don't see how you'll avoid that."

"Kids are malleable."

"That's shit. This is all shit." Kali stepped away from him. "Now that it's getting hard, complicated, you're walking."

Lincoln let out a short laugh. "Getting hard?" He spread his arms. "Kali, it's been hard since the beginning. This, compared to some of what's come before. This is easy."

"Leaving us?"

"No." Lincoln shook his head. "No, I mean these complications. Life, right now. But," he hesitated, searching for the words, for why he was doing this, how ... "Maybe we were put in each other's lives for a reason, when we needed each other most. We were broken. I was broken. But we've grown. We're both doing so much better. You're embracing your new life, finding your strength. It's amazing, inspiring, how you've handled this diagnosis. How you're looking toward the future, even though you don't know what that future's going to hold."

Her gaze seemed locked on his as her expression softened. "You're to thank for a lot of that."

"And you're to thank for where I am, the fact that I can see a future again. That I'm excited about my prospects. That I spent the last few days with my family." Lincoln smiled. "Loving you, both of you, it gave me back my life. Or, rather, a new life."

"Love?"

Lincoln inhaled deeply. "You know I love you. Both of you."

"Both of us. Yeah." She looked away, her jaw twitching the way it so often did. "And is there a time line on this? Like if in so many days or weeks or months I'm not with Derek you'll try again? Come knocking on my door?"

Lincoln swallowed. If he was letting her go, he had to let go. "No."

Her shoulders rose quickly then fell, the most elegant shrug he'd ever seen. "Well, I guess that's that."

His chest tightened once more; his throat constricted. *Say no. Take it back. Take it all back.* "I'll go say goodbye to Theo now. Maybe tell him I'll take him for an outing next Tuesday?"

"Sure." Kali's arms crossed under her chest. "Tuesday sounds fine."

CHAPTER THIRTY-THREE

Lincoln sat at the table, a massive platter in front of him.

"I'm telling you, man." Andrew grinned as he set his own plate down. "This is going to be epic. Best Shawarma in Dartmouth, no contest. Probably best in the HRM."

"Smells good."

"Lincoln. Buddy." Andrew sat across from him. "A little enthusiasm would be nice."

"Sorry." Lincoln pasted a grin. "That better?"

"That's fake." Andrew reached for the pop and poured them each a glass. "You'd been doing better, actually seeming like a person again. What's the deal?"

The deal was it'd been weeks and he couldn't get Kali out of his head. The other day he'd been walking on Portland and saw a woman in a third floor window—barely a silhouette, but the way she moved ... His breath caught and he stood transfixed as she walked out of view, his stomach cramping with hope and regret. Was it her?

He'd balled his fist and punched into his opposite hand. If she'd moved out she would have told him, wouldn't she? This month's rent had shown up in his email. Money he didn't want.

Still, he wondered. A certain lilt of a woman's voice, a slow turn of a head, or the flash of a red cardigan, they all left him unravelled.

"Lincoln. You there?"

"Yeah. Sorry."

Andrew placed his hands on the table. "You've got to move on."

"Tomorrow's her next doctor's appointment. She'll know at the end of it whether the radiation killed the tumour. Whether she's safe ... for now at least."

"Hope she's safe. Hope for the best, and move on."

"Yeah." Lincoln picked up his fork and took a first bite. "You're right. This is good."

Andrew sighed. "When'd you last see her?"

"About two weeks ago. Just for a minute, picking up then dropping off Theo."

"That when she told you she didn't think you should see him anymore?"

"Yep."

"So she's cutting it off?"

"Uh huh."

"And Derek was there?"

"I heard him. Didn't see him."

"So take that as a sign. You did the right thing. They're going to be a family. You gave Theo that. You did good. And like you said, you were both there when you needed each other. Realizing another person's life is as important to you as your own is huge. Transformative. Be thankful and move on."

Lincoln laughed. "Since when did you become a

philosopher?"

"I've always been a philosopher."

Lincoln pointed to Andrew's plate. "Stop worrying about me. Eat. This is some epic Shawarma, like you said. Shame to let it go cold."

"You don't have to tell me twice." Andrew picked up his fork, and they ate in silence.

When his plate was half empty, Andrew paused for a drink. Setting the glass down, he looked at Lincoln. "You staying here or in the tree tonight?"

"Here." Lincoln took a large bite and let out a little moan. "I've got a meeting with this marketing guru in the morning. If things go well, she wants me to meet some big shot based in Montreal in a few weeks. And then a distributor. She wants to brainstorm best ways to take the business online."

"You want that? An online business?"

"If it means being my own boss, maybe." Lincoln took another bite. "This is ridiculous."

"I know." Andrew grinned.

"Anyway," said Lincoln after swallowing. "I still want to focus on highly customized tree houses, but she's saying the market for that is too small here, that I have to be willing to reach a national and most likely an international market with it if I want to go anywhere. Niche and exclusive."

"And what do you think of that?"

"For the money it makes sense. But I also like the idea of being able to make something unique and wonderful for the average person, not just the elite."

"I feel that." Andrew gripped Lincoln's shoulder and gave it a squeeze and shake. "The Alexander way of business."

"The Alexander way." Lincoln took another bite of the

chicken and rice. "Exactly."

THUD, THUD, THUD, THUD.

Dr. Johnson grinned, his large hands clasped in front of him. "It's good, Kali. Very good."

Kali released the breath she hadn't known she'd been holding.

"We have every reason to think the tumour's dead. All that growth in the last scan, it's clear now. It was just swelling. And there's a strong chance what's left is scar tissue."

Thud-thud-thud. Kali's heart pounded harder, faster. "A chance."

"We can't know for sure. That's why you'll have the regular check-ups in the schedule I outlined earlier. I don't want to give you false hope. But this reduction in size, it's promising. It's about the best scenario we could hope for."

Kali nodded. She closed her eyes then opened them slowly. Could she see more of the room than the last time she sat here? A bit, maybe. But not much more. "My sight?"

"You're seeing Dr. Manning next week, correct?"

Another nod.

"She'll do an assessment. I expect you'll see some improvement, but probably not much. As I said, there's scar tissue."

"That could be residual tumour."

Dr. Jones flattened his hands on the table. "It could be, yes." He paused. "How have your symptoms been?"

"Better, definitely." Kali thought over the past weeks. So much better, in fact, that at times she'd hardly thought of them.

Dr. Jones leaned in. "Smile, Kali. This is good news."

Smile? The air in the room seemed thick and uncertain. A reason for hope, but don't hope too much. Tumour dead, maybe, but sight still impaired.

Kali took another long breath. With all that'd been going on she'd hardly had time to ruminate over this appointment. To let the fear fester and spread. The tumour had stopped growing, that much was certain. For now, at least, the invader was no longer winning. Lincoln would be thrilled. Ecstatic. He'd want to celebrate, take them all to dinner.

If he knew. He wouldn't know.

"Kali."

Kali made the corners of her lips rise. "This is great. Wonderful. Good news, like you said."

"Day by day, Kali. With this type of diagnosis, that's how you have to live. And today, you've won. Today, you've beat this thing."

"The battle though, right." Kali glanced to the window. This meant she could do that assessment at Westwood. If it went well, maybe go back to her old job ... if she wanted. If. "Not the war."

"Every battle won brings you closer."

"In a war that might not be won till I die?"

Dr. Jones leaned back in his chair, his brow furrowed, his eyes looking concerned. "Kali, how have you been doing, outside of this?"

Lincoln was gone. Derek was back. And she loved Derek. She did. In certain moments she could even imagine what it would be like to be with him again. To feel his large hands encasing her body, the strength of him as he pressed his weight down into her ... and all the other things too, things she was already experiencing from time to time. His laughter. The little tidbits of newfound knowledge he came home excited to share with her, the feel of his hand grazing the small of her back as they turned to enter a room.

But then the memory of other moments would emerge—the four years of life without him. The fear that at some tragedy, he'd bolt again.

Lincoln, that's who she wanted to tell this news to. Lincoln, who'd been with her through it all. Who was firm. Steady. Or at least had been.

"Kali?"

Kali inhaled, then let the breath out slowly. "Life's been interesting. Intense. A lot of changes." She pushed her chair back from the desk. "Are we done here?"

"No more questions?"

Kali shook her head.

"Then if you're done, we're done." Dr. Jones reached for a card from a little holder on his desk. "Remember, if you need someone to talk to, support is available." He handed over the card. "It's covered through the hospital, if that's a concern."

Kali looked at the card, multiple letters after the name. "I think I'll be all right. I'm part of a ... support group, I guess you'd call it. At the CNIB. They've helped a lot."

"That's great."

Kali stood. "Thank you." Her smile was genuine this time. "For the good news."

"I love to give it." Dr. Jones looked to his monitor. "You'll be getting an appointment date in the mail for another checkup sometime in the next eight to twelve weeks. If you have any sudden reemergence of symptoms before that, though, give my office a call."

Kali slung her satchel across her shoulder and set her headphones around her neck. With a nod, she stepped out of the room. This battle was won. For now, at least, she was safe. But it didn't feel like a victory, not in the way she'd hoped.

In the waiting room she looked to where Lincoln had stood five weeks earlier, remembered the way his arms felt as they wrapped around her, and how moments later, with the mention of a limp, everything had changed. She'd go back and tell him now, if she could. Explain it all right then, instead of pushing him away. She'd give them a chance.

But you couldn't go back, only forward. And if she wanted to go forward, she needed more information. She needed to understand how to make it right. She needed to figure out exactly what it was she wanted. Kali pushed through the hospital doors. She needed to talk to someone who knew Lincoln better than she did, who understood the way his mind worked.

At the bus stop, Kali pulled out her phone and texted Derek. *Results were good. Something came up, though. I may be a few more hours. That okay?*

He replied almost instantly. *Sure, no problem. Take your time. And that's awesome!*

Kali stepped onto the third bus to arrive, hoping she wasn't crazy.

CHAPTER THIRTY-FOUR

"Oh." Marilyn's eyes widened and her brow raised. She paused before breaking into a smile. "Come in, sweetheart, come right in."

Kali smiled back, the tingly feeling in her arms and flutter in her chest increasing at Marilyn's welcome. "Thanks."

Kali held out the flowers and sympathy card she'd picked up on the way over. "Again, I'm so sorry for your loss."

Marilyn took the offering with a smile then stepped to the side to make way for Kali. She stood waiting as Kali unlaced her boots. "Cup of tea?" Marilyn asked once Kali was standing upright again.

"Uh, sure. Thanks." Kali followed Marilyn down the hall to the kitchen. She sat on the island as Marilyn pulled open a cupboard full of options.

Marilyn turned with a grin. "I've got it all."

"Uh, regular is fine."

Marilyn tilted her head. "How about an Earl Grey de la crème?"

Kali shrugged a yes.

"I used to be a plain tea gal too, but Rachel got me started on these loose leaf teas. I was skeptical at first, but now I'm a convert." After scooping the tea into two strainers, Marilyn leaned against the counter as the sound of the heating water became audible. She crossed her arms, her intense gaze making Kali shift. "You look good."

"Thanks."

"Better colour to your face."

"Yeah?"

"Definitely."

Kali swivelled to take in the framed photos above the kitchen cabinets and around the room: an array of the Fraser children at various ages, with a few of Marilyn and a man Kali recognized from the funeral as a pre-Alzheimer's Alexander.

"Oh," Marilyn's brow raised again, "I should have asked if you wanted coffee. I hardly drink it anymore myself, so I don't think of it."

"Tea is perfect." Kali swallowed and bit her lower lip. Awkwardness hung around her like a thick fog. What was she doing here? Coming to the home of a woman who'd just lost her husband to, what? Ask advice, get the inside scoop on her son, simply not feel so alone? "How have you been doing ... since?"

Marilyn crossed her arms and leaned against the counter. "I've known this day was coming for years, of course. Sometimes even prayed for it." She looked past Kali. "But it's still hard. In some ways it's a relief, no longer having to see him suffer. In other ways I want just one more day, one more hour to hold his hand, to try to see the man he once was."

Marilyn shrugged as the kettle clicked. She poured the steaming water into two large mugs. "Milk or sugar?"

"Black is fine."

Marilyn grabbed what looked to be a timer, set it, then set the timer, mugs, two spoons, and a small plate on a tray. Tray in hand, she gestured to the patio door. "We won't have many afternoons like this left. Care to take this party outside?"

Kali eased off her stool and made it to the patio door in time to hold it open for Marilyn. An unseasonably warm breeze greeted them as the sun shone brightly on the patio. Marilyn set the tray down on a table between two chairs and opened the lid of an ottoman to pull out two knit blankets. "Just in case."

Kali sat in the chair closest to her and sighed at the array of colours in the yard. Rich green of the grass, bright blue of the sky, deeper blue of a lake at the far end of the property, and breathtaking reds, oranges, and yellows of the leaves.

"It's nice, isn't it?"

Kali shifted in the seat so she could see Marilyn. "Beautiful."

"I sit out here a lot." Marilyn's voice quieted. "When Alexander showed me this plot of land it was fall. He stood me right where this patio is and let me take in the view. There weren't as many trees then, and not as big, but it was still breathtaking. He promised me this patio and afternoons and evenings sitting out here hand in hand, the kids running in the yard."

Kali stared at Marilyn, who looked straight ahead at the view. "And was it like that?"

Marilyn turned to Kali, the warmth of her smile competing with the sadness in her eyes. "It was. For a time. And even now, with nothing but the view, this is my favourite place on the property to sit."

Kali looked back out at the view then jumped as the timer

dinged.

"Time to take the strainer out if you like the 'perfect' cup," said Marilyn, with air quotes. If you want it stronger, feel free."

Kali removed her tea bag and leaned back in the chair. She shifted again to Marilyn. "I'm sure you're wondering why I'm here."

"Oh, I think I have a pretty good idea." Marilyn glanced to Kali then directed her gaze back to the yard. "My son, who thinks too much, thinks life is more complicated than it is. As a result, he's got it in his head that he's not good for you, or not good enough, or the timing isn't right, or some such thing." Marilyn gave her head a slight shake. "He's either ended it between you or created some unclear distance, and you want to talk to me about it."

Kali's brow furrowed. Part of her wanted to laugh, the other scream. "That's pretty much it, yeah."

"What I don't know," said Marilyn, taking a sip of her tea, "is why he feels this way or how you feel."

Kali let out a long stream of air. She wasn't exactly sure why she was here, but here she was, and if she was going to ask this woman's advice, as weird as that seemed, she'd better give her the full story.

So she did.

"AND IS DEREK WHY YOU and Lincoln were only 'trying it out' in those weeks after the New York trip?" asked Marilyn almost twenty minutes later.

"I don't know." Kali's tea was almost done, but she sipped the last few lukewarm drops to give herself a moment to think. "Not the hope that he'd come back. I'm pretty sure of that. But his existence? The fact that he was out there in the world somewhere not with me, not with us, the fact that he left ... probably."

"A trust thing?"

Kali nodded.

"I get that. But that's not going to change unless you change it. Not with Derek. Not with Lincoln. Not with any other man who may or may not enter your life in the future."

Kali nodded again, her feet pulled up under her and the blanket tucked snugly around her legs. Still, she shivered.

"Should we head inside?"

Kali shook her head with a laugh. "I don't think it's the cold."

"The unknown future." Marilyn chuckled. "It's enough to make anyone shiver."

"I was starting to trust, I think. Lincoln was so patient, and so kind and ... dependable. But it was like we were pretending. Or I was. Not that I didn't feel for him. I did. I do. But it was this safe little bubble we were in, where I didn't have to commit."

"We always have to commit. At some point."

"But maybe if we'd had more time, I could have. If Derek had come back a year from now, even six months from now."

"But he didn't."

"I know. And so is there a reason for that? Was it some sign Lincoln isn't the one for me?"

"And Derek is?"

"No. No." Kali shook her head as she gazed past Marilyn to the yard. "I'll admit, at times I've wondered. And I know he wants to give it another try. But I think what we had, in that way, it's dead. I don't know that it could ever come to life again. There's too much history. Too much pain. Even if some of that pain was misplaced.

"I love Derek. I do. And maybe love is stronger than I think. Derek certainly thinks we can work through these past four years. And Lincoln seems to think so too. He thinks he owes it to Theo to get out of the way or something. Give Derek and me a chance. Give our family a chance."

"As you said." Marilyn sighed. "Personally, I don't believe everything happens for a reason. The world is messy and chaotic and basically off kilter ... but I do believe reason can come from every experience, good or bad. You just need to look hard for it. You need to take the time."

"So what's the reason for Derek coming back and Lincoln leaving?"

"I can't tell you that. But if you really take the time," Marilyn grinned, "listen to your heart and all that woo-woo jazz, I think you'll figure it out."

"Woo-woo jazz." Kali laughed. "That's what it sounds like. I'm not exactly a listen to your heart type of girl."

"Maybe you should try it."

"Maybe what it's telling me is that I shouldn't be with either guy. That I should be alone, and that's the best option."

"That's possible." Marilyn tilted her head and set her mug down. "You were alone for a long time. Think you prefer it?"

"I like not relying on anyone. I like only have expectations of myself."

"I know what that's like." Marilyn's eyes crinkled. "Can get kind of lonely."

Kali hesitated. "It can."

"And honestly, sweetheart, sounds to me like you saying that, it's coming from a place of fear. Of being in danger of letting your past define your future."

"Well, we're supposed to learn lessons from the past, right? Isn't that the wise thing to do?"

Marilyn leaned forward, a hand to her chin. "Maybe. In recent years, I'm more of the belief the past is a story we tell ourselves, and behind each of our lives are all these stories we tell about who we are, what we've done, what's been done to us, what we believe. If we let them, these stories control what we see, how we act, the choices we make."

Marilyn turned her gaze from Kali. "All the things in life that happen, they're part of our story, but we're each our own author, which means every event, emotion, everything and anything, can be rewritten or reinterpreted any way we choose. A tragedy can be a gift. A victory or blessing or seeming miracle can be a curse."

Marilyn looked back to Kali. "Everything that's happened to you, you've written into your story. You told yourself your husband abandoned you, while he told himself he did it for you, for love, to provide for you while protecting you from himself.

"You told yourself you could survive on your own. So you did. Then you got this horrible news; you were going blind, and you told yourself you couldn't do it anymore, that your life was over." Marilyn's smile broadened. "And then you told yourself it wasn't. You did some rewriting.

"All of it, Kali, our life, is just a huge conglomeration of stories. How we live is all based on the stories we tell ourselves." Marilyn paused. She reached her hand to rest on top of Kali's. "And that's the amazing thing. Our stories can be re-written. When we tell ourselves different stories about our past, about what we want our future to be, our whole lives change."

Marilyn gave Kali's hand a squeeze then let it go. She settled back against her chair. "So I guess the question is, what story are you going to tell?"

CHAPTER THIRTY-FIVE

Over the next weeks Marilyn's words kept flowing through Kali's mind. The question was there when she got ready in the morning—*what story are you going to tell?* As she made dinner—*what's the story?* While she sat in the park, Marvin beside her, watching Theo and Derek play and laugh. *Kali, what story are you telling yourself?*

The question seemed simple enough, but it wasn't. And the difficulty in answering that seemingly simple question forced her to search herself even deeper. It made her acknowledge her role in the anger and sadness and frustration she'd let herself live with the past four years. It made her consider the possibility that the reason Derek hadn't stayed in their lives was as much about his pain and rash, irresponsible choices as it was about her pride and inability to be open to making it work. His interpretation of what had happened could be completely different from hers, and neither one of them were necessarily entirely right or entirely wrong.

Perhaps the most compelling thing about Marilyn's words was that Kali had known them all along; she'd spoken them to

Theo weeks ago, in another form, but somehow not seen their importance or how they could apply to not just her current situation but the past as well. *The bad things, when they happen, they don't have to be as bad as you think ... we have a choice about how bad we let them be*. She'd had a choice about everything, but most of the time she'd made the wrong one.

"Mommy. Mommy. Watch."

Kali clapped as Derek held the back of Theo's swing and ran underneath him, making the boy soar.

"Again!" Theo squealed amid bursts of laughter. "Again!"

Kali turned to her right at the feel of Marvin's hand on her knee. "This is good, Sweetness, isn't it? Really good."

Kali smiled at him, something in her on the verge of breaking.

"Having the family together again. Seeing my boys. My girl."

"It's great." Kali kept her gaze on Marvin as he stared at Derek and Theo. His transformation alone was enough to convince Kali of the truth of Marilyn's words. He'd changed his story, clearly. Stopped seeing himself as nothing but a failure, an outcast, a burden. He was living with Derek full time now. His hair was trimmed short, his clothes clean and hole free. His must-have items now sat on shelves in his closet. The rest, along with the cart, had disappeared. He volunteered twice a week at a local shelter instead of being an occasional guest when the weather forced him inside.

"Beatrice would have liked this. Jason too."

"Definitely." Kali stretched out her hand to give Marvin's a squeeze then turned back to their 'boys.'

That's what it had seemed like the past couple of weeks. That they were a family. Unified. There for each other. And they were. But each night Kali had gone back to her own apartment. Lincoln's apartment. Twice, Theo had gone to Derek's place, leaving Kali to spend the night by herself for the first time in four years.

She'd entered the apartment that once seemed cramped only to feel small in a too large space. As the night wore on, she'd thought about her story. She'd made mistakes. Then she'd made the best of those mistakes. The best she knew how, anyway. She'd written herself as someone strong. Someone who could make it on her own, and seen that as a positive. But what had the desire to make it on her own done? Left her tired, angry, bitter, virtually friendless.

Had the stress of it all led to the tumour's rapid growth?

No.

She wouldn't write that storyline. But without a doubt, it had led to the fact that on her first night alone in years, she only had one friend she could possibly call to hang out.

But she didn't want a friend. Not that night. She wanted something more.

Theo appeared before her, his grin broad and quick. His voice sure. "Daddy says it's time to go."

"Oh." Kali pulled Theo into her lap. He was almost too big for this. He would be soon. "Then I guess it's time to go."

She raised her gaze to Derek, who was more handsome now than the day they'd met, who looked at her, in some ways, even more intensely than he had then. Who, day by day, was showing himself as someone reliable, someone who'd rewritten his own story. "You work in a couple of hours, right?"

Theo wriggled his way off of Kali's lap and, free from his weight, she stood.

"That I do." Derek's hand fell naturally on Theo's head and the boy leaned into him. "We could get together for a late dinner if you'd like. I have some pork chops thawing in the fridge."

Kali shook her head. She'd only been in Derek's place for a few minutes, twice. He'd invited her more than a dozen times. "We already have dinner plans."

Theo tugged on Kali's shirt. "No, we don't."

"We do," said Kali. "We're going to Shelley's house. Then you're going to stay and play with her kids while Mommy has her meeting."

"Oh yeah!" Theo grinned. "I forgot."

"That for the Dinner in the Dark thing?" Derek's head tilted.

"Dining in the Dark." Kali lifted her satchel from the bench and whipped out her cane.

"You decide who your plus one is yet?"

"Shelley's busy." Kali pressed her lips together. She hesitated. "Would you like to come, Derek?"

His smile erupted. Firecracker style. Just like Theo. "I'd love to come. When is it, again?"

"Friday night."

Derek turned to Marvin. "Dad, can you—"

"Happy to. What do you say, little man? You and me, Friday night?"

Theo's head bobbed back and forth. "Okay."

"Okay." Derek rested his arm across Kali's shoulders and gave a squeeze. "This should be fun."

"Seeing what my life may be like one day," mumbled Kali. "Yeah, should be a blast."

Derek turned her toward him. "Is that how you see this?"

No. It wasn't. That was her old story. The woe is me story. She was excited about the experience, about seeing the event she'd spent the past several weeks working on turn into a success. Going with Derek, in that romantic atmosphere, where their fingers may graze, where their conversation would likely be whispered—that's what she wasn't sure about. "I don't know why I said that." Kali rested her cane against the bench and bent to tighten the velcro on Theo's shoes—an excuse to escape Derek's casual embrace.

Derek's face tightened. He saw the ruse. She was sure of it. But she'd told him this relationship they were building was about Theo. Only about Theo. And then she'd invited him to an event that would be full of couples ...

"Well," Kali stood and brushed her hands unnecessarily on her hips, "you better get going or you'll be late for work."

Derek's face relaxed slightly. He turned to Theo and held his arms out. The boy leapt into them and they had a squeeze before Derek set him down again. "I'll see you tomorrow, buddy, okay?"

Theo grinned and Kali wondered for about the millionth time what their lives would have been if some little boy never ventured too close to the black rocks at Peggy's Cove. But he had, and everything that happened since couldn't be erased. She could rewrite her story, yes, she could change how she interpreted the past. But she couldn't rewrite the past. She couldn't bring Jason back. She couldn't pretend the years from that day to this hadn't happened.

CHAPTER THIRTY-SIX

Marvin turned to Kali as Derek walked away from the park. "What are you two up to now, Sweetness?"

"Heading home. I've got some work to do." Kali kept her gaze on Derek as his figure shrank in the distance. She couldn't rewrite the past.

"For this dinner?"

"No, actually." Kali broke her stare and turned to Marvin. A smile worked its way onto her face. "For my assessment at Westwood. I've been researching with the help of Alika from the CNIB. I think I have a much better chance of getting my job back than I thought."

Marvin nodded. "That's wonderful. And you want this job back? I thought you said ..."

"I think that was fear." Kali gestured to the path. "Walk with us?"

Marvin nodded and fell into step beside Kali and Theo.

"This was the dream job. It'll be more difficult, of course, but it's still something I love. Something I miss."

"You mentioned working at the CNIB?"

"And I can still do that. Volunteer. My supervisor at Westwood said it's likely they'd start me off on part time hours if all goes well. Even after I'm full time, I could help out at CNIB on weekends. If I decide I want to do something more permanent with them in the future, I could. But for now, I think showing myself I can do the work I did before would be really good for me."

Marvin let his head hang and shook it with a grin. "You're a wonder, you are, Sweetness. A fighter."

Kali's chest rose with a long draw of breath. "I don't know that that's always been a good thing. But sometimes it is."

"It is now." Marvin rubbed his hand on her back a little awkwardly. "I like the way you and Derek are fighting too, to make this work. To be a family."

Kali cast her gaze in front of her.

"Even if you two aren't together the way you were, you can still be a family."

Kali kept walking, her brow furrowed.

"It'd be great if you were. Wonderful. But even if you're not," Marvin paused, "even if you're with someone else, a family isn't one specific thing. It's people who love each other and ... and work together. Who are there for each other when life gets hard or messy."

Kali looked to Marvin. "You think so?"

"I've had a lot of time to think about it." He gave a little nod. "That's what family is."

Kali turned her gaze back to the path as they approached a cross-walk. "This is your turn."

"I'll walk you two home."

Kali took Theo's hand, looked both ways, looked again, then ventured into the street.

"That Lincoln," said Marvin, "he knows what family is."

"He abandoned his family for a long time."

"And created a new one."

"Lincoln?" Theo tugged on Kali's hand, his eyes wide and excited. "We see Lincoln today?"

"No, sweetheart." Kali turned her head back to Marvin. "You haven't asked about him, about why he's not around."

"He's not around because Derek is."

"And you see that as someone who knows what family is? Sounds like the opposite." Kali paused as she stepped back onto the sidewalk. "Things got messy and he left."

Marvin pushed his lips together and narrowed his gaze. "You think that's why he left?"

At times she did. At times his excuse of doing what was right for Theo, of giving Derek and her a chance to make it work sounded like bull. But then she'd remember the look in his eyes as he said it. The first time it may have been the mess. The last time, it wasn't.

"My boy loves you, Kali. That I know. And I love my boy." Marvin took a shaky, rattling breath. "And from what I know of the two of you, if you can work through your issues, start slow, build up what you once had, it'll be good. Better than good. I want to see that. I'd love to see that. It would make this old man go to his grave happy."

"Shh." Kali looked to Theo, skipping beside her, hopefully oblivious. "You won't be going to your grave for a long, long time."

"Maybe." Marvin turned his head to Kali with a soft smile. "Anyway, that'd make me happy. But only if it makes you happy. You're my daughter too now. My family. Your happiness is just as important to me as my son's.

"Whatever you do, whatever you decide in this life, do it for you, decide it for you. And don't be afraid." Marvin gave a little shrug and shake of his head. "I know what it is to live your life in fear, Sweetness. I've wasted half of mine that way. It's not worth it, even if you think it's the right thing." He gave a firm shake of his head. "It's not the right thing."

"You think I could be happy with Derek?"

Marvin kept silent for several steps. "Maybe we can be happy no matter what, just like we can be miserable no matter how good our lives look." Marvin let out a long, heavy cough. "Sorry, Sweetness."

Kali rubbed his back. "You got a cold?"

"Something like that." They turned the corner and Marvin took a deep, shaky breath. "I had two beautiful boys. I had a wife I loved till her dying breath and who loved me. I had a good job. But I was miserable. I lost it all. I betrayed her love and her trust, giving up like that."

"Marvin."

"I did. We all know it."

"You were hurting."

"I'm still hurting. But now I'm living too."

Kali stopped in front of her porch steps. Lincoln's porch steps. "You giving me permission or something, to choose a life other than one with your son?"

"You don't need my permission." Marvin ruffled Theo's head. "I'm just hoping you give yourself permission. Ever since my boy walked out of your life you've been living for your son's. Live for yourself too, Sweetness. That's important."

Kali frowned. She gestured to the stairs. "You want to come in for a bit? Have lunch?"

"Nah." Marvin waved his hand. He looked to the concrete then back at Kali. "It's hard, you know? Having a roof over my head, walls around me." He gestured to Theo. "He makes it worth it. And my boy. And you. But sometimes I feel like it's all closing in on me, like it's going to crush me. I'm trying though. Really trying. I know I need to, this way of living ... it's better."

Kali pressed her lips together before responding. "You were on the streets for a long time."

Marvin nodded. "They were my home." He gestured to the streets and buildings in the distance. "I miss the city, and I think maybe the city misses me. Today I'm going to walk it."

"You sure?"

Marvin winked. "Makes me happy."

CHAPTER THIRTY-SEVEN

Kali ushered Theo upstairs and let her hand trail along his back as they made their way into the apartment. Theo plopped onto the floor and undid his shoes, his teeth biting his bottom lip, his tongue slightly out at the corner. Kali sat down across from him as he looked at her, eyes wide.

She reached a hand to his knee. "Did you have fun with Daddy today?"

Theo nodded then brought his attention back to his shoes. He yanked the first one off and set it with the row of shoes by the door.

"You like Daddy, right?"

Another nod.

"More than Lincoln?"

Theo's head tilted. He was silent for a moment. "Different." He bent his head again and worked on the other shoe. Kali waited until it sat beside the first shoe.

As Theo was about to stand, Kali put pressure on his knee, indicating he stay. "What do you mean by different?"

"Mmm. I don't know." Theo rocked. "Daddy's Daddy and

Lincoln's Lincoln."

"Okay." Kali's brow furrowed. "You said once that Lincoln was kind of like a daddy. How would you like that, if Lincoln were to live with us and he and Mommy were together and he really was like your daddy?"

Theo shook his head, his face scrunched up with confusion and mirth. "Lincoln already lives with us. It's already like that."

"He hasn't been though, much, has he?"

Theo's face fell slightly. "He's busy because his daddy died. Then he's coming back, right?"

Kali took a deep breath. "He's not planning to, no. Remember he came in a couple of weeks ago to say goodbye. To tell you he wouldn't be seeing you so much."

Theo nodded, his face concerned.

"He doesn't live with us anymore."

"But I still see him. We went to the park and to the burger place and then," Theo tapped his chin, "swimming. He took me to the swimming pool."

"I know. But you haven't seen him in a long time, have you? Almost two weeks."

"I don't know!" Theo's eyes narrowed. "I'll see him again. He said I'd see him again. And when he's done being busy with his dead daddy he's gonna live here again."

"He said that?"

"I ..." Theo's mouth opened and closed. "I don't know. Yes. Yes. He said. He said so. He told me."

"I don't think so, honey. I think maybe you're confused."

"I'm not confused. You're confused."

"I told Lincoln I didn't think it was good for you to see him anymore. That it would confuse you."

"No!" Theo grabbed a shoe and hurled it at Kali's chest. She caught it before impact.

"Theo."

"No. You're stupid. That's stupid. Lincoln's coming back."

Kali rubbed her hands on her knees and took a deep breath. "That makes you very upset, doesn't it, the idea that Lincoln's not coming back."

"He is coming back." Theo yelled. "He's going to be like my second daddy. Or my first daddy. He's first. You said."

"I didn't—"

"You said he'd live with us and be like my real daddy."

Kali reached her arms forward and placed her hands on each of Theo's hips. She pulled him closer. "I didn't say that. I asked if you would like that."

Theo crossed his arms tight in front of him. "I would."

"Would you rather live with Daddy though?"

"Just Daddy?"

"What if it were Daddy and me and Grampie and you?"

"And Lincoln."

"No. Not Lincoln. But you like Daddy, right?"

Theo's lips pursed.

"Theo."

He nodded. "Daddy's fun. I like Daddy."

"Do you love him?"

Theo shrugged.

"Do you love Lincoln?"

Theo nodded.

"You love Lincoln."

Another nod. His lips trembled. His eyes glistened. "I want Lincoln to come back. I thought Lincoln was coming back."

Kali pulled Theo into her lap.

"Make Lincoln come back. He can be my daddy."

Kali rocked Theo against her, her heart aching, then shifted him so she could see his face. She wiped away the few tears that fell with her thumb. "I'm sorry, honey. I shouldn't be talking to you about this."

"You should. You should bring Lincoln back."

"But we've been doing okay, haven't we. Just me and you, then seeing Daddy and Grampie?"

Theo nodded.

"You love Grampie, right?"

Another nod.

"And maybe you'll love Daddy too, sometime soon."

"I don't know him so well."

"But you're getting to, right?"

"Uh huh."

"Daddy loves you. So much. He came back for you."

"And you."

Kali smiled. "Mostly you." She squeezed Theo tighter and smoothed her hand over his dreads. "I'm so sorry, baby, that you don't know your daddy better. He wanted to know you. He wanted to visit and I, I kept him from you ... I was scared."

Theo's eyes widened. "You were scared of Daddy?"

"No. No." Kali looked up to the ceiling. Lately it felt like she couldn't get anything right. She adjusted Theo again so she could look him in the face. "I guess I was scared that he'd love you so much he'd try to take you away from me, but that was silly. So silly. He loves you like crazy but he'd never take you away."

Theo's brow furrowed. "You sure?"

"So sure." Kali smiled and cupped Theo's chin. She eased

him off of her lap, stood, then offered a hand to help him up. "You must be hungry."

Theo nodded, a hand wiping under his nose.

"Time for lunch?"

"Uh huh."

Kali squeezed Theo's hand then released it. "You go play with your cars. I'll make grilled cheese."

Theo turned without a backward glance. Kali rubbed a hand on her neck. She'd made her son cry. She'd tried to get answers out of him she needed to answer for herself. Theo loved Lincoln. He missed Lincoln. That much was clear. But he'd love Derek too. She was sure of it. Like Lincoln said, kids were malleable. Kali glanced into the living room, where Theo sat crouched on the floor, completely engrossed in his cars. Theo would be fine. No matter what, he'd be okay. He had his Dad back. That's what was important.

"AND YOU CAN BUILD this anywhere?"

"Not anywhere, no. I need a tree. The right kind of tree."

"Right." Twizzler turned then leaned against the fencing Lincoln had built with Theo in mind. She smiled, her grin lighting her face. "It looks even better than last time."

"Thanks." Lincoln leaned against the logs making up the tree house's outer wall, fighting a grin himself. "I'm sure you get this all the time, but—"

"Twizzler is my real name. My given name." Twizzler shook her long wavy red locks and flashed a smile. "My father had a sense of humour."

"And you're carrying on the joke."

She raised an eyebrow.

"You could keep your hair short. Dye it."

"This is my hair, and I like it."

Lincoln's grin escaped through the corner of his mouth. "I respect that. It suits you, anyway."

"The name or the hair?"

"Both."

Twizzler gave a crisp nod then pulled out her camera. "I think I've got enough shots up here. I'll take a few more from the ground, then we're done."

Back on the forest floor, Twizzler tucked her camera away after some final shots. "The key now is to find interested buyers, preferably people with visions of their own, so you can work with them, create a portfolio of potential styles and designs, from simple and rustic to elaborate and classy."

"I'm guessing mine's the former?"

Twizzler let her head bob side to side. "Closer to the former, but really somewhere in between. The finishing work you've done, high end customers will want that and more, but you said you also want to appeal to the Dad who wants a man cave, the family who wants a fun retreat for their kids. They may not care so much about the double layer you've done, the natural trunks. Plain old lumber should suffice."

"Okay."

"My job is to focus on what you want. Help you make this the business you want it to be."

Lincoln raised an eyebrow.

Twizzler waved a hand. "I know when we first met I had all these visions and I laid them down hard. I know your family. I know Joseph. I may have let that influence who I thought you'd be and what you'd want. But if this is going to work, it's got to work for you. You want the main focus to be you designing houses individually, that'll be the main focus. You want to actually be there doing the work a lot of the time, that's what you'll do. You'll make less, but you'll make a name. Niche can be good."

Lincoln looked up to the tree house and bit his lip. "I'm okay with pre-designed too. I liked that combo thing we talked about. Basic structure but with options for people to personalize it. And I'm okay with hiring contractors for the work. Just not right away. I want to make sure I have something solid before I start to grow. I want to control that growth, not let it get away from me."

"You want a business that supports your life, not one that becomes it."

Lincoln gave a slight nod. "Yeah."

"You will have to travel."

"I know."

"But we'll start as close to home as we can."

Lincoln gave another nod. "You have someone in the Valley?"

"I do." Twizzler grinned, her green eyes sparkling. "But I really want you to meet with the Montreal guy first. Get started there. He's a name maker."

"I don't know. It's not exactly close to home."

"It's closer than Germany, where I think you could eventually have a lot of interest." Twizzler finished fastening the cover to her camera case then slung the bag across her shoulder. "Listen, Lincoln, if this guy wants to hire you it'll be a big job. More than that, if he likes it, which he will, he'll want to show his tree house off. This one job could make your career. It may make you busy enough that you don't have to advertise for years."

"Won't that put you out of a job?"

Twizzler crossed her arms and sighed. "I'd get a cut then move on to the next client until you need me again."

"Anyway," Lincoln leaned against his truck, "I don't want to be busy for years, I want—"

"To do a full day's work then go home and rest. I get it. So you do the design. You hire contractors. You get them started—you're out there for a fews days—if you want to make sure they're doing the work the way you want to do it, then you take a trip every couple of weeks."

Lincoln cringed.

"Get your foreman to send you daily pictures. You can make it work. You said you were fine with travel."

"I am. But contractors on my first job. Contractors without me there?"

"So stay. Do it there. A few months of hard work if you do it alone. Far less if you hire a team you'll oversee. You don't have anything holding you here, do you?"

Lincoln took a deep breath and lifted his arms as his shoulders shrugged. "No. You're right." He pushed out a smile. "I'll meet with him. See if we're in alignment."

"You'll be in alignment. I'll book the flights tomorrow. In one to two weeks is good?"

Lincoln nodded.

Twizzler pulled out her phone, pressed a button to show the time, then brought her attention back to Lincoln, a grin on her face. "All right, back to civilization."

CHAPTER THIRTY-EIGHT

Kali stood in front of the mirror, turning first one way and then the other. She smoothed her hand over her hips. Was this the right choice? Did it matter? The majority of the evening would be spent in the dark. Not only would no one care about her outfit, most people wouldn't see it.

But Derek would.

She wanted to look nice. But not too nice. Not like she was trying to look nice, or good, for him.

"Mommmm-eeeee!"

"I'm almost done, sweetie."

"I got to peeeeee."

"Okay. Okay." Kali took one more look at the simple burgundy dress then opened the door. Theo burst in, pushed past her, pulled his pants down, and hopped on the toilet with a sigh.

A chuckle burst out of Kali. "You really had to go, didn't you."

Theo nodded, his hands crossed over his knees. "Daddy's here."

"Already?"

Another nod.

"And you let him in? What did I tell you about letting people into the apartment."

"He's not people. He's Daddy."

"Still." Kali gave one last look into the mirror, adjusted the flower clip in her afro, then turned back to Theo. "Don't forget to flush and wash your hands."

Theo put a hand to his forehead, salute style. "Aye, aye, captain."

"Where do you get this stuff from?" Kali shook her head and made her way to the hall.

Derek stood when she entered the living room, a bouquet of assorted flowers in his hand. "You look nice." He stared at her the way she'd used to love. The way that had made her say yes all those years ago. "Of course, you always look nice."

"You didn't need to do that." Kali gestured to the bouquet.

Derek shrugged. "Seemed appropriate."

"This is a work thing. A volunteer work thing."

Derek held up the flowers. "You have a vase?"

Kali turned to the kitchen. "A water jug will have to do." She reached into the cupboard then turned to see Derek behind her, his free hand outstretched. "I'll do it."

Kali was about to protest then raised her hands in a motion of surrender. "As you wish."

She perched on the counter, watching. He filled the vase about a third full, reached for the little packet of white powder flowers always came with, tore it neatly, then grabbed a long wooden spoon and gave the mixture several twirls. Next, he filled the sink with several inches of water, cut each stem with a knife, and put them in the vase. Once they'd all been transferred, he took a moment to rearrange them, propping the tallest stems in the middle, the shortest on the outside, and making sure not too many of the same bloom were beside each other.

This was different. This wasn't the Derek she'd remembered. That Derek would have offered to do it, but he'd have probably done it under running water, maybe with scissors, even though Kali had told him early on knives were the way to go. He'd have plopped all the flowers in the vase at once, and that would be that ... only he probably would have forgotten to put the water in first, so he'd hold the stems to the side and squish the flowers in their vase under the faucet, wetting the leaves in the process and splashing water everywhere.

"What?" Derek turned to Kali, his head tilting with a soft smile.

"Nothing."

"No. What?"

Kali smiled back. "You're so methodical now."

Derek laughed. "I'm an army boy now. Or was." He handed the vase to her. "M'lady."

Kali took the vase and crossed past him to the living room. She cleared a spot and set the flowers on the centre of the coffee table. She stared at them then bent down to sniff.

"Gotta make time to stop and smell the roses."

Kali turned to Derek. "Thank you, they're lovely."

"You're lovely."

She turned from him and grabbed her purse and cane. At the street she looked up and down the road, her brow furrowing. "You didn't drive here?"

Derek pointed to the Lexus two houses down. "Borrowed

a friend's."

Kali opened her mouth to protest, to say he didn't need to go to the trouble, that this wasn't a date. But maybe it was. And maybe that was okay. He clicked the key fob twice, walked to the passenger door, and held it open for Kali. She folded her cane, slid into the leather seat, and buckled up.

Derek slid in beside her.

"You know how to drive stick?"

"Do I know how to drive stick?" He glanced over at her, shook his head, then started the car and pulled away smoothly. "I'm a mechanic, Kali."

"I know." She stared ahead.

"But I suppose it's a fair question, not a lot of people do, and you've never seen me."

"Mmmhmm."

He reached across and squeezed her knee. "Relax, okay? This is going to be a fun night. A good night."

"I know. And I am."

Derek drew his hand back. "I hope so. I'm excited. I hear the food at this place is amazing."

"It's supposed to be, yeah."

"And it'll be especially cool, knowing you helped put it all together."

"Uh huh." Kali turned her gaze to the side window. Why had she lied? She wasn't relaxed at all. The scent of Derek, a smell she'd never forget—the faintest hint of grease, the deodorant he always bought, and something else, uniquely him-caressed her nostrils. He looked good tonight. Really good. And the feel of his hand on her knee—strong and sure, felt even better. She stole a glance at him, eyes on the road, hands in the ten and two position. She'd fallen for him once.

Was she capable of it again?

IN THE RESTAURANT FOYER, the crowd led Kali to push up against Derek's chest. His hand rested on her upper arm, just barely, as more people entered. Most were sighted and buzzing with excitement, but Kali could recognize those who weren't; the way they clung closer to those they knew or tried to carve out little pockets of space for themselves.

"Kali, hi!" Alika approached with her familiar large smile. "You look lovely."

"You too." Kali turned slightly. "This is Derek. Derek, Alika. She pretty much runs the CNIB."

"Oh," Alika laughed and waved a hand in front of her, "barely." She extended that hand to Derek and gave a hearty shake. "We hope you enjoy the evening. Is this your first?"

"Dining in the Dark? Yeah."

Alika winked before turning away. "It'll be an experience!"

Derek leaned down to Kali's ear as Alika left to greet someone else. His lips were so close she could feel the wind of his breath on her ear lobe. "She's bubbly."

"She is." Kali shifted away as the restaurant manager stepped into the crowd.

"Welcome." The manager's voice rang clear and confident. "And thank you for coming to this event. We're excited and honoured to be hosting CNIB Halifax's 6th Dining in the Dark experience."

A small thunder of applause erupted throughout the room.

"For those who've never done this before, you're sure to get a treat. Pay attention to the guidelines to help make this the best experience for everyone. For the veterans among us, please listen closely as well, as some things may be different this year.

"We'll be taking you into the dining room in groups of six. From the moment you cross through those curtains, you'll be in complete darkness and will be until the end of the evening. First you'll meet Shana over here—Shana, give the crowd a little wave."

Heads turned as a young woman in uniform stepped out from behind her podium and waved to the crowd.

"Okay." The manager clapped his hands together. "Shana will give you a choice of two meals—Vegan or Meat. Each will come with an appetizer and a dessert. You won't be told what it is, but never fear, we've taken into account the allergies everyone listed when you bought your tickets. If someone purchased a ticket for you, be sure to let Shana know of any allergies and food restrictions. Next, we ask that you give her any electronic devices with a light—so watches, fitbits, your cell phones. We don't want to ruin the 'dark' experience for anyone."

"This is intense," Derek whispered beside Kali.

"It's got to be," she whispered back.

"Finally," continued the manager, "you'll don one of these lovely aprons." He gestured to a server to his right wearing a black smock. "As some of you know, blind eating can get a little messy."

A round of chuckles went through the crowd.

"And then you'll be taken to your table. Place your hands on the shoulders of the person in front of you and trust your servers to be your guide.

"Oh, one last thing," continued the manager, "if you need to use the facilities, we ask that you use them now. We'd rather not have people groping through the darkness for the restroom." More chuckles. "But if you must, simply let your server know and he or she will guide you out. We won't make you do that in darkness."

The manager clapped his hands and rubbed them together, his face alight with a grin. "Everyone ready?"

CHAPTER THIRTY-NINE

Kali and Derek, along with Heather and her sister and a couple Kali recognized from the CNIB, were the third group to line up for Dining in the Dark. Kali placed her hands on Heather's shoulders as Derek's softly gripped her own.

"You good in the lead?" asked Heather of the woman in the couple. Linda. The name came to Kali, though she couldn't remember her partner's name. From what she did remember, they were both blind, the woman completely, the man legally, and had met in a life skills group.

"You know it." Linda responded with a laugh. "I don't even need this guide."

"She's blind?" whispered Derek.

"Fully," Kali whispered back, though she imagined in this close vicinity, most likely everyone in the line could hear them.

"I can see some differentiations in light." Linda called back. "No shapes."

"So this is your every day experience," answered Derek as Kali winced.

"It is indeed."

"Waiter, can I be seated next to her? I'm sure she'll have some helpful tips."

"You bet." Linda laughed, easing Kali's tension. "I'll take this young gentleman under my wing."

As they passed through not one, but two heavy curtains, all light vanished. Kali knew Heather's head was less than eight inches in front of her, but she couldn't even see its outline.

"Wow," Derek breathed, "the whole meal like this."

"It's dining in the dark." By the sound of Heather's voice, Kali could tell she'd turned back to respond to Derek. "So it's got to be dark."

Once the waiter had pulled out a seat for each of them, doing a bit of maneuvering to place Derek beside Linda, his voice towered over them. "We won't be serving the first course until everyone is seated. Take a few minutes to familiarize yourself with your cutlery, your plate, your glasses—which are to your right. Wine and water." He paused. "And if you don't all know each other, introduce yourselves. By the end of the evening, you may feel like old friends."

"Oh, sorry." Derek chuckled nervously as his hand grazed Kali's. "Was reaching for my glass."

"Reach with your fingertips first." Linda's voice carried above the low murmur in the room. "Slowly and gently."

Kali listened to the directive and found her plate, forks, knives, and water glass. It'd been weeks since she'd played her game of starting the day in darkness, but more came back to her than she would have imagined.

"If it gets too complex." Heather's voice. "You can always

use your fingers. I don't know how many times I've searched my plate for something with a fork and just ached to dig right in, letting my senses guide me."

"Really?" her sister asked. "You could."

"You say that," sighed Heather, "but I'm pretty sure I'd gross out everyone at the table."

"No one to gross out tonight!" A man from another table chimed in, making Kali acutely aware that anything said tonight would be heard by more ears than usual.

After familiarizing themselves with the items on the table, including some melt in your mouth garlic bread, they made the introductions.

"And Kali," asked Heather's sister, Elaine, "how do you and Derek know each other?"

Kali looked in Derek's direction. How could she have not thought of an answer for this question? She took a sip of wine, marvelling at the taste. Focus. What could she say, and could she say it before—

"We're married."

Kali swallowed, about to explain.

"Separated though, for over four years now."

"Oh." Elaine let out a little cough.

"Still amiable though," said Linda. "That's lovely. Do you have children?"

"One boy," Derek answered. "I was away for most of that time. In the army. But I'm back now and we're doing the best we can."

Silence around the table.

"That's wonderful," said Elaine, "and admirable."

"What's admirable is Kali." From the sound, Kali could tell Derek had turned his head in her direction. "Taking care of Theo on her own all those years, raising him to be the amazing boy he's become. And now being gracious enough to let me back into their lives."

Before anyone could respond, the sound of their waiter filled their ears once more. "The first course. I will be serving on your right."

A wave of warmth flowed through Kali. He could have said anything, framed their situation any way. She fumbled for his arm, found his hand, and gave it a squeeze. He squeezed back before she let their fingers drop.

UNCERTAIN, NERVOUS laughter erupted throughout the room as people took their first bites, tried to guess what it was they were biting, and compared tastes and textures to see who had gotten what. The first course was fairly simple. Soup or salad depending on your meal choice. Still though, determining the contents proved more difficult than Kali imagined, as did getting the hot liquid onto her spoon and into her mouth without any spills. But it was good. So good. And better without seeing the food or her dining partners. All she had to focus on was the food. She barely spoke. Others did, but her contribution to the conversations around the table wasn't necessary. She could sink into the darkness. Contribute when she wanted, or stay silent.

As the waiters cleared the first course and the second arrived, the laughter and chatting increased. Several light arguments ensued.

Kali wished she could catch Heather's eye, offer a smile of knowing. They'd had the restaurant change it up this year. Rather than simply two meals, there were five. Three meat options and two vegan. So it wasn't as simple as those who'd come before expected. Even with that advantage, Kali couldn't quite decipher her meat option. She'd decided not to know, trusting instead the manager's skill in choosing the best dishes.

"Fish." Derek's voice was warm and excited beside her. "Mine is definitely fish. I know that." He let out a soft little sigh. "Salmon, I think, and some of the best salmon I've ever had. The texture, the taste, it's like nothing I've ever experienced.

"Linda, this isn't new for you. Is it the lack of vision or is this the best fish you've ever had too?"

"Mine is definitely not fish." Linda's voice carried over the chatter from the other tables. "Some kind of poultry. Not chicken. I don't think chicken, but—"

"Duck, maybe?" asked Heather. "Mine seems quite oily. Duck is oily, isn't it?"

"Duck. Yes." Linda laughed. "It could be duck."

"What about your side?" asked Derek. "I wonder if those are the same? Mine seems kind of like rice, but not quite. It's sticky. There's some kind of sauce, and bits of something sweet."

"Mine's like that too," piped Linda's husband, Steve, "but I don't think I'm eating fish or poultry ... it's some kind of shaved meat. Maybe beef or pork?"

"Kali, what's yours like?" Derek leaned toward her.

"The shaved meat it seems." Kali took another bite. She laughed, feeling light and free, then uncertain as Derek's arm brushed up against hers, only the hairs tickling her skin. A shiver ran through her. "I have no idea what it is, but it's good."

"Trade bites?"

They laughed with nervousness and excitement as their forks crossed and clinked, as they groped around each others' plates for the right sampling, using directives, mostly from the face of a clock, to guide each other.

"You two are loving this!" Linda exclaimed from beside Derek.

"It's an experience, that's for sure." Derek's voice lowered, the mirth exiting it. "An education, too. As interesting as this is, I know when it's done I can step back into the light, navigate the world in the way I always have. It's fun because I know it won't last. If it did ..." He hesitated. "I hope it doesn't seem insensitive, my excitement about this experience. My enthusiasm and—"

"I know." Linda cut him off. "The event is meant to be fun. But also to open people's eyes to the struggle, the reality, while showing how capable we still can be."

"Seeing the smocks at the end will be evidence of that," said Steve. "The sighted are sure to have far more accidents."

"Were any of you born without vision? Or limited vision?" Derek's voice came out strong and clear.

"I lost mine when I was two," said Linda. "I remember a few vague images. Some colour."

"Twenty-six for me," said Steve. "Almost overnight. It was the scariest thing I've ever experienced. Now I see in my dreams. Besides that it's fairly limited. Shapes. Light. Some faint colours."

"Mine happened slowly," added Heather. "Is still happening. If I'm lucky I'll have a few more years."

"More than a few, hopefully," said Elaine. "Your doctors thought by now it'd be gone. But you're a fighter."

"That I am." Heather offered an uncertain chuckle.

Derek's fingers reached along Kali's arm. They trailed up her flesh until they found her hand. They squeezed, his thumb giving a little caress, then drew away.

They'd hardly talked about Kali's tumour. He knew the extent of her vision loss, knew it was stable for now, but there were no guarantees.

"I hope it's not too intrusive to ask," said Linda, "but I could hear you have a limp. What's your story?"

"Oh," Derek's voice shook slightly, "I know what it is to have something you took for granted be lost in an instant. A literal instant for me." He spoke briefly, giving little more than the necessary details. His time in the military. The mission. The unexploded IED bomb. How lucky he was; how his comrade wasn't so lucky. "Losing a leg is nothing to losing a life."

"Do you think it was worth it? What we were doing over there? Worth the casualties, the, OWW!" Steve's question stopped mid-sentence.

Again, Kali could hear Derek's smile. "I'll be honest; I didn't sign up for any great belief. When it comes to the politics of war, I know less than I should. Is it right, wrong? Those questions are too complex for me to answer. All I knew was I wanted to help people, do something good to make up for some of the bad. To try to feel I had purpose and was contributing the best I knew how." He paused. "Would I do it again, knowing what I know now? I'm not sure. But I helped people. Many people. To them, I imagine us being there was worth it. I was never in a combat role. I can only speak to my own experience."

Before an awkward silence could settle, Heather clapped her hands and rubbed them together (or at least that's what it sounded like). "What do you think dessert will be? That's what I'm most excited about."

"Talking about exciting, do you know what would be fun?" Linda let out a little laugh. "Make it dining and dancing in the dark next year!"

Heather guffawed. "I'm not sure if CNIB could handle the liability insurance for that."

"What?" Kali could almost hear Linda's grin. "I can dance."

"With a sighted partner leading," returned Heather.

"Partnered dancing, yes, I suppose." Another laugh from Linda. "But it could just be a dance party. Everyone gets their little square of floor. Oh!" Linda's voice picked up in excitement. "We could tape something down that was raised or textured so people could feel if they were leaving their square. It would truly give everyone the chance to dance like no one's watching."

"But with the energy of the crowd," said Derek. "I'd be down with that."

THE CONVERSATION continued with laughter and questions and moans of delight over dessert. Kali had forgotten how easy Derek was in a crowd. How he made people laugh, was aware of their insecurities or uncertainties, and put people at ease despite them. How attentive he was, even to strangers. She had forgotten the swell of pride at being the woman he chose to have by his side. Not that she was by his side tonight, not in that way. But it was close enough, and it was nice. Really nice. Incredibly nice.

The waiter's voice. "Are we all finished?"

After everyone around the table agreed, their waiter

instructed them to stand and put their hands on the shoulders of the person in front of them once more. Derek's strong hands on Kali's shoulders felt familiar, reminding her of those early months of pregnancy when he'd rubbed out the knots she kept getting from hours with her head stuck in a text book. They reminded her of other things too. Touches she'd strived to forget.

Kali breathed deeply as they pushed through the first curtain and the intensity of the darkness eased. Her heart raced. Her extremities felt numb. Was it the memory of what had been or the start of what could be?

The light hit her like a slap in the face, making her squint and turn her face away, but there was nowhere to turn. Derek's gasp followed a millisecond after her own, and his hands dropped from her shoulders. They mingled in a half crowd, half line as they waited to return their food splattered smocks and pick up their devices. Once they'd made their way through, Derek hugged Elaine, Heather, and Linda goodbye and shook Steve's hand. Kali stood beside him, smiling at them all and offering her farewells.

And then they were in the street, walking to the borrowed car, Kali's purse in one hand, her cane in the other and Derek keeping pace. He hesitated several spots up from the Lexus. "It's still early and a lovely night. You want to keep walking? Maybe go to the harbour front?"

"Oh." Kali turned to him, standing before her, tall and vulnerable and so handsome. "It is a nice night."

He smiled, that half smile that used to make her stomach flip, his head tilted. "I'm asking for a walk, Kali. Nothing but a walk."

"Okay." She smiled back and they turned toward the

harbour. On the boardwalk, the normal hustle of the day had settled into couples and small groups of friends meandering, speaking in soft voices to not overpower the gentle lapping of the water.

"How long do you think it's been since we walked here together like this?"

Kali glanced at him. "We were here less than two weeks ago, to show Theo the—"

"No." That smile again. "Just you and me. Just walking."

"Five years, maybe."

"Four years, nine months, and ..." he hesitated, "three days."

Kali walked on. She remembered now.

"We were walking along, fingers interlaced. I was rubbing your wedding band. I used to love to do that."

Kali kept silent.

"A couple walked by pushing a stroller. And then you said it, your voice so soft and uncertain I wasn't sure I'd heard you. 'That'll be us soon,' you said. At first I thought you meant one day, you know? Then I looked at you."

"And swung me around," said Kali, her voice as soft as it had been that night.

"And I kissed you."

Kali kept her gaze ahead.

"And kissed your belly." Silence. "That was a good night."

Moisture built behind Kali's eyes. "It was."

Derek took a long breath. "The things I'd say if I thought you wanted to hear them."

"Derek."

"Things like there's still time."

"Please."

"We could have more children."

"Don't."

"Like I'm sorry. So sorry. But we've wasted enough time, it doesn't make sense to waste more."

Kali turned to him. She held a hand up between them, her chest tight, her whole body on edge.

"Things like I love you. I've never stopped."

Kali closed her eyes and shook her head.

"I have to say that, Kali. I love you. I know you must know. And I'm sure, so sure, that if you let me, I can make you love me again."

Kali looked at him, their gazes locking. "Derek, I'm sorry. So sorry for all the time I made you miss with Theo. It was wrong. Awful." Kali closed her eyes and put her head down, fighting the tears. She still held her hand up, Derek's chest pushing into it now as he moved closer. She thought of the way he had been with Theo since returning: patient, kind, loving, fun. Even the way he was tonight: chatting, laughing, showing genuine interest in the people around them, showing genuine respect for her. This was a good man. A man who loved her and loved her child. And she'd stolen from them. Stolen hugs and laughter and four years worth of memories. Even if he'd been away for months at a time, Theo could have known his father, recognized his father. Derek could have known his son.

Kali brought her gaze back to Derek. "I'm so sorry. If I could change the past I would. I'd let you know your son."

Derek put his hands on Kali's shoulders. "We're not talking about the past right now and we're not talking about Theo. We're talking about you and me."

Kali shook her head. "It's too late."

"It's not."

Her head continued shaking.

"Is it because of him? Lincoln?"

"No."

"He's gone now. I talked to him, explained it all, got him to agree it was best if he stepped out of the picture so you and I could try to make it work."

"You what?"

"I talked to him, asked him to step back. To let us be a family."

Kali backed away. "What'd he say?"

Derek's brow furrowed. "I shouldn't have even mentioned his name. This is about us. I love you, Kali. I love Theo. I'm not asking for a yes. I'm not asking for now. I'm asking for hope. I'm asking if you think there's the slimmest sliver of hope that one day you could love me again the way you did."

"No." Kali's head seemed to spin. The whole boardwalk seemed to spin. How many glasses of wine had she had? "I don't know. You asked him? You initiated talking to him?"

She turned away and took several steps. Derek had asked Lincoln to leave. It hadn't been simply Lincoln's idea. The father of her child had asked Lincoln to walk away. And he did. He walked away. Without a fight though? Without argument? Had it been what he was hoping for? An excuse. Or was he just that selfless?

Kali spun back toward Derek, ready to question him, but his arms were around her before she could speak, his lips cutting off her words. He pulled her against him, her body pressed tight, so familiar and yet so foreign. Their lips parted, his tongue exploring, hers responding, and it all came back. The nights of slick sweat and heat and an ecstasy she'd never known existed. The comfort, the safety, the only man she'd ever opened herself up to. He released her at last and they stood staring at each other, their chests heaving.

"That's not nothing." His voice was hoarse, full of passion and yearning. "That's hope."

CHAPTER FORTY

Over the next days the kiss ran through Kali's mind again and again. It didn't erase the past. It couldn't. But Derek was right; it spoke of a possible future. It proved not everything they'd shared had vanished.

"Kali." Allison leaned back in her seat. "I've got to tell you, I was doubtful. But I think this is going to work."

Kali let her breath out slowly. She'd walked into Westwood this morning hopeful yet realistic. Now hope soared. "You think it will work?"

"An assessment is just that, obviously. It's not being on the floor. We'd need you partnered for the first few weeks, someone shadowing you to ensure you can do the job safely and efficiently. I'd also need to get clearance on the cost of the equipment."

"Oh," Kali folded her hands, "will that be difficult?"

"No." Allison grinned. "Not at all. The worst that I can see happening is it takes longer than we'd like. The red tape, you know. But approval shouldn't be an issue."

"Okay."

"So," Allison leaned forward, "are you ready to come

back?"

To Westwood. Was she ready to come back to Westwood? She was terrified. Uncertain. But she was ready. Incredibly ready. "Yes." Kali's smile spread until it overtook her face. "Definitely."

"Great." Allison walked around the desk and put a hand on Kali's shoulder. "We've missed you. Your patients have missed you. And I have to say," Allison perched on the edge of her desk, facing Kali, "I'm incredibly impressed at your fortitude. Not everyone would fight the way you have. Some people would let a circumstance like this break them. I've seen it dozens of times. The road ahead of you is going to be hard. It'll be frustrating. Things that used to come easily will be more difficult now. But I also believe in time you'll hardly notice."

A tingling made its way through Kali. Allison wasn't wrong. It would be difficult. Even in the assessment, Kali could feel the tension as it took longer to check her pretend patient's vitals, scan for bedsores, and maneuver around the room so that she didn't bump into anything. The worst, perhaps, was accessing medicine. She could stare straight in front of her, missing half of it. It seemed like nothing, the effort to shift your head in order to see the full picture. But it wasn't nothing.

"Plan to come back two Mondays from now. I'd rather you start with your own equipment. That should give enough time for clearance, purchasing, and arranging a shadow. We'll start you on half days."

Allison hopped off of the desk. "A new phase in your life. I'm excited for you." She stuck out her hand and Kali stood to meet the vigorous shake.

A new phase.

Kali walked out of the room half in a daze. It'd be frustrating at times. Difficult often. But worth it. Kali smiled. Those words spoke to so much more than her career.

Frustrating. Difficult. Worth it.

Kali pushed out of Westwood's doors and into the parking lot. She crossed the lot and stood at the bus stop. A new phase. A new life. A new story.

She didn't have to be afraid anymore.

She'd been a single mom and powered through; her son was incredible. She'd had a tumour, she'd lost a significant amount of her vision, but she hadn't broken ... not irrevocably, anyway. She'd lived without love. She didn't want to, not anymore.

Kali waited for the bus door to open. The driver smiled at her, a rare occurrence, and she smiled back as she showed her card then found a seat. She'd let fear overtake her, cripple her, close her off. But she didn't have to, not anymore.

The memory of Derek's kiss tingled on her lips. It'd been incredible. Beautiful. It'd taught her something—she'd forgiven him. Maybe not completely, but enough. More than enough. He was Theo's father. He was here. Whether she wanted it or not, he'd always be in their lives in some way or another. She'd never keep Theo from him again. Kali touched her lips. She *wanted* him in their lives.

He was a good man, despite his poor choices, and it wasn't fair to keep him waiting in this limbo any longer. He deserved her answer and deserved it now. She loved him, and it was cruel, keeping someone you loved in this kind of limbo.

Kali stepped off the bus and walked the three blocks to Derek's apartment. She inhaled then let the breath out slowly. He was her husband. He could be again. They'd made vows, and she'd meant them, every word.

She stood in front of his building. She needed to be sure, certain, before she knocked on his door. She took another breath. They could live a good life. A long life. Forgiveness may have to be given again and again. Trust would have to build up slowly. But it was possible. More than possible. She knew that, felt it in her bones. She and Derek could have a future. They *could*. She knocked three times. Waited.

CHAPTER FORTY-ONE

A

"Hi."

"Hi." Kali's smile wavered. She bit her lip and seemed to tremble.

Lincoln swivelled so he was facing her full on. His gut twisted with uncertainty. "How'd you find me?"

Her shoulders rose and fell. "It took some searching. Some calling around. And then it came to me." She smiled again and let out a nervous laugh. "May I sit?"

"Yes. Sure. Of course." Lincoln pulled out the computer chair next to him.

"Okay." Kali swallowed and sat. "How have you been?"

Lincoln ran a hand through his hair, noting the way Kali looked in the direction of several of the library's patrons. "Kali, what is—?"

She brought her gaze back to him. "How's the business?"

Lincoln sighed. "Good, actually. Coming along. I have a marketing manager and am heading to Montreal next—" Lincoln stopped. "Kali, what are you doing here?"

She gestured to the door. "Can we go outside? More privacy, you know?"

"Yeah, okay." Lincoln crossed in front of her then held open the door as she passed under his arm. Cinnamon and coconut. He breathed her in, only now realizing how much he'd missed this scent. Kali sat on a step leading to the library's small lawn and tucked her feet underneath her. Lincoln hesitated then sat several feet away.

Kali folded her hands in her lap and looked down at them. "I've been thinking a lot these past weeks, about life. About the stories we tell ourselves."

Lincoln took a breath, his brow furrowing. "Stories?"

"Your mom phrased it like that, actually. I went to visit her a while back."

"Okay." Lincoln shifted, one part of him needing to tell her to leave, the other part frantically memorizing every feature in case she did.

"A lot of the stories I was telling myself, they were of anger, weakness, being a victim, being a martyr. Almost none of them, though, were what I want my story to be."

Lincoln pushed out a breath. She was here. Why, he wasn't sure. But she was here. She'd searched for him.

"I just came from Derek's."

Lincoln's hands clenched onto his knees. Here to tell him she had made her choice? To thank him, maybe, for stepping back?

"I love him." Kali looked to her hands and nodded. "I forgive him, as much I'm able. Which," she looked up, head tilted, "I think is enough."

Lincoln clenched and unclenched his hands, the knuckles whitening then filling back with colour. "Enough?"

"To make it work. To start a new life, be a family in the way he wants."

So this was it, the final goodbye. Lincoln's hands relaxed.

"But there's just one problem. That's what he wants. And it doesn't make sense, me making massive life decisions based on what other people want or other people think is best for me." She smiled—scared, hopeful, uncertain.

Lincoln's throat convulsed, his breath held.

"I love Derek." She paused, her smile growing. "And we could make it work. But I don't want it to just work because that's the simpler choice, the more logical choice. I want more than that. I want you." She paused again. "I'm in love with you."

Lincoln kept silent, not believing the words.

"That sounds so crazy, doesn't it?" Kali let out a short laugh.

Lincoln shook his head, swallowing.

"That I love him, but it's not enough. It doesn't matter. My husband. My son's father." Kali looked to the lawn. "Derek seemed to think it was crazy when I told him. He thought I was just afraid to give us another shot." Her gaze locked on Lincoln. "But I'm not. It's not about fear." Another soft laugh. "For once."

Kali shifted closer. "I've let fear make so many decisions, let it write my story ... fear of being alone, of being the statistic of a single mom, of being rejected, of the tumour, the blindness, you. I let you push me away, the way I'd been pushing you away, because I was too scared to take any action." She rubbed her hands together and turned her gaze to the bus that groaned to a stop up the street. Several people walked off and made their way past them to the library doors. She turned back. "I told him I'm filing for divorce."

Lincoln inhaled.

"I already contacted a lawyer." Kali picked up a fallen leaf from the lawn and twirled it in her fingers. "He's Theo's father. Theo's blood. Not mine. Those promises we made, we can honour them in other ways, by working through ... all we have to work through, by being friends and giving Theo both his parents in the best way we're able.

"I'm sorry I didn't do it sooner. That I let that fester between us—the lie about Derek's existence, the lie that I was a single, available woman when in so many ways I wasn't." Kali blew out a strong gust of air and bit her lip. "I'm sorry I didn't tell you about him. I was scared. But I'm not anymore. Well, not as much." She laughed self-consciously, a hand to her neck. Her gaze zeroed in on Lincoln. "I've been so indecisive. But I want you to know this isn't a test or an exploration, me saying I choose you. It's an intention. I want to see this work. I am committed to making us work."

Kali lowered her gaze then brought it back up to Lincoln. "In love. I never thought I'd say that about someone again. Maybe that was childish. Maybe it was naive." Her laugh was louder this time, with a lightness the others lacked. The sound seemed to kick start Lincoln's heart. It raced. She smiled, and the words began to sink in. "I choose you." The softest smile. "It's not too late, is it?"

Lincoln's heart thumped so hard he was hardly sure he'd heard her. "Too late?"

"You can say no if you want. I'm not going back to Derek, either way. You won't be the reason Theo's parents aren't together. I'm the reason. It's my choice." Kali rubbed a hand along her thigh. "He's Theo's dad, and I couldn't be happier that he wants to be in his son's life." She shrugged one shoulder. "Theo couldn't be happier." She paused. "He loves you more, but Derek's his dad. The love will grow. So, we'll work something out. Some kind of joint custody or visitation rights. I don't know yet. We didn't figure all of that out."

Kali bit her lip. She let her shoulders rise and fall in the way that made Lincoln's breath stop. "You haven't moved on, have you?"

"Moved on?" Lincoln stared, incredulous.

"Yeah. You gonna choose me too, or what?"

Lincoln laughed. The type of deep belly laugh he hadn't had in weeks. His hands tingled as he placed them along the outside of her thighs, drawing her closer. "Are you sure?"

She bit her lip, her uncertainty vanishing into a grin. "I'm sure."

Lincoln nodded, pulling her closer still and leaning in so their foreheads touched. "Yeah," he whispered, inhaling the scent of her, imprinting this moment in his mind—the crisp breeze, the goosebumps that travelled over his body, the strength of her thighs underneath her soft leggings. "I'm sure too."

"Really?"

Lincoln blinked to clear his vision. "Oh yeah." He pressed his lips together then breathed deeper the scent of her. "I'm still a little broken though, still figuring it all out. You know that, right?"

Kali put a hand to his cheek, her smile reaching her eyes. "Me too."

Lincoln mimicked her movement, raising a hand from her thigh to her face. "So, what's next?"

Kali bit her lip again, grinning. "I think a kiss would be appropriate. And then," she gave a little shrug, "we figure it out. Together."

And yet we hold on.
We hold onto it all, as if by doing so we hold onto ourselves.
We tell ourselves a story:
We matter. This matters.

What beauty.

THANK YOU!

Hello, Dear Reader,

I hope you enjoyed *The Stories We Tell*.

And thank you for taking the time to read my work. I'd greatly appreciate it if you also took the time to leave a quick review. Reviews are incredibly important, especially for independent authors like myself. They let other readers know whether or not it's worth taking a chance on an author and help us get marketing deals, which can extend our reach and mean we're able to provide you stories for years to come! If you've never left a review before, it's very simple. Head over to your favourite retailer and/or Goodreads, do a search for *The Stories We Tell* by Charlene Carr, choose your star rating, then you'll be asked to leave your review. It could be two words or two hundred, as long as it's honest.

Thank you again for taking the time to read the *Behind Our Lives Trilogy*. If you'd like to read more of my books, visit charlenecarr.com. While there, you can also sign up for my mailing list and get the first two books in my Women's Fiction series as free ebooks!

All the best,

Charlene Carr

ACKNOWLEDGEMENTS

A huge thank you to my husband for constantly supporting my work. To my mother, for her keen eye on the many versions and revisions - this would be an entirely different process without you! To my beta readers, who read my works in their early form, with metaphorical bloomers showing - your feedback is invaluable.

I would also like to thank the clients and staff of the CNIB St. John's. Sylvia Staples, Jeana Bowen, Kelly Picco, and Kim Thistle-Murphy; thank you for sharing your experiences with vision loss and allowing me to draw from your words to create authenticity. You opened a window to a world I otherwise would have had to create from imagination. Kathleen May, Cindy Antle, and Lynsey Soper, thank you for opening the doors of the CNIB and educating me on the services your organization offers. I so appreciate your generosity with your time.

Thanks, as well, to Dr. Linda Magnusson and Dr. Teri Stuckless for your medical consultation and your enthusiasm for helping my work be as realistic as possible. If anything in the story does not make sense medically, that is wholly based on my lack of attention to detail or failure to ask the right questions. Your help and generosity have been a gift.

Finally, thank you to my readers. You're the reason I do this. You give me the motivation to keep on. I hope this story has given you hours of enjoyment.

ABOUT THE AUTHOR

Charlene Carr is a lover of words. Pursuing this life-long obsession, she studied literature in university, attaining both a BA and MA in English. Still craving more, she attained a degree in Journalism. After travelling the globe for several years and working as a freelance writer, editor, and facilitator she decided the time had come to focus on her true love - novel writing. She's loving every minute of it ... well, almost every minute. Some days her characters fight to have the story their way. (And they're almost always right!)

Charlene lives in Dartmouth, Nova Scotia, is a brand new mom, loves dancing up a storm, and enjoys using her husband as a guinea pig for the healthy, yummy recipes she creates!

Charlene's first series, *A New Start*, is Women's Fiction full of thought, heart, and hope.

If you would like the first two books in her Women`s Fiction series for free as ebooks, sign up for her mailing list at: www.charlenecarr.com/freebooks

Made in the USA
Lexington, KY
06 April 2019